Love at FIRST SPARK

HELEN B. AITKEN

Love at FIRST SPARK

HELEN B. AITKEN

Editing by: Lynne Pearson, www.allthatediting.com
Formatting by: bbebooksthailand.com, paul@beebee.asia
Cover Design by: Dineen Miller, https://subscribepage.io/DineenMillerPortfolio

ISBN: 979-8-9901067-5-8

Love at First Spark is dedicated to readers who love romantic suspense and firefighters. And to my personal assistant, Debbe Johnson, who laughs at my jokes and has the monumental task of keeping me sane and somewhat organized. What did I do with my calendar, Debbe? I lost my head, again—where did I put it? I don't know what to do without her.

Chapter 1

MITCHEL STRONG WORKED a thick lather of shampoo and lemon juice into his short black curls for the second time, getting it in his eyes. "Yow, that stings!" Acrid smoke particles mixed with unknown organic matter were difficult to remove, a reminder that fighting a farm fire gave the gift that kept giving, without the benefit of a barbecue.

He tilted the shower head to spray cold water into his eyes, then shivered as a charred feather fell on his foot and quickly kicked it away, barely managing to stay upright. Quickly adjusting the temperature to rinse his hair before the hot water ran out, he lathered a natural bath sponge with sage and citrus shower gel. He unapologetically took every opportunity to pamper his body now, knowing there would be times when he wouldn't get that luxury.

The wail of a commercial smoke alarm penetrated the shower's interior. He turned off the water and listened closely. "What the hell? Is it coming from next door?"

Snatching a beach towel from the cabinet, he sprinted out of the bathroom toward the kitchen;

without any clean clothes, the towel would have to do. He grabbed a fire extinguisher from under the sink before rushing outside. Following the sound, he ran through an arched wrought iron gate, into the neighbor's expansive backyard, and toward the kitchen, where black smoke wafted out of a window.

"Anyone here?" He yelled loudly, banging on the door before trying the doorknob. It turned in his hand. Mitch barreled inside while yelling, "Anyone home? I'm coming in. Your kitchen's on fire."

Flames engulfed an unidentifiable object inside a large frying pan sitting on a commercial stove. Smoke rolled upward in waves. Mitch aimed the extinguisher, squeezing the trigger as hard as he could. It jammed open, shooting out a continuous fog that extinguished the fire. Yet it filled the room with a white cloud that covered everything within a ten-foot radius, even reaching the ceiling. He pulled on the trigger again, using both hands, before it finally shut off. *Another faulty trigger. How was this possible?*

He barely heard a voice screaming at him.

"Have you lost your mind?" A tall woman emerged like a ghost, wearing goggles and a white lab coat, each hand covered in an oven mitt. She clutched a long spatula in one hand and a dinging timer in the other. "Look what you did… *That* was my dinner." She fanned her face and spat out some of the inhaled powder, coughing until she covered her nose and mouth with her lab coat sleeve.

"Your smoke alarm went off, so I ran over. You're welcome, by the way." Unable to find another oven mitt, he doubled over the end of his beach towel and used it to pick up the frying pan before heading out the patio door.

Following him, the apparition screamed between

coughs, "Where are you taking that?"

"Outside to clear out the smoke," he replied, then placed the frying pan on the ground. As he straightened, the towel slid completely off, trapped under the pan.

The phantom wiped her goggles with an oven mitt, her eyes widening, and her mouth dropping open. If she hadn't noticed before, she certainly did now. He was barefoot, bare-chested, and bare everything. Once her eyes refocused on his face, she frowned. "Who are you?"

He casually grabbed the towel and wrapped it around his waist. "I'm Mitchel Strong, but my friends call me Mitch, your next-door neighbor. I, um, moved in a week ago. Are you Bree or Prissy?" He walked toward her and extended his hand as if this were the most natural way to introduce himself.

"I'm Bree, and I'm furious with you." She ripped off the goggles, and white dust blew across her face into her vibrant red hair.

Mitch stared, mesmerized by the deepest green eyes he'd ever seen. He moved closer and gently wiped the white dust from her lips, but his fingertips lingered a little too long. "You've also got a little here…" He stroked her cheek, and an electric spark traveled down to his toes. Her lips quivered. He couldn't move or speak. *What kind of spell did she cast on me?*

Bree cleared her throat and blinked repeatedly. The magic disappeared, leaving her face flushed, as she quickly wiped it as best she could. "I know I'm a fright, but staring isn't polite."

He backed up a step. "I'm so sorry… under all that dust, I think you're the most beautiful woman I've ever seen." *Why did I say that?* His mouth had overrun his brain. Again. As usual, without any filter. "I… I can help you wash it off with a warm washcloth, or maybe help you in the shower—"

Her face turned bright red. "No thanks... but... I appreciate the offer."

The smoke alarm continued to blare.

"Maybe another time." Mitch smiled from ear to ear. "What's with the outfit? Are you a mad scientist or something?"

"Mad? No. Scientist? Yes. Um, did you just come back from the beach?"

A fire truck's siren interrupted the conversation, then cut off as the truck stopped in front of Bree's house. Moments later, fists pounded on the front door, and a man's deep voice yelled, "Bree, are you in there?"

She rolled her eyes, coughed again, and yelled. "Come around back, Hank."

Mitch froze. *Hank? My captain, Hank? Why's he here, and how does she know him?* "This should be interesting."

Five firefighters in full gear raced through the side gate and into the kitchen. Hank looked around before issuing orders. "Mac, turn off the alarm. Jerry and Steve check the damage, close the doors, and seal off the air ducts. Frank, check out Bree. She used a fire extinguisher again." He turned away from Bree and spotted Mitch casually leaning against the open door. "What are you doing here? Um, did you just come from the beach?"

"Captain." Mitch straightened. "I was showering when I heard an alarm go off, so I ran over with a fire extinguisher."

"Right," Hank smirked. "I guess it's a good thing you came quickly. By the way, you're still dripping."

Heat rushed to Mitch's face. "Sir, how did you know about the fire?"

"Bree's smoke alarm is hardwired to ring at the station. She tends to..." He cleared his throat, "need our services on occasion. However, she's good at putting out fires on her own. Isn't that right, Bree?"

"Y-yes, Hank." Her gaze drifted to the floor.

Steve Chambers approached Hank to give his report. "Looks like someone was trigger-happy with the fire extinguisher. It's one big mess, about a two-day clean."

Mitch winced.

"Hmm." Hank crossed his arms. "I'm sure Mitch will be glad to use his day off to clean things up, won't you, Mitch?"

"I can manage," Bree said. "No need to ruin his day off. Since you're here, I have a large pan of lasagna, garlic bread, and cookies that Prissy made, so you'll save me a trip to the station if you can take it with you."

Hank beamed. "Of course. We love your cousin's cooking. Tell her thanks. The guys will be eating well tonight. Uh, Bree, I'd feel better if you used the kitchen only under her supervision. This is the second time this month we've had to come over. The guys need training for more than kitchen fires. What do you say?"

"I'll take it under advisement," Bree answered, forcing a smile. "Thanks for coming, guys. I'll walk y'all out."

Mitch was in no hurry to go home. The water heater needed time to recover, and this would be the perfect opportunity to learn more about Bree and her fire habits. He stretched out on a lounge chair, hands behind his head, and closed his eyes. *Yep, this should be interesting.*

"BREE?" DOORS INSIDE the house opened and closed. "Bree?" Her cousin's voice got louder when the kitchen door flew open. "You did it again!" Prissy barreled through the kitchen and out the door to the patio, coughing and fanning her face.

"What did you incinerate this time? Oh, no. Chicken." Prissy looked down at the scorched pan with the efficiency of a coroner identifying body parts.

Bree pointed a long spatula at the smiling, towel-clad man relaxing in the lounge chair. If it had been a gun, she would have already killed him. She tried to think of the right thing to say. "Um, well… you see…"

"Please tell me that you thawed out a six-month-old bird you found at Sale Mart and not my hand-fed, range-free, sang-to, twenty-five-dollars-a-pound French Bresse chicken from the Chicken Ridge Farm in Kentucky?"

Bree cringed. "I suppose that makes about a hundred and fifty dollars of chicken I ruined, but I meant it to be a surprise birthday dinner for you tonight. I'm so sorry. I will replace it. How about I take you out to dinner?"

"Not so fast." Prissy held up a hand like a traffic cop. "My kitchen, my rules, and my burned food. You leave me no choice. You will compensate me for your past, present, and future kitchen disasters with a Bresse rooster and five hens, along with an extra-large chicken coop for the backyard that I'll order today. It'll look perfect near the pond."

"That's kind of harsh, don't you think?" Mitch

asked.

"And you are?" Prissy focused on the nearly naked man.

"This is Mitchel from next door," Bree said.

"Just Mitch," he corrected.

"This is Just Mitch from next door. He created the mess in the kitchen."

"Not *Just Mitch*. Mitch." He rose from the chair, leaving part of the beach towel behind. However, what came up with him managed to cover the best parts. Two sighs and two pairs of eyes followed his full height. Mitch stuck out his hand. "You must be Prissy."

"I'm Pricilla Matthews, but I prefer Prissy. Bree's my first cousin."

"Dirk told me you were beautiful, and I agree wholeheartedly."

Bree groaned and stalked back to the kitchen in a huff.

"Wait, Bree. I'll help you clean up the mess. After all, I made it." Mitch jogged to the door, fisting the towel closed.

Prissy lifted the chicken and her favorite two-hundred-dollar All-Clad frying pan to the garbage can, then dropped it in while humming "Taps."

"What kind of mad scientist things were you doing while simultaneously burning freakishly expensive chicken?" he asked.

Prissy yelled after him. "Bree's not a mad scientist, she's a scientist with numerous degrees, and technically you should address her as Dr. Kelly, Ph.D. in Physics." Prissy followed them into the kitchen. "So, Bree, *what were you* doing while my Bresse chicken was being cremated?"

"For the record, I was distracted for only a moment before the smoke alarm sounded." Hands on her hips,

Prissy waited for her to continue. "I… um, well, I was calculating the rise in air temperature by the speed at which the crickets rubbed their wings together. It's called chirping. It was extraordinary." She cleared her throat. "I promise you, Prissy. I set the timer."

"The oven timer?"

"Yes."

"The four manual timers sitting on the counter?"

"Yes." *Why is he still standing there? This is so humiliating.*

"Your cell phone and the two alarm clocks in the den and living room?"

"Of course. Don't you find chirping fascinating?"

"Whatever." Prissy sighed. "Help me open the doors and windows and blow this stuff out. This kitchen must be clean and sanitized to the point where you can eat off the floor. Exactly what were you trying to make for my birthday dinner?"

"Blackened chicken with Paula Deen's asparagus and hollandaise sauce, baked brie on sliced baguettes, a side salad with raspberry vinaigrette, and a beautiful birthday cake from Molly's Cakes with twenty-eight candles. And you have two beautifully wrapped birthday presents on the dining room table."

"First of all, blackened chicken isn't burned. The spices coating the chicken are blackened. Although I appreciate the thought, you are banned from the kitchen without adequate supervision. Is the rest of the meal in the refrigerator?"

"Yes. If you were to teach me how to cook, I could finish the dinner—"

"Your interest in learning is inspiring, but *I* will cook dinner after the kitchen's cleaned."

Bree let out a long breath. The gourmet kitchen looked like a snow blower had gone out of control.

After Prissy graduated from the Cordon Bleu three years ago, the kitchen had been remodeled with top-of-the-line stainless steel Wolf appliances, a gas range with a fire-suppressing hood, double ovens, two dishwashers, a Sub-Zero refrigerator and freezer, an ice maker, and an undercabinet beverage center. Storage cabinets went from floor to ceiling, and the pantry could have stocked a small grocery store. There was a small island with a marble countertop for making desserts, and a larger island covered in quartzite, which surrounded the stove. It was used for preparing and packing food or serving a buffet. From the studs to the floor and everything in between, every part of the kitchen had to meet state building codes and health standards for a professional kitchen, so Prissy could cook and cater out of the home until she got her own restaurant up and running. The nine-month process was brutal.

But Prissy was right. There were so many surfaces and crevices that needed cleaning. Bree winced. *I really did it this time.*

Mitch jumped into the conversation. "Ladies, why don't we dine outdoors tonight and make it a real birthday party? I'll invite some firefighters and EMTs from the station, and Prissy can invite her friends. We'll have lots of beer, cheap hot dogs, hamburgers dripping in grease, and you can bring the birthday cake, say, seven o'clock?"

"Perfect," Prissy said as Bree muttered, "No, thanks." They eyed each other.

"Great. I'll get dressed and be back in ten minutes to help clean." Mitch sprinted out the door, gripping the towel with one hand as the women continued to argue.

Chapter 2

FULLY DRESSED, MITCH retraced his steps to Bree's house by going through both backyards. Although he was invited to Dirk's house in Morehead City, North Carolina, several times during college summer breaks, he had never been inside Bree's brick three-story Colonial Revival mansion or even known that Bree or Prissy lived there. He wondered why Dirk had never mentioned them. He took a few minutes to admire the two-hundred-acre estate, surrounded by four-foot-high hedges.

In the early twentieth century, the Well's stately home was the only house at the end of Dogwood Lane, lined with hundred-year-old live oaks, cedars, and pines. Twenty or thirty years later, four other two-story brick homes had been built on both sides of the street, including Dirk's house next door. However, due to hurricanes and structural decay, three of those homes had been demolished. When the land went up for sale, Stanley E. Well bought it and expanded his property. He added a four-car garage with a storage area and laboratory, a pool, a guest bungalow, and beautiful gardens around a freshwater pond.

Dirk's brick, two-story colonial home was a quarter the size of the Well's house and property, but it had four bedrooms, three bathrooms, a spacious family room, a modest kitchen, and a mudroom that connected to an attached garage. His grandparents built it, but his parents inherited it when he was about eleven. Over the years, it was remodeled and well-maintained. After his parents retired to the Charlotte area, Dirk and his two siblings, Brandon and Alexa, were gifted the house. Dirk had emotional ties to it, and the backyard was great for barbecues and touch football. Since he worked in the area, he lived there, but Brandon and Alexa had their old bedrooms when they visited. He'd told Mitch that he planned to buy the house from his siblings and then make additional renovations if he received a promotion.

Mitch stepped through Bree's kitchen door, which was guarded by two large box fans working hard to remove the white haze from inside, but created a snowing effect on the patio. He held a bucket filled with his homemade cleaner, a large spray bottle, super-absorbent microfiber towels, newspapers, gloves, and goggles. He wore rain boots, cargo shorts, a black Station 18 T-shirt, and a bandana tied around his head, like bikers do under a helmet. Cleaning up after a fire was as crucial as putting one out, and he had vast experience with both.

To his surprise, Bree rolled out a professional-grade, three-tray stainless steel cart stocked with cleaning products, rags, a wet vac, a whisk broom, a large microfiber mop, and a squeegee mop. An orange utility jumpsuit, commonly worn by cleaning crews, replaced her lab coat. Goggles covered her eyes, and a red bandanna covered her hair. She passed Mitch a heavy-duty mask and goggles before donning yellow dishwashing gloves.

Although Prissy had vowed not to help, she appeared wearing rain boots, a straw cowgirl hat, the shortest pair of jeans he'd ever seen, which could double as bikini bottoms, a three-button shirt knotted in the front, and looked like a chic version of Daisy Duke.

Mitch whistled. Prissy struck a pose, and Bree rolled her eyes. "Being in the same room with two beautiful women makes this my lucky day."

"Quite. However," Prissy said with her hands on her hips, "I'm only here to inspire and direct the cleaning because, with all this mess, my culinary career is on the line." Bree cringed.

Mitch finally realized the differences in the cousins' priorities; Prissy's enormous kitchen was designed for efficiency and functionality, with the best commercial appliances. While Bree owned the best commercial cleaning equipment, with the dings in the cart, she used it frequently. What a paradox. It would be fun figuring out these two ladies.

Bree swept her hand toward the front of the cart. "I have everything, but I will lean on your expertise since you're the specialist. What should we do first?"

"We'll vacuum up the powder from the walls and floors as much as possible. Unfortunately, the particulates will settle overnight, so we'll repeat this process tomorrow. Then we spray the smoky areas with my secret solution and wipe it off. Newspapers work best on the windows, and the other surfaces are cleaned as usual."

"Sounds good. Tell me why you used so much extinguisher powder to put out a simple frying pan fire?" Bree asked.

"The trigger got stuck and nearly emptied the canister before I could unjam it. That's the third one this month that's done it. I'll take it back to the station and have the maintenance crew look at it. Maybe they can figure out the reason for the malfunction, and then I'll contact the manufacturing company."

"Which company made it?" Prissy asked.

"SEcure Well," Mitch said.

Bree's eyebrows scrunched together as she stared at Prissy. "I'd like to see the extinguisher, please."

"Sure. I'll go get it."

He returned to be greeted by Prissy, Bree, and a large man who didn't speak to him. Bree took the extinguisher. "Thanks. Come with us, Mitch."

They walked from the kitchen into what he assumed to be Bree's office. The spacious room was divided into three zones: her office, which held a large antique desk surrounded by wall-to-wall bookshelves; a modified lab space; and a cozy seating area in front of a large fireplace. She headed to the lab area and positioned the canister underneath a tall, lighted magnifying lamp. "Look here. A piece of wax is lodged between the trigger handle and the canister opening. Joe, see if you can remove it."

The man used very slender, long-nose pliers to remove the wax. "There's something else here. It looks like a BB. I can't get to it without breaking the trigger housing. Mitch, do you mind if I break it?"

"No, go ahead." Mitch watched him take it apart as Prissy videoed everything on her phone.

Joe performed the surgery under 'hushed scrutiny'. He lifted out a tiny metal ball for all to see. "Bree, this wedged the trigger open so the canister would empty its contents. It's been sabotaged."

"You said this was the third one this month that discharged this way?" Bree asked, turning her serious gaze on Mitch.

"Yeah. We got new fire extinguishers three weeks ago from SEcure Well, and I brought this one home to test. What's going on?"

Bree took out her phone and photographed the partial tag attached to the canister's neck, as well as the letters scribbled on it. She enlarged it. "Prissy, can you read this?"

"Looks like NW."

"That's what I thought. Joe, do you concur?"

"Definitely."

I hate being ignored. "What is NW?" Mitch asked, waving at Bree to get her attention.

"It should be the inspector's name, and the numbers on the tag indicate that this one was produced in Beaufort, North Carolina. Joe, get a crew over there to do a complete investigation and update me ASAP." Joe nodded and walked out of the lab, talking on his phone.

"Mitch, we need to talk to Hank," Bree said.

"He's off today and won't be in until tomorrow's second shift. I don't understand what's going on. What do you know about fire extinguishers?"

She nodded. "By then, we should have more information. Let's clean the kitchen, and Prissy and I will explain."

MITCH PICKED HIS jaw off the floor. "You *own* SEcure Well? Wow. So, you were dressed like a mad scientist because you develop safety products?"

"Uh… Uh-huh. I'm working on a unique concept now, and if I can get it to work properly, it will revolutionize commercial smoke alarm systems—"

"Unfortunately," Prissy interrupted, "there have been some product development leaks. *"Miraculously,"* she used air quotes, "our competitors introduced identical items into their lines at a lower price before we could put them in our catalog or on the website. Fire extinguishers are the backbone of our fire safety line. If they fail to work properly, the public will lose trust in our products. This is very serious."

"Prissy's right. The fire safety line is losing money, and we're suing one company for industrial espionage in court. However, resolving the issue may take years. Any rumors or stories from investigative reporters about faulty fire extinguishers could damage our reputation, causing our stock to plummet and potentially leading to bankruptcy." Bree used a large dry microfiber mop to wipe the walls. Periodically, the dust would kick up, and they would cough.

"My new smoke detection system will get us back on track if it remains secret and our security teams catch these culprits. For now, we will continue like we normally do and go on the offensive, hoping no one is aware that we know about the tampered extinguishers." Bree pointed her finger at Mitch. "I am relying on you not to say anything, not even at the station."

"Of course. It's in mine and every firefighter's interest to solve this mystery."

"Thank you for bringing this to our attention, Mitch, even if my kitchen had to become a disaster area," Prissy said. She picked up a handheld compact vacuum cleaner and ran it across the countertops and the stove. Within a few seconds, the filter was full and had to be dumped.

Mitch winced. "Sorry about the mess. I'm also intrigued by Bree's inventions and would love to hear all about them."

"Perhaps one day." Bree shifted the conversation from espionage to more friendly topics. "How long have you been a firefighter, and did you know Dirk before now?"

"We went to East Carolina University at the same

time, majoring in Criminal Justice. He focused on emergency management while I concentrated on fire investigation. We roomed together during our junior and senior years, and while he moved home after graduating, I worked at a Greensboro fire station for five years. We kept in touch, and when there was an opening here, I jumped at the chance to complete my certification in arson investigation. Now, Dirk is my supervisor until I take the exams."

Mitch climbed a tall stepstool, then gently moved a vacuum tool brush across the ceiling. "I came a few times to see Dirk over the summers, but he never introduced me to you two."

Prissy huffed. "That was his stuck-up phase. I think he was jealous that Bree and I spent more time with Brandon and ignored him. Just because I'm two years younger than Bree, he always called me a baby." She lifted the stove's burner grates, sprayed cleaner everywhere, then vigorously rubbed the surface.

"Well, the baby has grown up. Does he ignore you now?"

Bree snorted. "No matter how much she tries to get his attention, he doesn't give her the time of day, and it drives her crazy. She's been in love with him for years."

Prissy smirked. "One day, he'll come to his senses. Until then, I'm having fun, so it's his loss."

"Dirk's a good guy, but guys can be clueless. I know I am."

Bree and Prissy laughed as they worked. Mitch told stories from the firehouse and about the people he met on the job. Prissy worked without complaint, carefully dismantling the professional appliances and fixtures, then showed Bree how to clean each area before reassembling them.

"Is there anything you *can* cook, Bree?" Mitch asked.

"Well…" She stood to her full height, which brought her close to his eye level, and pondered the question. "I can use the toaster oven. It has a timer." She looked toward Prissy and shrugged before continuing, "One day, I want to master the microwave and the stove, but as Hank suggested, I need supervision and a comprehensive manual to study." Prissy vigorously nodded. "Realistically, my time and expertise are needed elsewhere, and Prissy is too busy to instruct me."

"I might be persuaded to show you a few things." Mitch grinned. "Firefighters take turns fixing dinners for the crew, so I've picked up the basics, and I promise to supervise you if you like… that is, if Prissy lets us."

"That's sweet." Bree glanced at Prissy. "If you have the time, I'll take you up on it, but you may regret offering."

He patted her hand in reassurance, and she grinned.

Mitch turned to Prissy and swallowed hard. "Uh… are you serious about raising chickens out back?"

"Of course. I hope to raise enough of them to become the star ingredient in my chicken dishes. I intend to make Bresse chicken *the* standard for chicken, just as connoisseurs have made Wagyu the standard for beef. I will become the Bresse culinary queen." Prissy threw her arms wide in a dramatic flair.

"But, they smell, and they peck, and they… they fly. Aren't you worried about them taking out someone's eyes?"

"Hardly. I don't foresee entering the poultry business, except to have enough chickens to create a demand for my future restaurant. I'll only raise twenty-five or thirty here, and later, move them to a proper facility overseen by a manager and crew. They are, after all, the most delicious-tasting chicken in the world."

"That sounds… delicious." *How big would a coop need to be for thirty chickens?* His breathing was shallow but rapid. "About tonight, when we stop for lunch, I'll take care of the party plans, and you show up at about seven, okay?"

"Sounds great," Prissy said.

MITCH INITIALLY THOUGHT that being in one room with two beautiful women was terrific. However, when Prissy and her entourage appeared carrying a cake, he was dumbstruck. They were all dressed fit to kill in short, tight dresses and stacked sandals. Prissy introduced her friends to Mitch, and in turn, he introduced the firehouse men to the women. They were knockouts, but they weren't Bree, not even close. He looked behind them, trying to find her. "Where's Bree?"

"I'm not sure she'll make it. She got a phone call just as we were leaving to walk over. Business. It's always business, and I'm glad she handles it all. She gets so engrossed in it, and it bores me to tears." Prissy strutted over to the sound system and cranked up the music. Beer and wine were handed out, and impromptu dancing began.

Mitch handed the grill honors to one of the guys and headed to Bree's house.

"Knock, knock. Bree? It's Mitch. I'm coming in." He found her in the dining room with Joe, looking at pages of documents. "Hey. I know you've been working, but it's time to take a break and have some fun. I'm here to walk you next door."

"Are you going to be her escort for tonight?" Joe's deep voice caught Mitch by surprise.

"If Bree would like me to be. What do you say? Want to be my date tonight?"

"Joe, I don't think it's a good idea. Thanks, Mitch, but I should finish some work before I go to bed."

"She would be pleased to go with you." Joe faced Bree, stony-faced. "Go, have some fun. Mitch and I will talk while you get ready." Joe pulled her out of the chair and led her toward the staircase.

"When did you become so bossy? Okay, I'm going. I'll be down shortly, Mitch."

Joe motioned for Mitch to sit. "Since you know about Bree's company, you should also know that her security has increased. Given the fire extinguisher sabotage and other incidents, we must assume she is at personal risk until the company returns to normal. Here's my business card. Call me if you ever need me."

Mitch took the card for Joe Bell, Assistant Chief of Security, SEcure Well, and tucked it into his wallet.

Minutes later, Bree appeared wearing black slacks, a white, short-sleeve cotton sweater set, and ballet flats. She had pulled her hair above her ears into clips, leaving it to fall gently along her shoulders, exposing a porcelain neck adorned with a gold necklace that held a pendant with multiple emeralds, which matched her eyes.

Mitch stared. Compared to the other women at the party, she was perfection. "That was quick. You're even more beautiful without the lab gear."

Bree blushed, and Joe hid his grin.

"One last thing, Bree. Here's a new piece of technology—to be worn at all times." Joe placed a black silicon watch on her wrist. "It's equipped with a GPS that transmits constantly, and four action stems. Press this stem to automatically record any conversation, which is then transmitted back to us. And this one is a built-in silent alarm that's speech-activated by the word

Xena. Press the stem now and say 'Xena.'"

"As in Xena, the Warrior Princess?" Bree asked.

"Of course. She's your favorite character, so you'll never forget. If you say 'Xena,' we come running. Literally, I'm just a word away." Joe patted her hand.

"Xena."

"Now it's activated."

Mitch snickered. "Wow. Bree has a fantasy heroine. Do you dress up like her? Because I would pay money to see that." He ducked just in time as a coaster flew past his head. "So, Joe, what do the other two watch stems do?"

"They set the time and the calendar." Bree swatted Joe's arm for being cheeky, which caused Joe to crack a smile. "I'll be here when you drop Bree off before midnight."

"Or she turns into a pumpkin?" Mitch asked.

Joe crossed his arms over his broad chest and lowered his voice. "Or armed security crashes your party."

Bree rolled her eyes, and Mitch sobered.

THE PARTY WAS in full swing when they arrived. Bree thought her heart would beat out of her chest. *There are so many people I don't know. I shouldn't be here.* Teams were playing cornhole, couples were dancing, and food was coming off the grill in massive quantities. People found places to eat standing up, sitting in lawn chairs, or around the fire pit. Each guest had contributed to the enormous cache of food covering the long table: hot dogs, hamburgers, shrimp skewers, steak bites, potato chips, popcorn, and other items Bree couldn't identify.

It was the most festive party she'd ever been invited to. In fact, this was only her third adult party before her thirtieth birthday that wasn't geeked out. Perhaps she should consider this time an opportunity to expand her knowledge of social interactions. She studied exchanges between males and females, as well as the interactions between females, and the behaviors of the male species. Their body language indicated who was on the make and who was there only to have a good time. Fascinating.

Mitch poured her a beer from the tap before escorting Bree around the backyard.

"Heey… Mitch." The synchronized, singsong voices came from blonde, modelesque twins who had to be six feet tall. They wiggled their fingers at him.

"Sherry. Berry. Good to see you two. Have fun tonight."

"Part of your fan club?" Bree's stomach quivered at Mitch's deep laugh.

"Nah. Most of the firefighters have dated those two… in fact… I did the last time I visited Dirk, about a year ago. They're hot but too hot for me to handle. I ran like a rabbit." He shook his head and laughed at himself. "I'm more of a take it slow, cuddly kind of a one-woman guy, not a—"

"I get your drift. Let's get a hot dog." Bree blushed.

"Sure. I bet guys are just knocking down your door, and you have to use Joe and Bob to beat them off."

She snorted like a pig. "Hardly. I'm not like Prissy."

"Don't be modest. You're the hottest woman I've ever seen, and with the perfect equipment. Maybe you need the right guy who can show you how to use it."

"Do you *ever* filter what comes out of your mouth?"

Mitch laughed, sneakily putting his arm around her

as they walked.

"The short answer is, 'no.' It's part of my irresistible charm." He shrugged. "People come to expect it."

"That'll take some getting used to," she said.

"I think you're already used to it, and you're glad I live next door to keep you on your toes… *I'm* certainly glad I live next door to you."

"Are you Irish? Because you're slinging the blarney, and I know blarney when I hear it."

"Bree, you're priceless." He swooped in and hugged her to him like a pillow. His hard chest could have crushed her, but instead, he fit to her like a glove—one that smelled of sage, citrus, and all Mitch. If she could bottle it, she'd be a millionaire again. Maybe she was in the wrong business.

Mitch introduced her to the guys from his fire station. Although she didn't recognize all of them, everyone knew who she was… the "fire starter." They made little jokes and teased her while she quietly stood among them, smiling at their banter, her face growing hotter and hotter. Being the center of attention was mortifying, made worse because Prissy chimed in, laughing at all their teasing.

She didn't have any comebacks, so she stood there until Mitch realized her discomfort and steered her away to get a beer and more food. "You know, they wouldn't tease you if they didn't like you. But if it bothers you, tell them to go pound sand."

"You're repeating two of the most classic phrases in response to bullying—I've heard them all. I used to be teased unmercifully in high school and college for being 'brainiac red'. I thought it would get better when I got older, and other people matured. Perhaps I shouldn't think this way, but I want to even the score."

"How?"

"I'll think about it." She raised her left eyebrow,

and the corners of her mouth turned up.

The music ramped up as the guys hooted and hollered. Bree turned to find that Prissy had removed her shoes and gotten up on one of the tables to dance. It prompted her to sing, and immediately, the booing began because, sadly, Prissy couldn't carry a tune in a bucket.

Laughter erupted, and Bree felt humiliated for Prissy's sake. She looked at Mitch, her eyes silently pleading for help. He understood and started singing the happy birthday song at the top of his lungs, weaving through the other guys and elbowing them in the ribs to join in.

"*Happy birthday to you, dear Prissy. Happy birthday to you.*"

Dirk magically appeared with sparklers to add to the cake. Prissy was helped off the table, squealing in delight. She grabbed the sparklers to make air designs. When they fizzled out, she dropped them into the trash can of water Dirk handed to her.

"Come on, everyone, let's eat birthday cake." Prissy cut slices and served everyone without a second thought.

Steve Chambers moved close to Prissy, holding an object in each hand behind his back. "I have a birthday gift for you, but you must choose. Left hand or right?"

Prissy squealed again. "Right hand."

He brought his right hand around and squirted her with silly string, then immediately squirted her with men's shaving cream from his left hand. Prissy ran away from him, screaming. Steve chased her around the yard as everyone yelled for him to douse her. He did.

Bree was mesmerized. She watched the silly string project thin, colorful strings in semi-solid streams away from the can while the shaving cream's foam expanded over a wide surface. What if the two could be combined? Interesting. She watched until all the string and foam had been exhausted, and the entire yard, including Prissy, wore the combination. *Time to go. I don't want to see how she handles this.*

Bree turned her back on the melee, faced Mitch, and yawned. "I've had fun tonight, but I have a busy day tomorrow. It's pumpkin time."

"Come on, I'll walk you home," Mitch said.

Joe opened the door before they got to the porch. "Right on time."

"Joe, I need two cases of silly string and at least a case of five different kinds of men's shaving cream brought to my laboratory as soon as possible. Can you do that?"

"I'll get on it right away. Is Prissy behind you?"

"No. The party is still going on. Leave the door unlocked."

"Not my problem. She knows the rules, and my top priority is you, Bree."

"She's going to be angry if you lock her out. It's her birthday, Joe."

"I'm sure she had a great birthday. She'll be fine."

"Well, it's your head, and I'm staying out of it," Bree said as he retreated into the hallway, giving her some privacy. "Tonight was fun, Mitch. Thanks for dragging me out."

"I'm glad you came. I'll see you tomorrow morning to finish cleaning, and I'll bring breakfast if you make some coffee."

"That could be a problem… Prissy only lets me use the single-serving coffee machine." Bree looked around and whispered, "But she just bought a new espresso machine. I'd love for you to show me how to use it, so take your pick. I'll supply the coffee."

"Sure thing. See you about eight." He kissed her on the cheek and retreated.

Bree leaned her back against the door, touching the place where Mitch had kissed her. *Just a friendly kiss. Nothing more. I don't think I'll wash my face until the morning.*

Chapter 3

AS IT WAS his habit never to be late, Mitch arrived fifteen minutes early, looking the same as he had the day before. He carried his five-gallon bucket of tools in his left hand and in his right, another five-gallon bucket containing a small breakfast picnic. He managed to use his elbow to ring the doorbell and was surprised to see another security man, about forty years old, dressed in all black, open the door.

"Mitch, I presume. Please come in. Bree will be down shortly." He led Mitch to the dining room, where the table was set for four people. "I'm Bob Turner, Bree's chief of security. Since you're here, I'd like to take your fingerprints as a precaution."

Mitch flinched but nodded. *Overkill?*

On a side table, Bob had set up a wireless digital system, similar to the one used by the TSA to screen future passengers. Mitch placed both hands on the pad and then individual fingers after completing the initial scan. The prints were downloaded, and within a minute, a bell chimed, and a green light flashed.

"You've been vetted, which makes my job much easier. Since you will be in Bree's company, I'd like you to wear a watch like hers." He lifted his wrist, showing a larger version. "It's for her safety, and I would feel better knowing that when you're with her, there are other eyes on her."

"Of course, but I can't wear it at work."

"Noted. The code word for Bree is Xena, while Prissy's code word is Rambo."

Mitch snickered. "I get the Warrior Princess, but Rambo?"

"Just like she'll detest this watch, Prissy detests Rambo movies, so it's perfect," Bob said.

Bree walked into the dining room dressed in cleaning clothes. "Whatever you brought smells fantastic. Bob, would you pour us some juice? If Mitch shows me how to make coffee, we can eat in a few minutes." Bob nodded and headed to the kitchen.

Mitch leaned into Bree to kiss her cheek, "Mornin' sunshine."

"You are such a flirt. I'm sure you act like this with every woman you encounter, so I'll ignore your shenanigans."

"I believe you are mistaking me for some of your other gentleman friends." He smiled broadly. "However, I need coffee. Come on. We'll read the manual together." She laughed as he reached for her hand, and she pointed at the black watch.

"Looks like Bob put you on the payroll. You don't need to accept any responsibility for me, but if you wear it willingly, I'm grateful. Thank you."

BREE, BOB, AND Mitch had nearly finished cleaning

the kitchen as Prissy entered wearing jogging pants, an oversized gray T-shirt with Dirk Sullivan's name over the firehouse's logo, wedge sandals, and carrying a grocery bag stuffed with a multi-stained dress. Her hair jutted out in disarray, with bits of silly string still evident. She headed straight for Bob and poked him in the chest.

"I celebrated my birthday last night, and Joe locked me out of the house. I had to crash on Dirk's couch. *His couch.* Joe is on my shit list, and I'm not fond of you for setting those stupid curfews. We are grown women, and I have an active social life. Midnight during the week and one in the morning on the weekends aren't working for me, so I'm telling you to change it!"

"I can't do that. Bree's life may be in danger. By default, yours may be as well. Until everything is cleared up, it has to stay this way."

Bree ducked her head, knowing she was the real target of Prissy's anger.

"You can order them to stop this. I'm not like you, Bree. I have needs. I have a life, and I want to control it. Do something, because if you don't, I'll move out." Prissy crossed her arms over her chest.

"Gentlemen, would you excuse us for a few minutes?" Bree pulled Prissy into the dining room and lowered her voice. "Please, be reasonable. You're an owner, and you need protection too... I understand you're frustrated with the restrictions of living here, but hopefully, it will only be for a short time. Try to be patient. A lot is riding on this."

"You have no idea about life. You don't date." Prissy's voice got louder. "You don't have to be seen or mingle with the right people, like I do. You're insulated so tightly in an unrealistic cocoon that I'm surprised you know what year it is. This isn't fair to me, and if you think I need protection, tell me why no one knew where I was last night."

"We knew," Bob said as he and Mitch entered the dining room. "I had two men positioned outside Dirk's house all night, and they signaled me when you were heading home. Unfortunately, I had to pull those two men from another job to watch you. Right now, I don't have the manpower to keep you under surveillance after curfew."

"I'll give you a week to hire and train my security team because that's the only way this will work," Prissy snapped back.

Bob looked at Bree, and she nodded. "I'll get on it this afternoon. Until things are settled, though, you'll need to wear this tracking watch." He handed Prissy a stainless steel and gold-tone watch. "It's waterproof, so you can wear it in the shower."

Prissy groaned. "At least it's not hideous like the one Bree's wearing. Don't look at me like that, Bob. She never wears a watch, and you and Mitch are wearing something similar. I may be a chef, but I've got eyes. Just show me how it works."

Bob demonstrated the functions. "Your code word is 'Rambo.' If you say it, the cavalry will come to your rescue."

Prissy rolled her eyes. "Fine. I'll take a long, hot shower and a nap before I get ready for my catering job this evening. This kitchen better be ready by three o'clock to use… and stay out of my way!"

THE FOLLOWING AFTERNOON couldn't have been sunnier for Mitch. There was a spring in his step, and

Bree was the reason. He entered the fire station wearing the standard uniform of black utility pants and a Station 18 T-shirt, eating the last few bites of an extra-stuffed burrito, and sipping an iced tea from Taco Bell. Steve held his hand up to stop him in the engine bay. "You're wearing sour cream."

Mitch stared down at the blob on his shirt and laughed. "Some days, I don't get to taste the sour cream. Today I got everything but this dollop." He scooped it up and sucked it off his finger. "It's my lucky day."

"I hope you have a clean shirt before Hank-the-hammer sees you."

"Good point. I'd better grab my gym bag. Be right back." Mitch finished his dinner and dropped the remains in the nearest garbage can. He hurried to change, knowing that he had to get things ready for Bree.

Bree. She was like fresh air—clueless to her beauty, sweet, intelligent, and fun to be around—without demanding anything from him. Fortunately, his month's evening shifts had ended so he could work when she worked and spend long evenings with her. Thinking about her and seeing her in the station would be the highlight of this twelve-hour shift.

Steve followed him into the lockers. "You know, Prissy is one firecracker."

"She's something, all right. What happened last night after I walked Bree home? When I returned, Prissy was gone, and the yard looked like a food bomb had exploded."

Steve snickered. "Prissy grabbed the birthday cake and threw it at me, but hit Dirk in the face with it." He let out a deep laugh. "Dirk grabbed me by the shirt, and I knew I was in for a pummeling, but Erik and Randy picked up the cooler filled with ice water and dumped it over the three of us. I've never heard a girl scream like that—like the cross between an air raid siren and a banshee… Prissy's dress left nothing to the imagination, so Dirk pulled a Houdini with the plastic tablecloth and wrapped it around her as he walked her into the house. Then the party broke up, and we all went home." Steve rubbed his chin thoughtfully. "I'm glad I don't have to see Dirk for a few days. Maybe he'll cool off by then."

"No, you're dead meat. When you least expect it, his retribution will be epic. I'd sleep with both eyes open." Mitch slapped Steve on the back and headed to Hank's office.

He knocked on the door before poking his head inside, seeing papers strewn over the desk. "Hey, Captain. I'd like to speak to you. Is now a good time?"

Hank Morgan motioned for Mitch to enter his office and close the door. He didn't stand up from behind his desk but signaled for Mitch to sit in the only chair that wasn't covered with gear samples and catalogs.

"Looks like it's time to do an inventory of all the worn and damaged items needing replacement. At my last station, we had company reps demonstrate new products that we added to our gear. I'd be happy to give you some recommendations."

Some items could be bought immediately, while others were too expensive and were put on a wish list for the county and generous sponsors to fulfill. It was a tedious process, but that was part of the job. Hank nodded. "Good to know. I hate going through catalogues and the paperwork. It's always the paper-work that's the killjoy." Hank stretched his back and took a long sip of coffee.

"I'm glad you stopped in, Mitch. Since you're living next door to Bree Kelly, I thought you might want to know more about her. She and her cousin Prissy own SEcure Well, the company that makes our fire safety products. Our station is named after her grandfather, Stanley E. Well, who provided the money to build it."

"Interesting."

"There's more. She's… weird."

Mitch cleared his throat. "Excuse me?"

"Her full name is Enya Brianne Kelly. Get this, her first name means, wait for it… 'fire.'" Hank snorted. "Perhaps her parents knew she was a fireball waiting to happen… Have you ever seen red hair that color? It's like it could instantly burst into flames." Hank laughed as if he'd made a great joke. "Meeting her, you'd think she'd have a terrible temper, but instead of freaking out, she's docile and easily manipulated. No wonder her cousin, Prissy, gets away with everything she pulls."

Hank shook his head and continued, "I guess the only reason her security takes her seriously is that she pays them well. There's no telling when she's going to burn her house down or blow it to kingdom come with those inventions of hers. If I were you, I'd stay as far away from her as you can. Now, what is it you wanted to talk to me about?"

Mitch's heart raced, and his blood pressure rose while trying not to explode. "Captain, I appreciate your honesty, but I will only say this once. When you're in Miss Kelly's presence, I expect you to act like a gentleman, and if I ever hear you speak negatively about her again in my presence, I'll report your actions to the Fire Chief."

Mitch walked to the door before turning to address his superior. "Miss Kelly will be here shortly to test our fire extinguishers, which her company manufactured, and since there isn't anything going on in the classroom, I'll set everything up there. And she'd like to speak to you afterward."

The captain's cursing echoed through the closed door as Mitch walked away.

He willed himself to calm down before he called Bree. "Hey, Barista Bree, everything will be ready for you when you get here. I'll find the fire extinguishers from SEcure Well, track down the purchase invoices, and Hank will be available to talk. Could you also bring me some of Prissy's delicious triple chocolate espresso cake? Hello? Bree?"

Click.

Mitch snickered. *She's so much fun to tease.*

It took him less than an hour to gather everything for Bree's crew to examine. While he worked, he thought about Hank's snide comments, which angered him even further—she was so much more than Hank or anyone knew, and now he was determined to learn more.

Bree, Bob, Joe, and two other SEcure Well men arrived carrying large black plastic cases. Dressed in a black pantsuit and flats, Bree carried in a large turquoise box with Prissy's catering company logo stamped in gold.

"Miss Kelly, it's nice to see you." Hank reached out to take the box, but she pulled it away from him.

"Uh, sorry, this is for Mitch… as requested. Whether he shares it with anyone else will be up to him."

"Thanks, Bree." Mitch accepted the box gleefully. "Please tell Prissy the guys on duty thank her too. I'll just put this in the break room with a note not to touch it until I say so."

"Good luck with that. Everyone knows that box. By the time you get there, there won't be anything left… I might also sneak a bite," Steve said, moving next to Mitch.

"In that case, I'll hang on to it until Bree's finished."

Hank motioned for Steve to move along as the rest of the group walked toward the classroom.

Mitch turned back to Bree. "You didn't bring any of that gourmet coffee to go with the cake, did you?" Joe snickered and got the evil eye from Bree. "Never mind. I'll drink the swill we brew here."

"Oh, for Pete's sake. Joe, can you grab that thermos in the backseat? Mitch is so needy."

Mitch sidled in close to speak privately. "You're very thoughtful. I bet you made the coffee. Didn't you?" She blushed. She'd taken copious notes as he had walked her through the steps for using the machine, and had no doubt committed them to memory.

"Yes, but," she leaned into him and whispered, "Prissy was home, so Joe supervised."

He whispered back, "One day you'll make it just for me… it'll be so good." He winked at her, and her cheeks flamed.

Mitch led the team to the classroom, where Hank stood waiting. A dozen fire extinguishers had been laid out over four tables. Each SEcure Well member put on latex gloves and went to work. Bob passed out plastic evidence bags and took photos of each canister before, during, and after the surgery. Whoever tampered with the canisters had put a lot of time and effort into figuring out how to do it.

Steve had followed Mitch up the stairs and waited beside him to watch what was going on. "I assume the men in black work for Bree. Right? What kind of sneaky stuff are they doing?"

"They're checking out our fire extinguishers."

"I can see that. Why?"

"It beats me. Maybe a routine check."

"Uh-huh. I smell something stinky."

Hank lifted his chin at Steve and tilted his head toward the door for him to leave. Hank closed the door and joined Bree. "What's all this about, Miss Kelly?"

"I'm sorry that this is official business, Captain, but it's possible that the firehouse received several faulty fire extinguishers. My team will examine the ones you have, and we'll replace any defective ones. Hopefully, it won't take too long."

Bree turned and walked toward Mitch. He directed her to a chair and handed her a file folder. She scrutinized the paperwork while the men discovered that every canister was defective and bore partial tags with the inspector's initials, "NM," scrawled across them. Bob and Joe boxed up the defective canisters and replaced them with newly inspected ones carrying authentic tags.

Bree turned to Hank. "I think it would be better to speak in your office. Mitch, I'd like for you to join us, too." Hank's right eyebrow rose.

Mitch trailed behind Bree, Bob, and Joe to Hank's office in silence, then closed the door. "What did you find out?"

"All of the fire extinguishers came from a group that shouldn't have passed an inspection. These could have been life-threatening if Mitch hadn't shown me the canister used to put out the fire in my kitchen. He should be commended for being proactive, and I intend to write to the county fire chief and the mayor about his actions." Hank's eyes widened, speechless.

"Currently, we're tracking every canister in that manufactured group before any problems arise. I assure you that each one will be located and replaced. Captain, you have my phone number, and this is my chief of security's card, Bob Sullivan. Please call either of us if you need anything or have issues with any of our products. Do you have any questions?"

"No, but I appreciate your commitment to correcting this situation. If I can help in any way, let me know." Bree nodded and then stood. He extended his hand to shake hers and the other men's hands before they walked out of the office.

Mitch followed Bree and her contingency to their cars. "Why didn't you tell Hank about the sabotage?"

"The less he knows, the better. We don't want the person who did this to find out we're on to him. Any well-meaning conversation can quickly turn into damaging gossip that can spread around the world, potentially tipping off our guy, and consequently, our stock will plummet. If that happens, we may never find out what's happening or who's behind all this."

"That makes sense. Did you ever find the inspector?"

"There's no inspector with the initials NM at the plant. We'll have to dig a little more, but my team will find him. Thanks, Mitch, I owe you."

He smiled. "Since you owe me, I'll see you early for breakfast after my shift ends." He shut her door and waved her off.

Chapter 4

MITCH KNOCKED ON Bree's kitchen door, holding a dozen assorted doughnuts. He could see her sitting at the kitchen table, eating a bowl of cereal. The door was unlocked, so he walked in.

In front of her were five different cereal boxes, all high in sugar and typically designed for children. One contained dehydrated marshmallows, another sugar-coated fruit, another strawberry puffs, and another was chocolate.

"I see you like the breakfast of champions… do you mix them or eat them individually?"

Bree didn't look up or acknowledge his presence. He moved closer, but her eyes were closed. She was sleep-eating. This was a first. Should he talk to her, or should he leave her alone? Would she choke? *What should I do?*

Bob quietly entered the kitchen and placed his index finger over his mouth to silence Mitch, then motioned for him to follow him into the hallway.

Mitch pointed his thumb over his shoulder. "That's not normal, is it?"

"It is when she has a lot on her mind and works

through the night. I keep an eye on her so that she doesn't choke. I'll give her five more minutes before walking her to her bedroom and letting her sleep for a few hours. We have a long day ahead, and based on the information that comes in, Bree might want to visit some of the warehouse facilities, which means a road trip. Why don't you come back for lunch?"

Mitch nodded, then tiptoed out. He wished he could stay, but she had Bob and Joe to look after her. He snagged two cream-filled doughnuts and a jelly-filled one, leaving the rest in the box on the countertop. He ate two donuts before walking through his back door into the kitchen. He grabbed a carton of milk, poured a glass, and carried it and the other doughnut to his bedroom. When everything was consumed, he fell onto bed with his phone alarm set for noon. Before long, he dreamed of cartoon characters dancing around Bree's cereal bowl, throwing pieces into her mouth while her eyes were closed.

A CRACK AND a resounding boom woke Mitch, not his alarm. He sat up, realizing it was thunder and lightning, and that it was raining cats and dogs. He had slept for about three hours. He yawned, stretched, and flexed his left wrist, wincing at the arthritic ache. His hand and wrist were swollen, and his fingers were stiff. He massaged it, took a pill, and hopped into a hot shower.

Nothing seemed to alleviate the ache, not even ice—he faced a long, painful shift because of the low barometric pressure. Mitch repacked his duffel bag, adding a large bottle of acetaminophen and a black elastic glove with Velcro straps that could be tightened around his wrist. After tossing the bag into his truck, he headed to Bree's house, dressed in yellow rain gear with the Station 18 logo.

"Knock, knock. Coming in."

"Hey, Mitch. Missed you for breakfast, but you're just in time for lunch." Bree glanced in his direction. "You're soaked. Hang your jacket in the mud room and grab a towel. If you're muddy, take off your shoes. Prissy will make you swab the deck if you ruin her clean floor."

Bob tipped his chin toward Mitch as Bree served large slices of lasagna to him, Joe, and a couple of other men dressed in black uniforms with the SEcure Well logo embroidered on their shirts—all bootless and walking around in their socks.

Mitch stifled a yawn. "This smells amazing. I love lasagna and don't mind helping you eat all this." He leaned closer to Bree, and when no one was looking, he kissed her cheek. "Hey, beautiful. After I got off work, I needed a nap and got my gear ready for my shift in a few hours. I also brought back your thermos."

He held two thermoses, one twice the size of the other. "I'm returning your thermos, and I hope you won't mind if I fill mine up." He gave her a cheeky grin. "Are you having a meeting? I can eat and run, or pack a doggy bag and go?"

Bree snorted. "We're having a meeting, but you might find it interesting. Stay if you like. And I *insist* you eat with us and fill your thermos before you go."

"I'm hooked on your coffee. It's the expensive stuff and would probably cost me half a day's wage, so I'm just going to come over every day and drink yours. That is, if I'm welcome to."

"Of course, but I also *insist* you make enough for Bob, Joe, and me." She grinned.

After everyone had been served, they moved to the dining room. Bree sat at the head of the table with Bob and Joe sitting on her right side, leaving Mitch to sit to her left. Prissy was seated at the opposite end, and beside her sat two guys Mitch had never met, highly focused on using both hands to devour everything in sight. There was little talking except "I need another napkin," or "Pass the tea." Mitch mused that if it had been any quieter, he would have been eating alone.

"Prissy, as always, everything is delicious," Bree said, wiping her mouth with a napkin and placing it on the table. Prissy waved her off. "Does anyone need anything else before we begin? Seconds, thirds, or fourths in Joe's case? We'll start our meeting in five minutes. Cake, cookies, and carafes of coffee are on the table, so help yourself as we talk. Everyone, this is Mitch. He's a firefighter and my next-door neighbor. You may speak freely since Bob cleared him. Joe, please introduce Chris and Roy."

"Mitch, Chris is a surveillance specialist with impressive computer skills, and Roy specializes in electronics and explosives and is a tactical leader during recovery operations, among other things. Generally, Chris and Roy work in the security division of SEcure Well, but they'll be helping us until our problem is solved." Chris and Roy acknowledged Mitch with head nods.

Mitch reached for the saltshaker with his left hand and winced. He flexed his hand and slid the shaker toward his right hand before using it. His movements escaped no one, yet Bree refrained from commenting.

She cleared her throat to start the meeting. "What do we know about the facility with the faulty canisters? Have the surveillance videotapes been helpful? Do we know when they were sabotaged and if there are more?"

"It occurred over a three-day holiday weekend," Chris said. "I've analyzed the videos, and from his height and build, it was a man operating alone. He knew enough to erase the security videos but didn't know about the redundant videos stored in the cloud in case of fire."

"Can you identify him?" Prissy asked.

"Unfortunately, no," Roy said. "He wore a white technician's jumpsuit, ski mask, and blue surgical gloves. His face is distorted, and there are no fingerprints. However, he carried a small black tool bag with the SEcure Well logo on the side, used a forklift to bring down a pallet of canisters at a time, and opened them individually on a table. He took his time figuring out how to disable them, but once he did, it only took about five minutes each. Chris confirmed he tampered with two hundred extinguishers, that we know of."

Mitch whistled.

"Please tell me the fire extinguishers are still in the warehouse," Prissy said.

"I wish I could." Chris grimaced. "Video stamps show that he started this six weeks ago on the front rows of pallets in one section, which were shipped out the next week. Later, he picked random spots in the warehouse to remove the pallets—nothing sequential."

"So, shipments were sent to different regions of the country at different times," Bree said. "He wanted us to feel this for a long time. Can we determine where they went and when?"

Chris looked at his hands. "For most of them. Without going through this facility row by row and matching shipping labels with invoices, we won't know for sure. I've got a team working on the facility's videos to check the pallets, locate the boxes, and track the ones sent out."

"What's the bottom line for this?" Bree asked.

Bob looked from one woman to the other. "We estimate that it will cost about fifteen thousand dollars to fix the problem in this facility. We can't shut it down without alerting the saboteur." He cleared his throat. "Unfortunately, there are four other warehouses to check. Roy, you're up."

"I'll take a small group in on Friday night and work all weekend, putting dummy labels on the ones that have been compromised. They'll be shipped and stored at another location, then we'll send perfect canisters to the customers. The customer will never know. Our perpetrator will think he's done his job, and we'll also install additional video equipment in places that might catch this guy if he decides to pull the same stunt again."

"I've got another team scanning the other facilities' videos, and we'll go back up to a year if we need to," Chris said. "We should know in a couple of days."

Bob picked up the discussion. "Based on Mitch's information and what we know, we believe this man is a company employee. We're doing background checks on every researcher and company executive, but nothing has been flagged. The saboteur may have also stolen company secrets, so we've expanded the list to include those with R&D access and will conduct a more thorough investigation. Finally, we'll increase security around this facility should the perp return."

Joe interjected, "We need to interview supervisors and managers, get their reactions, see what they know. We can conduct this under the guise of a workplace satisfaction survey and gather ideas for improving conditions. Prissy and Bree should be there to validate the cover story. Food would help, too." Prissy sighed as he concluded, "Let's plan this for Friday morning."

"I'm free on Friday," Mitch offered. "I could tour the facility and ask questions from a firefighter's standpoint. Count me in." Bree mouthed, 'Thank you,' and he flashed her a grin.

Everyone turned to face Bree. "It's a good plan, and thank you, Prissy, for making food for us to take." She hesitated for a moment before speaking again. "The Chirp is ready for the next phase of testing, and I need to know who I can trust to work with me. Bob, bring me what you have on the researchers. If you have no further questions, please help yourself to more food while I clean the kitchen. If anyone wants food to go, let me know."

Mitch and the other men stood as Bree exited. He spoke softly to Joe and Bob. "Have you looked into some of the men attracted to Bree? It could be some guy who's not happy with being turned down, or maybe she broke things off, which may have caused all this."

"There aren't any," Prissy said. "Bree doesn't date, and even if she did, no one can get past her body-guards." She looked directly at Bob and then at Joe, scowling.

"That's not true," Joe replied. "One of the re-searchers, and an accountant, asked Bree out. She went out with both a few times. They're at the top of our list." Joe turned to Chris and Roy and spoke softly enough that their conversation wasn't overheard.

Mitch picked up several plates and headed to the kitchen. He rinsed the dishes and put them in the dishwasher while Bree packed plastic take-out contain-ers for the refrigerator and to hand out.

"I'm glad you know how to make yourself at home," she said.

"It's nothing. Prissy cooked, you served and packed up food for me." He flexed his left hand.

"What's up with that?"

"It's from an old baseball injury."

"Don't you mean an old football injury?"

"No, smarty-pants, it's from a college baseball

injury. The happiest day of my life was being selected to pitch at Arizona State University. In my sophomore year, I got hurt, one of those freak accidents where I rounded third base while a runner was going home. He tripped, and I couldn't stop, so we both got caught in a pileup with the catcher. My wrist got stepped on, and two players fell on my arm. I had three surgeries, a year of rehab, and lost my ticket to the major leagues. That was the worst day of my life."

"I'm so sorry to hear that." Her voice conveyed genuine sympathy.

"I can tell the weather from my left wrist. On warm days, the arthritis is hardly noticeable or there's no pain at all, but with rain coming down like today, it hurts like hell."

"Doesn't that limit your firefighting abilities?"

"Some, but thankfully, I'm right-handed, and it's not enough to keep me sidelined. At least, not yet... Besides being charming, I'm also tough and resilient... I'm Batman."

"Don't forget modest and reserved."

Mitch lifted her off the ground and twirled her around. She squealed. Everyone rushed in as Bree slid down Mitch's body, laughing.

Prissy pushed through the security contingent. "Oh, it's you." She huffed and turned back around. The other men cleared their throats. Joe snickered then slapped Bob on the back while he and the others walked away.

Bree and Mitch finished the dishes and cleaned the kitchen. Despite the meeting, it felt like a family meal, and although he'd only known this group for a short time, he felt welcome and at home.

They sat at the kitchen counter, sipping decaf coffee and sharing a slice of carrot cake while chatting. He openly flirted, watching as Bree blushed easily and frequently. He stole a bite of her cake while she tried to keep it to herself. Her easy laugh made his heart sing.

"Hank tried to warn me off you," Mitch said, "but I'm really attracted to women with red hair and green eyes. You have the reddest hair and the greenest eyes I've ever seen, and I'm head over heels for you… Don't laugh. You wound me… Never mind. I'll stop, but you are so much fun to tease.

"With everything going on around you, how do you stay calm? Hank says that for a redhead, you don't have a temper…" She whacked his arm. "Hey, don't hit me… that hurts." He held his arm tightly against his chest and poked his bottom lip out.

Bree hopped off the barstool and crooked her finger for Mitch to follow her to the west wing of the house. Next to Bob's office was a small gym that she told him used to be her grandfather's workroom. A large blue workout mat covered the center, and two big punching bags hung from the ceiling. In the far corner was a weightlifting area, and in the opposite corner, there was a treadmill, a stationary bike, and another machine for arm and leg workouts. She pointed to each section. "I exercise."

Bob popped his head into the doorway. "Don't let Bree fool you. She handles herself well and can be a formidable foe. Long hours of practicing Tai Chi keep her grounded and centered. However, when things become too much, she works out and goes several rounds with either Joe or me. We both have significant bruises to prove she's a fighter." Bree's face turned red.

"So, Xena the Warrior Princess was both accurate and metaphorical. It suits you." Mitch's phone alarm went off. "Rats, I've got thirty minutes to get to the station. I'll grab my doggy bag and thermos and head out."

He and Bree returned to the kitchen in silence.

Mitch gathered his things, and Bree held the door as he walked out.

"This is my last evening of twelve-hour shifts this month, which means I'm off Thursday, Friday, and Saturday. Then, I start daytime twelve-hour shifts on Sunday for a month. My evenings will be free unless they need me to work on something special. If you're not busy, we could hang out together… that is… if you'd like to."

"That would be fun, if you behave."

Mitch raised his hands in surrender. "And go up against Xena? Not a chance." He kissed her cheek before sprinting to his car, then he entered the station with a smile on his face. Bree. He couldn't stop thinking about her.

BREE DIDN'T HAVE time to wonder if Mitch's proclamation of being 'head over heels' for her was the truth. She couldn't figure him out. He was the opposite of every man she'd spent time with. He wasn't geeky, but easygoing, and probably the sexiest man she'd met in the last ten years. The hunky men she employed didn't make her heart flutter or make her interested enough to spend time with them. And that also bothered her. Why would he want to spend time with her? She knew how people talked behind her back, and that most men didn't want to be associated with brainiac women who were also powerful. She needed to stop thinking about Mitch and get back to her work. *Focus, Bree.*

She entered her office and looked at the oil painting of her grandfather hanging above the fireplace.

"Don't remind me, Gramps… the company comes first." *Why did he always scowl at me?* "I know what I need to do. One day, you'll send me a sign that I've made you proud."

She sighed heavily while pacing in front of her desk, from one end of the room to the other, ignoring the pattern her shoes made on the carpet. Bob knocked on the door and entered. "You're going to wear it out."

She didn't smile. "Come in. Everything is weighing heavily on me. I didn't want to say anything at lunch, but when you do the background investigations, please do a deep dive into Prissy's associations."

"You can't mean that!" Prissy stormed in. "I'm not a criminal, and neither are my friends."

"Probably not, but what about the men you've dated recently, or people you've had run-ins with? We can't take the chance."

"This is absurd. I'm already being tracked and can vouch for my friends."

Bree stood ramrod straight and stared Prissy down, her tone solemn, her voice calm and direct. "There's too much to lose, and it's time you act like a responsible adult. You own twenty-five percent of the company. I can't do this alone. We know nothing about your friends, the men you've met, or even your catering clientele. We need to know who came into your life before our research material was stolen and the warehouse was sabotaged. I also need to see if it was my fault." Beneath all Prissy's bravado and bitching, deep down, Prissy wanted to know, too.

"From now on, we must be proactive and cautious, so please don't argue with me on this. The sooner the background checks are completed and we address this issue, the sooner you can return to your life. You *will* cooperate with Bob and Joe and help them create a timeline. Do I make myself clear?" Her chin lifted higher, waiting for the backlash she'd expected.

Prissy rushed to wrap her arms around Bree and then abruptly let go. "You've never spoken to me like this, and I've never known you to be so scared. For me. For you. For the company. I'll do as you say until all this is resolved, but when things are settled… You can kiss my ass."

Bree wiped away a tear and huffed out a laugh. "Deal."

Chapter 5

FRANK LASSITER PARKED his car away from the streetlamp and surveyed the area before getting out. It was nearly eleven o'clock at night, three vehicles were in the parking lot, and things were quiet. He approached the back entrance of the large office building for Guardian Systems, the direct competition for SEcure Well and the company that stole Bree's secret designs. He rang the buzzer and looked up at the camera above the door. It clicked open.

He cautiously walked up the hallway into a small foyer that exhibited photographs of the company's division heads, the CEO, and CFO, surrounded by the words, "Guardian Systems, Your First Line of Defense." The head of security waved him into the CFO's office, then stood outside with his back against the door.

Mark Stokes rose from his seat and motioned for Frank to take one of the club chairs across from the matching leather sofa occupied by the CEO, James Fuller.

"What is so urgent that you'd come here in person?" Stokes demanded before sitting down.

"Station 18 received faulty fire extinguishers, and Bree Kelly took a contingent of men there to inspect their other canisters. The rest were also defective, so she replaced them with new ones. The company has initiated an investigation at the warehouse. Since I wiped the video, it will take months for them to find the additional tampered extinguishers, and they'll panic thinking their other facilities have been sabotaged. This means at least a year of scrutiny before they send out more extinguishers."

Frank wiped his forehead. "Bree will assume other products have been tampered with, leading to a domino effect. With a few well-placed stories, the shareholders will hear and demand Bree's resignation at the annual meeting. I've done what you've asked and now I'm through with all of this."

"Not so fast," said Stokes, holding up his hand. "We need proof that Bree is in a tailspin, because they've not stopped the lawsuits." He paused for effect. "Their *accidents* did nothing to deter them, despite bleeding money on court continuances, and now they've increased their personal security."

"What accidents? Never mind. I don't want to know, and I don't want to be involved."

Fuller stopped puffing on his foul-smelling cigar. "You're already involved, Lassiter. Steady, now. Just do as we say, and your dirty hands won't get filthy." He grinned, raising a glass of amber liquid to his mouth.

Stokes leaned forward to rest his arms on his knees. "You're the CFO. Convince them it's in their company's best interest to drop the lawsuits because we can keep it going for another ten years, but they can't." He spoke slowly and clearly. "Don't forget you also owe us the schematics for the next thing she's working on. When we get that, her company will be finished, and we can buy her out for pennies on the dollar. Until then, you're still on the payroll. Now get out."

The door opened, and Frank practically ran out of the building, regretting ever getting in bed with the people. With the lawsuits and now tampered fire extinguishers, the SEcure Well coffers needed filling, and Bree had to be working on something to handle it. This had to be his final act for Guardian Systems. Maybe Angela could help with that. Eventually, Bree would need her researchers to test items. Yes, Angela would be his best hope. *Dating her wasn't that repulsive, and she's so needy. She'll tell me everything with the right stimulus, just like she did the other two times. It's incredible how the right drugs can make you pliable and then forgetful.* He smirked. If that didn't work, Bree would be his target, but he'd have to find a way to get rid of her guards. *They act more like guard dogs. Maybe a thick juicy steak laced with something.* He laughed out loud at his quip.

Chapter 6

SOMETIME AFTER MIDNIGHT, Station 18 received a call reporting a fire behind the supermarket off Highway 70, involving two of four metal dumpsters sitting side by side. After they were hosed down, Mitch was tasked with scooping out the interiors to ensure that nothing inside was smoldering. Then he was told to climb into the other two dumpsters to check for incendiary devices, specifically, lit firecrackers allegedly tossed in by teenagers cruising the streets.

Mitch swallowed his pride and carried out his job in front of a crowd that included neighborhood watch members, a newspaper photographer, two reporters, and the New Bern TV station. Steve pointed out Mitch to the media and explained what he was looking for. Luckily, after waiting an hour for something to happen, the press finally left Mitch to finish his work, grumbling all the way to their vehicles about the stench they had endured.

Assuming this was his initiation into the 18th, Mitch went along with it. For now.

Four hours later, back at the station, Mitch was barred from crossing the bay door. Steve threw him a black garbage bag and the world's smallest bath towel. "Hose down your gear and let it drip-dry outside. Then drop all your clothes in this bag, including your shoes, before you hit the shower."

Mitch's walk of shame included whistling, taunting, and throwing trash at him. When he reached his locker, he saw that his shampoo was gone. In its place, someone had left him a sliver of Dial soap. He took a long shower, praying that the soap would last, but it disintegrated in his hand. "Dang it." Suddenly, the hot water shut off, and for now, he was destined to stay stinky.

He dried off as best as he could before opening his locker door. All his clothes were gone. "Son of a biscuit eater." Every locker he tried to open was locked, except for one. "I bet Steve did this. One day, Steve. One day."

The last locker belonged to Dirk, and as his housemate, he had taken pity on him... or maybe not. Dirk's duffel bag was inside, containing only a V-neck midriff T-shirt that left most of Mitch's torso exposed, and lightweight running shorts with slits on the sides that opened almost to the waist. At least he could get dressed. Barely. As he walked out the bay door, no one was to be seen. "Cowards," he yelled out, then cringed, hearing the clicking of a cell phone taking photos. "Perfect. Just perfect." He knew that when he returned to the station, the photographs would line the lockers and lounge area like wallpaper.

Pretending it was just another day at work, he picked up the garbage bag of clothes and strolled out of the station barefoot and went commando. He threw the garbage bag in the back of his truck, rolled down the windows, and hung his head out as he drove away. Even he didn't want to smell himself.

At home, he remembered that aside from his two

suits and winter clothes, everything else was dirty. If he timed it right, he could wash a load, have breakfast with Bree, and then start another load while the first one dried. Ten minutes later, he could be back at Bree's house. For the first time in six hours, he smiled.

He carried his laundry to the washing machine but couldn't find any washing powder. He checked the kitchen for dishwashing detergent, and there was nothing, not even the cheap green stuff. Mitch shook his head. He stood to his full height, took a deep breath, and nearly puked. There was only one thing he could do: bring three loaded laundry baskets and the garbage bag to Bree's back door, including his foul-smelling body, and hope it didn't jeopardize their budding relationship.

"Knock, knock. It's me, your friendly next-door firefighter needing your help."

"Come in, Mitch." Bree's smile faded when he remained outside. "What's the matter? Oh my God! You reek. Stay right there, don't you dare come any closer. What happened to you?"

"Grocery store dumpster fires. I had to clear out two, then crawl into two more. Did you know that rotting fruit is slippery? The goo got under my coat and down into my pants. The first time I fell, it was funny. It was so funny when Steve climbed onto the fire truck and filmed it for YouTube. It was also funny as I fought off two rats and hordes of swarming flies the size of hawks. I swatted the blowflies so hard that I knocked off my helmet into a box of rotten tomatoes. Wouldn't you know it, I will probably be on the newspaper's front page and *Good Morning, New Bern.* When I got back to the station, I found maggots in my hair, and somehow, they had gotten into my under-wear. Did my coworkers take pity on me? Of course not. I stank so badly they made me ride to the station hanging off the back of the truck… downwind." He extended his arms wide and sighed. "It's been one of those days… Bree, want a hug?"

Snickering from the dining room erupted into full-blown belly laughter.

Et tu, Bob and Joe? Great.

Bree covered her mouth as her shoulders shook, then she couldn't hold back the laughter. Just when it seemed like the laughter couldn't get any louder or more humiliating, it did. Joe and Bob were clutching their sides as they entered the kitchen.

"It's not funny. Well, maybe in a year or two it might be, but Bree, please take pity on me. I have no clothes to wear. I don't have any laundry detergent, and I need a shower… with a real bar of soap. Bad. Can you help me?"

Bob said, "There should be some tar soap and a scrub brush you can use in the apartment, and while you wash, Bree and I'll handle your clothes. Joe might have something you can wear."

"Thanks, Bob. The really, really, stinky stuff is in the black trash bag outside. I'm not sure if my black boots are salvageable… I might need to burn them. Bree, you're an angel. I'll see you later."

"Thank goodness, Prissy isn't here. You'd be banned forever." Bree yelled as Mitch walked away, four feet downwind from Joe holding his nose. "As soon as you're squeaky clean, you can teach me how to make waffles…"

Mitch followed Joe to the apartment. It wasn't an apartment per se, but a bungalow guest house with three bedrooms, a living room, dining area, full kitchen, and a small office located behind the garage. Between the garage and the bungalow was an unusually shaped swimming pool; a long, narrow lane for laps attached to a rectangular pool that was rounded on the long side. The shape reminded him of something, but he couldn't put his finger on it. He'd figure it out eventually.

Joe entered a six-digit PIN on the keypad and led Mitch inside. Without giving him a tour, he took him to one of the bedrooms and pointed to the bathroom. "Everything you need is in the cabinet under the sink. I'll find a garbage bag for your clothes, then drop it off at the house. In the meantime, I'll loan you some workout clothes and flip flops—they'll be waiting for you on the bed. I'll be back in an hour to get you, 'cause you'll need all that time to de-stink. By the way, you have two maggots in your chest hair and one in your navel." Joe walked away smiling.

As predicted, it took Mitch an hour to get sanitized and dressed. Joe was drinking from a mug of coffee as Mitch entered the kitchen. "Thanks for the clothes. I'll return them as soon as I buy laundry detergent." Joe slid a cup of coffee Mitch's way. "This is a nice apartment. Do you live here?"

"Not all the time. I'm married with two kids, and much like your shift at the fire station, Bob and I usually work twelve-hour shifts that can overlap when Bree needs us for special projects. Unfortunately, over the past year, things have escalated to the point where one of us is always with her, and we've been staying in the apartment or the main house during our shift."

"What kinds of things?"

"Guardian Systems is the company SEcure Well is suing for stealing their industrial products. Their lawyers strongly advised Bree and Prissy to drop the lawsuit. They didn't come out and threaten them, but it was as if they did. Two weeks later, Bree's brake lines were cut while her car was in the driveway. We found out when Prissy stepped into the fluid wearing new shoes. She pitched a fit. Who knew shoes could be that expensive? We confirmed it after the SUV was jacked up. Bree hasn't been allowed to drive since then.

"Then, a week later, Prissy *accidentally* got locked in a walk-in freezer. A long metal spoon blocked the handle. Fortunately, one of her servers heard her beating on the door and yelling out. Otherwise… Now, she always carries a charged phone, and an undercover security agent is present at her catering events."

Joe refilled his coffee cup and sat down on a barstool. "Even though we act as their bodyguards, we're also Bree's companions and sounding boards during normal times. Sometimes, we assist her with the research and development of various products, but mostly we manage the security component of SEcure Well from here. It takes Bob and me to do that and watch Bree. Business is so good that we need to hire another person or ten to handle logistics and management, otherwise I'll never see my family."

"Wow. It sounds like Bree works doubly hard."

"She works too much. Once she can trust her research and development team to handle new projects without leaks, she can focus on her passion projects and let them shoulder the burden. When we catch the SOB sabotaging fire extinguishers and selling secrets, Bree can have a life and finally go on a vacation—she hasn't taken one in two years. She needs a little fun to distract her and keep her sane. So far, you've made her smile, but if I ever find out that you've taken away that smile… I assure you, smelly garbage will be the least of your worries. Are we clear?"

"Crystal, but you don't have to worry about me. Bree's amazing. If I ever act like a douchebag, I'll dump myself in the foulest stench possible."

Joe's face hardened. "That's not all. Bob will be first in a lineup of fifty security men who work for her, and they will take you apart piece by piece."

Mitch swallowed hard. "Um. Sure. Okay. I'll keep that in mind."

MITCH SMELLED ONE armpit, then checked the other, satisfied he was now Irish Spring fresh. He knocked on the kitchen door and walked in, calling Bree's name. Large vanilla-scented candles burned on each countertop. He moved toward the dining room and saw more candles there. Everywhere he looked, vanilla-scented candles were burning. Suddenly, he craved cookies. He called Bree's name again and headed down the hallway. Hearing voices, he followed the sound.

"I should talk with Mitch," Bree said. "Odors get trapped in the clothing fibers and can't be eliminated by detergent alone—he'll need a pretreating spray. I'll make a mixture of washing soda and some oxygen-enriched powder, and for the whites, soaking them in some bleach water will help." She held up a station T-shirt and was eyeing it critically.

"You sound like a commercial," Mitch said.

On a folding table in the laundry room, Bob and Bree had sorted his laundry into three big piles: white, dark, and light.

"Do guys always wash their underwear with their dark clothes?" Bree asked.

"I do," Mitch said. "I've been doing that since college. It saves time and water."

Bree tsked. "It's a terrible habit." She and Bob turned toward Mitch, each wearing a lab coat, goggles, and blue medical gloves. Bandannas covered their noses.

"Do you do everything in that getup?" Mitch asked.

"Only if something's dangerous or might leap out at me," she said.

"Ha, ha. At least you weren't dumpster diving. But I'm thankful for your help and will consider your suggestions. If you want to stop, I'll take over. After all, it's my stinky stuff."

"We've already started the process. The washer and dryer are going, so we can leave long enough for brunch. Prissy bought a new Belgian waffle maker, and I want to make waffles. And bacon. And sausage. And grits. I love grits." Bree was talking faster than usual and looked at Mitch with twinkling eyes. She and Bob peeled off their laundry outfits before washing up in the sink.

"Whoa Nelly. Will Prissy be home?"

Bree whispered, "Yes. But you're supervising me. Right? She can eat, and of course, Bob and Joe will be eating too, so we have to make sure they're edible. Tell me what we need, and I'll take care of it."

In just a few minutes, the countertop was crowded with everything a platoon of hungry Marines would devour. Mitch cleaned the new machine and then plugged it in to heat up. "When the light goes off, it's hot enough to put in the batter." He handed Bree a whisk for the batter, pulled out a skillet for the bacon, and another for scrambled eggs.

Sssssss. Mitch turned to find that Bree had poured the batter into the waffle maker and closed the lid. "Did you spray it first?"

Bree's hands dropped to her hips. "What do you mean, spray it? It's nonstick. Why do you need to spray it before you use it?"

"Even though it says nonstick, assume it isn't and overspray the surface."

"That concept needs further investigation. When I'm not busy, I'll work on developing a genuine nonstick formula for appliances."

"I'll buy stock in it, and together, we'll make millions. Unfortunately, the waffle maker needs to be cleaned, so we'll start over." Mitch unplugged it and then scraped everything into the garbage can.

"Bummer. Okay, show me how to make waffles, and I'll video what you're doing so I can go through it again. Once I perfect the procedure, I'll get inventive with fruit and chocolate chips. Hurry, I'm hungry."

Prissy walked in. "I hope the fire department isn't called this time." She pointed to the mess on the island.

"We've got it covered," Bree said. "If you'll make the coffee and pour juice, we'll be ready soon."

Mitch saw Prissy watching him guide Bree through the task. She didn't speak or give suggestions, but he knew that if he had done anything wrong, she would have yelled at both of them. Instead, she strained to see Bree responding to his instructions like a curious child hanging on to every word. Once Bree completed the task with a big smile, Prissy left the room without saying a word. He wished she had given Bree some praise, but it wasn't to be. Instead, he rewarded Bree with a kiss on the cheek and then turned her loose to make a large batch of waffles.

A few minutes later, Joe entered the kitchen carrying large boxes. "The silly string and shaving cream were just delivered. I'll put them in the lab. What else do you need, Bree?"

"I need an empty room completely covered in plastic, walls, ceiling, and floors. It doesn't have to be a sterile room, so the garage will be perfect. Let's eat in the dining room, and I'll explain."

The group filled their plates and took their usual seats as if they were having a business meeting. "I have an idea for a personal fire extinguisher and will need everyone's help to collect the data. Prissy, remember when Steve chased you around the yard with silly string and shaving cream?"

"How could I forget the most humiliating night of my life?"

"Sorry. I only mentioned it because if we could combine the qualities of silly string and shaving cream with the right chemicals, it could create a unique fire extinguisher that is simple enough for a child to use. It would shoot out of a slender, handheld container like a string, then expand into foam with an environmentally friendly propellant. It would be perfect for use at home, work, in the car, or in the garage. Let's call it The Hot Shot."

Everyone muttered, "I like this idea."

Mitch sat up straighter. "It must be light, easy to direct to a flame, be effective, and inexpensive. If you think you can do all this, I'm ready to help."

"I'll need to analyze the silly string and shaving creams, record data, and create a few prototypes to test on different fires. Mitch will probably call me a mad scientist, given the time and tests required for each stage. This would be a chance to create the next generation of fire extinguishers, small enough to use everywhere."

Smiling, Prissy leaned forward in her chair. "When do we start? I have a lag in my catering business for the next week. I'm on board."

Bree put her hands together. "Thank you, Prissy. As soon as the garage is prepped, we'll begin. I need to research the chemical compositions of our samples and consider which substances would be most effective. How about tomorrow?" Heads nodded. "Fantastic! We'll reconvene at breakfast. I cannot stress enough that this must remain top secret until the canister is developed. Bob, we will need extra security to keep prying eyes out."

"Will do."

The dryer's signal dinged. "Looks like another load is ready. Come on, Mitch, you can take Bob's place while he and Joe prep the garage."

Once they got into a folding routine, Mitch asked, "How did you become the primary owner of SEcure Well?" He'd found out on an internet search that her grandfather, Stanley Everette Well, was a mechanical engineer who revolutionized machine technology and frequently lectured at North Carolina State University, supervising select student projects.

"Gramps was an inventor. He married Eileen O'Donnell, and they had two daughters, Colleen and Brigid. Colleen, my mother, married my father, James Kelly. Brigid was Prissy's mother, and she married Preston Matthews." Bree took a T-shirt from the pile of clean clothes and folded it.

"We never met our grandmother. While Gramps was away on one of his project visits, his house burned down with Eileen inside. He never forgave himself for not taking her with him and swore that if there had been some alarm to wake her, she might have survived. So, his passion became finding practical solutions for putting out all kinds of fires.

"He restored this house into a family home and a lab for his inventions. He also wanted the family to feel comfortable here and encouraged us to come for extended visits because he hated being alone."

"How long have you lived here?"

"Since I was five. My parents died in a car crash, and he did everything he could to make me feel loved. He was my whole world. When I wasn't in school, we were inseparable." She smiled wistfully.

"Gramps was a genius. He gave me real-life problems to solve, and together, we tinkered with various inventions, hoping to find workable solutions. Nothing was off the table. Even though I was young, he expected me to make suggestions and allowed me to experiment. We celebrated with ice cream for every little success or solution."

"He sounds amazing."

She nodded. "During his lifetime, he amassed over two hundred patents, but his passions were fire suppressants and alarms. When I was eleven, Prissy's parents thought she should spend the summer with me while they traveled in the diplomatic corps to several African countries. Sadly, there was an uprising, and they were caught in the crossfire." Bree's voice hitched for a moment, then she shook her head.

"Pricilla Ann Matthews was raised as a little princess. She hated the outdoors, getting dirty, and at first acted like Gramps and I were her staff. It lasted only a few days, and he started calling her 'Miss Priss,' which evolved into 'Prissy,' and it stuck. Rather than detest it, she liked it so much that she insisted all the kids at school call her that." Bree rolled her eyes.

"She's two years younger, but she still rules the roost. Gramps and I spoiled her, and she did whatever she liked, including bossing me around… Old habits die hard." She laughed, then said softly, "I can't let anything happen to her, even if she's unbearable most of the time. Prissy probably doesn't realize it, but she's also an inventor in the kitchen. You know how gifted she is there, and before long, she took on the role of matriarch and blossomed into what you see today.

"When Prissy was in college spand I was in graduate school, Gramps died, leaving us the company. I believe he'd approve of what we've done, but I can't let anyone ruin our company or the family's reputation. It's all I have. One day, Prissy will become a famous chef-restaurateur, and I'll buy her share of the company so she can grow her business. I dread that day. Until then, I must protect us, what we have, and expand the business."

Mitch wiped a tear from Bree's cheek and hugged her tightly. She rested her head on his shoulder and cried softly.

"You're not alone in this. Whatever you need, I'll do my best to provide. We all will." He stroked her hair and kissed the top of her head. "Bree. I hate to tell you, but there's a maggot in your hair."

Bree pushed away and screamed, "Get it out, get it out!"

Mitch retrieved the maggot with two fingers and held it up in front of Bree's face. She screamed again.

Bob and Joe ran inside, guns drawn.

Bree threw smelly socks and dirty underwear at Mitch as Bob and Joe holstered their guns, shaking their heads.

Chapter 7

PER HANK'S ORDERS, the firehouse had to be sanitized. Everything needed polishing for inspection, and the equipment had to be checked, rechecked, and checked again. Hoses were rolled, and every vehicle was loaded with the correct supplies. There was a mandatory two-hour exercise session with an instructor in the exercise room, followed by a five-mile run in three groups over the course of the twelve-hour workday. Thankfully, no emergencies were called in.

Standing in front of his open locker, Steve wiped his face with a towel and wrapped it around his neck. "Who put a burr under Hank's saddle this morning? Was it you, Mitch?"

Mitch flinched. *It probably was my fault.* "Can't say I know."

"You'd think the state's fire chief was coming for an inspection. I haven't worked out this hard since playing high school football." He squinted at Mitch. "Why do I have a sneaking suspicion that you're behind it? Is this because of Bree's visit? Or was it because of you and *your girlfriend*, Bree?"

"What? Get real. Bree and I are just friends."

"Uh-huh. Just how friendly are you with Bree, hmm?"

"None of your business."

"That's it! You're hung up on the 'fire starter'." Steve smirked.

Mitch grabbed the towel around Steve's neck with both hands and twisted it. "You're a bully. Don't ever let me hear you call Bree that again." He quickly let go and stomped toward the showers.

"Well, what'd ya know? Strong man has the hots for Bree Kelly."

"Grow up, Chamber pot." *If he can see my interest in Bree, then who else can?*

Once Mitch showered and rubbed his aches and pains with a menthol topical analgesic, he had three hours left of his twelve-hour shift for study time. He entered the empty classroom to watch a video tutorial on arson investigations and a written quiz for his certification. He'd taken a few fire investigation classes in college, but needed firefighting experience before transitioning into that area of expertise. He had ten more units and tests to complete, and then he needed to review all the North Carolina jurisprudence manuals before taking the state test. *At this rate, I'll be an old man before I finish.*

Satisfied with the highest score possible, Mitch managed to sneak out of the firehouse before Hank could give him anything more to do. *Why am I sneaking out? This is ridiculous.* It was already eight o'clock and he was off duty. He looked over his shoulder once more before getting into his truck. It was a relief to find nothing inside to prank him. Lifting his arm to put the truck in gear, he winced in pain and continued to do so all the way home.

He should have just gone home to sleep, but instead, he parked his truck and headed to see Bree. "Knock, knock. Just me." He strolled into the kitchen, where a smorgasbord of breakfast items lined the center island. Immediately, his stomach growled.

"In the dining room," Bree hollered. "Help yourself."

The table was filled with the security guys he'd met before, and little was said while everyone ate. Mitch sat next to Bree. "Mornin'."

"You look like something the cat dragged in," Prissy said, smiling a little too brightly.

"I feel like it, too."

Bree reached over and patted his arm. "You don't smell like you've been swimming in garbage."

Mitch winced. "Hank went all GI Joe training today, and Prissy could serve dinner off our equipment." Joe and Bob never looked up but snickered. *And there's no reason to tell Bree what Steve said.*

Prissy got up from her seat to place a large envelope and a newspaper, opened to the last page of the first section, by Mitch's plate. "Looks like now you're a celebrity. I thought you might like some 8x10 color glossies to add to your scrapbook. Way to go."

He was confused until he saw the half-page article titled "Firefighters Respond to Grocery Store Fire." Multiple photos submitted by Steve Chambers showed Mitch rummaging through a dumpster. The writing was positive toward the firehouse, him, and their commitment to the community.

"Son of a… that jerk needs to learn some manners."

"On that, we agree," Prissy said. "He's immature *and* a jerk. One day, he's going to get it, and I want to be there to help dish it out."

"When it happens, I'll let you know." He high-fived Prissy. "Despite Steve's childish proclivities, we were putting out dumpster fires instead of something more important, like a burning apartment building."

"The article paints the firehouse and you, Mitch, in a favorable light. I wonder what Hank thinks of this?" Bree asked.

"Hank may have viewed this as derogatory, and the article may be why we were all worked to death today." He examined the color enlargements. "Thanks, Prissy, for these. Mom will love them." Prissy's smile fell. He knew he'd just deflated her attempt to be mean and would need to watch out for her next try.

"Once everyone's finished, grab some coveralls and goggles and let's head out to the garage," Bree instructed.

BREE LOOKED AROUND the garage and nodded in satisfaction. One bay was draped from floor to ceiling and covered on all four sides in plastic, so the group entered through a zippered area.

"This looks like a biohazard containment zone," Mitch said. "Tell me we're not working with something dangerous."

"It is, but for nothing dangerous," Bree assured him. "I've done some preliminary research on the silly string and each type of shaving cream. I must say that the shaving cream combinations are interesting, but they seem very masculine. I think my choice would be vanilla and cinnamon..." She stared into space, imagining other scent combinations.

"Earth to Bree." Prissy whistled. "Let's get this show on the road."

"Sorry. Our objective is to measure the distance the string covers during different time intervals. Then we'll monitor the shaving cream as it spreads outward in small, medium, and large spaces. Everything will be videoed and recorded, starting with the shaving cream."

She held up four different kinds. "We'll measure the diameter of the foam from different heights for each type over a period of three seconds. You will stand over a table three, six, and nine inches away, aiming for the black dot on the butcher paper. I will count down, three, two, one, and you will press the trigger. After three seconds, I'll tell you to stop. I am looking for the initial cream or gel that transforms into foam the soonest and remains foamy at the farthest distance. We will test each product five times, drawing a circle with a marker around each diameter, and then move the sheet to a different table. I am also interested in your evaluations based on the parameters I provided. I will demonstrate." She aimed a can of shaving cream, pressed the trigger, and counted.

"If there are no questions, Mitch, Prissy, and Joe take your positions."

After getting them situated, she raised a hand and counted off, "Three, two, one, go… Stop. Excellent."

The test was repeated until she was satisfied with the results, and the sheets were placed in a plastic tub to dry—the circles indicated the range of spread. "Next is the distance test. Along three walls, we set up distance markers where the string goes straight in a single shot. Then you'll move back from the wall to the next distance and repeat. I am interested in the distance when the string begins to drop. I will demonstrate."

She did so and looked at the others for confirmation. "This is easy. Mitch, Prissy, and Joe, take your positions. Three, two, one, go… Stop. Excellent." The test results were gathered, and Bree clapped. "Thank you all for helping me. I know this looked strange, but I'm very encouraged by what I saw."

"Are we finished with all this?" Prissy asked.

"Yes."

"Then take this!" Prissy used the rest of her silly string to attack Joe, then Bob. "That's for locking me out of the house on my birthday."

Not to be outdone, the men, including Mitch, chased and attacked each other with silly string. Bree laughed hard at the squealing and hollering. Mitch eyed Bree, and before she could react, he squirted her. Like Prissy, she squealed and ran around the garage. Then she picked up a new can and fired it at Mitch until it was empty.

"Is everything all right in here?" A deep voice resonated through the plastic barrier.

"Not Dirk." Prissy groaned softly. "He can't see me like this."

"Is Prissy in there?" Steve hollered through the plastic. "I found her gold earring on Dirk's sofa, and if she wants it back, she'll have to go out with me Sunday night. She knows how to find me." His snickers were sickening.

Prissy hissed, "What a jerk. Don't tell him I'm here. I'd rather poke myself in the eye with a hot poker."

Mitch carefully removed his goggles, unzipped the plastic, and stuck his face out. "Hey. We're trying to determine if we can use a shaving cream or silly string activity for the kids during Firefighter's Day. It's fun but would be too messy unless it's self-contained, so we decided not to use it."

"Silly String? Glad you ruled it out," Dirk said.

"Hank would pitch a fit. Well, I'm off to work. Don't forget we're having a barbecue on Saturday. Tell Prissy and Bree to come. My brother, Brandon, will be home for the weekend, and he'll want to see them."

"I haven't seen him in years. Is he still in the Marines?"

Dirk nodded. "Yeah, but he'll be getting out in six months."

Steve tried to peek into the containment room. "Don't forget to tell Prissy about the earring. I'll text her so she won't forget to call."

"Will do." Mitch zipped the plastic and faced the group.

Bree whispered to Prissy, "Brandon's coming home. It'll be good to see him again."

Prissy smiled. "He's a sweetheart. We should go to the barbecue and welcome him home. I need to find something to wear, and I'll even help you pick out something."

"Thanks," Bree answered a little breathless.

Prissy exited, leaving Bree to pick up the plastic tub and clipboard before turning to the others. "Thank you for the help. If you don't mind tearing this down, I'll need another room like this for the next round of testing in a week. See you later, Mitch."

LIVING WITH ANOTHER firefighter had its advantages and disadvantages. When they were on the same schedule, it was nice to pal around together, share the chores and cook at home, then continue bonding at the firehouse. Lifelong friendships were often forged that way. Mitch and Dirk had never served together, but having roomed together for their last two college years, living in the same house again, seemed like old times.

It could get lonely when their schedules didn't match and no one else was home. So, the station's crew usually volunteered to coach, work with non-profits, take on pet projects, or work out in the gym or dojo. Mitch preferred the small gym at the fire station. He also had his coursework, and his preferred pet project was Bree.

After the silly string experiment, he'd left the plastic cube confused, wondering if Bree had just given him the brush-off. She had been so excited to hear about Brandon. *Was she ever that excited about me?* He unloaded his truck and lumbered off to bed for a long nap. When he got up, the sun was low in the sky. He stretched, waking up after dreaming of some phantom guy and Bree having fun with Silly String. Her smile could light bottle rockets, but it was for the other guy. His stomach rolled like he was going to be sick.

He'd texted Dirk to bring home egg rolls and beer since he'd made a rice-and-beef stir-fry.

Dirk replied: *Steve wants to know if there's enough for him, too. He said he'd bring the beer and dessert.*

Mitch hit his forehead with his hand. Steve was such a busybody: *Fine. But he's also doing dishes. And tell him to bring the good beer this time.*

A smiley face appeared.

Another text from Dirk appeared: *I didn't send that. Steve, the fifth grader, grabbed my phone. We'll be there in fifteen.*

True to form, Mitch made enough food for six people, but firefighters could pack it away in a flash, as if it were their last meal. Dirk walked in, followed by Steve. "Smells good. I brought veggie egg rolls, six shrimp egg rolls, and sauce packets. Steve brought a cheesecake and two six-packs of Corona but forgot the limes. He said you wouldn't care."

Steve put most of the beer in the refrigerator, pulled out three frozen mugs that were always available, and opened three bottles of Corona.

Mitch pulled Dirk aside, speaking low. "I don't care about the beer, but I was hoping to talk to you about Steve and his penchant for eavesdropping, sticking his nose where it doesn't belong, and finding out why he's so interested in what Bree's doing."

"He's always been a prick, but he's interested in Prissy and she can't stand him."

Steve yelled across the room, "Mitch, what's going on? These beers won't drink themselves."

Mitch yelled back, "We're trying to decide if the eggrolls need warming. I think they're fine, Dirk. Let's eat."

Steve asked more than a dozen questions during dinner: "What were you doing in that white room at Bree's estate? Did you give Prissy my message? Was Bree in there with you, too? I didn't see any of Bree's security goons around. What are they up to lately? Are there problems at the factory that would get Bree to exchange the fire extinguishers from the fire station? Is Bree working on anything new?"

Dirk shot Mitch an inquisitive look but didn't say anything.

"You sure ask a lot of questions. What's it to you?" Mitch asked, frowning.

Steve shrugged. "I like knowing things, and maybe I can figure out how to get Prissy to go out with me if I can talk to her about what's going on with the business."

"She's out of your league," Dirk said. "And she's a man-eater. Guys disappear, so don't press your luck."

Steve shrugged again. "I like a challenge."

"Your funeral, man," Dirk noted.

After Steve left, Mitch cornered Dirk. "Remember when Bree and her security team came to the station? They tested our canisters, and all of them were faulty. So she replaced them with good ones."

"Routine checks are mandatory in her business. So what?"

"It wasn't routine. They had been deliberately sabotaged."

"Come on," Dirk scoffed. "That's insane. Why would anyone do that?"

"To ruin her company and buy it out. It's true, and this is serious. I'm telling you this because Bree needs our help to find out who's behind it and stop them. It could even be one or more people in our station house." Mitch held his hand up. "Wait. Hear me out. I've been doing some digging. After SEcure Well creates a prototype that meets their rigorous standards, they use our station to test it in real-world situations. We make suggestions for improvement, then test the final product again with an endorsement. Our crew is featured in the advertisement, and the station gets a hefty donation from the company." He took a breath.

"This is where it gets tricky, so keep an open mind. Bree's company is embroiled in two lawsuits against the same company for alleged industrial espionage. Someone stole and sold their designs to the company that made the products, bringing them to market six to nine months before SEcure Well could register the patents. They lost millions and millions of dollars, and the stock value decreased. Now, Bree is developing revolutionary products to keep the company afloat until the perpetrator is found. She can't trust her researchers and does most of the work at home. Here's the interesting part. The same three station crew members were on the initial and final testing teams for those stolen products, and they also knew about the faulty extinguishers—Captain Hank Morgan, Norman Anderson, and Steve Chambers."

Dirk shook his head. "This is absurd. What would any of them gain from the involvement? What would they gain from the money? Norman's brother was killed in an oil rig fire six years ago, and he takes a monthly leave of absence to work with Texas companies to develop better safety protocols and equipment. Hank wouldn't ruin his reputation because he's hoping to become the district fire chief. And Steve? I... I don't know."

"Exactly. I ruled out Norman for the same reason you mentioned. Hank has it in for Bree and doesn't respect her, so I'm leaving him on the list. But Steve's always snooping around to find out stuff. Every time you go over to Bree's house, like you did when we were testing out the shaving cream, or when there's a backyard party, he comes, invited or not, to see if Prissy will be there, and he's always asking lots of questions. So, after I tell the SEcure Well team my suspicions, they'll investigate."

"What about me? Do you suspect me, too?"

"No. You have one of the largest Superman complexes I've ever seen, and you'd never do anything to hurt Prissy or Bree. But you can help—observe and report. And I'm sure they would welcome your input during one of their morning meetings. I've been to a few, and the food is primo. I'll see how to get you an invitation, on the down low." He rubbed the back of his neck and breathed deeply. "I need to change the subject. Tell me about Brandon and Bree."

Dirk grinned, pointing finger guns at him. "Ah ha! You *are* infatuated with Bree."

Mitch shrugged.

"Good for her, bad for you. Her security personnel respect and love her more than they would if she were family. I take it they vetted you, but you'll never have any privacy away from her home. If your intentions aren't admirable, quit now."

Mitch swallowed hard. "I think she's terrific, and I can't stay away from her. But sometimes I don't know if she's just being nice to let me hang around. What do you think?"

"Hmm. It doesn't scare you." Dirk whistled. "You've got it bad, but you also have competition. My brother, Brandon, is five years older than Bree and stationed at Camp Lejeune with MARSOC. When he gets out, he's looking to hire on with SEcure Well, and Bree and Prissy have been in love with him forever. Good luck."

Imagining Bree in *his* arms, Mitch lightly sang, "Cheek to Cheek" while going upstairs to bed.

Chapter 8

THE NEXT NIGHT, Mitch called Bree to tell her he had the house to himself. "Pizzas are coming. Plus, I've got wine and beer, and plan to watch a Fred Astaire and Ginger Rogers movie. Would you like to come over?"

"I love old movies. Sure. We'll be there in fifteen minutes."

"We?"

"Yeah. Joe will escort me."

"O-kay, sure." It wasn't exactly what he had in mind, but there was nothing he could do about it.

Mitch looked around the house realizing he had to vacuum, dust, and make his bed. The back doorbell rang just as he finished his chores. He opened the door to usher Bree inside, but before he could close it, Joe cleared his throat.

"Sorry, pal, I have to do a complete sweep of your house," Joe said, walking in. "Is there anything I need to be aware of—incendiary devices, firearms, or dangerous chemicals?"

"Uh, no."

"That makes my job easier. Bree is wearing her

watch. You should wear yours too. I'll start upstairs and work my way down. If everything checks out, then I'll wait until the pizza guy does his delivery."

"Ignore the mess in Dirk's room. He's a slob. Bree, pick out what you want to drink, and I'll set up the movie."

Joe reappeared about fifteen minutes later. "All clear. And the pizza guy is at the front door."

"Hey, Mitch. How's it hanging?" A pimply faced teenager entered the house holding two large pizza boxes and a white paper bag. "Maggie made some cannoli for you and wants you to call her tomorrow. She's off on Saturday and wants you to be her date. You're all she talks about. I don't know why, but she does. Hey, who's the babe?"

Mitch shut his eyes and groaned. "Bree, this sixteen-year-old twirp is Billy DeAngelo, his family owns the restaurant, Il Cigno Italiano. Billy, this is Bree Kelly, who lives next door, and Joe Roberts."

Billy shoved the boxes at Mitch. He reached for Bree's hand brought it to his mouth, and kissed it. "Bella. Forget everything Mitch said. I'm more mature than he is. If you're ever looking for a romantic date with a nice meal, look me up at the restaurant."

Mitch handed off the boxes to Joe before taking Bree's hand from Billy. "Okay, lover boy. Take your money and get out of here."

Billy grinned at the extra-large tip Mitch handed him. "Thanks. What do you want me to tell Maggie?"

"Tell her thanks for the cannoli, but even in another five years, she'd still be too young for me."

"Got it. Can't blame a girl for trying. Ciao Bella."

Bree giggled. "He's adorable."

"Yeah. Adorable." *If I turned my back, the little gigolo would probably stab me and try to make out with Bree… Where did that come from?*

"Looks like you ordered enough pizza for a party. Joe didn't eat tonight. I hope you don't mind sharing with him," Bree said.

"Too late. He's already helped himself to a full plate and is sitting in front of the TV." He pulled Bree close enough to whisper, "Is Joe staying with us all night?"

She whispered back, "I'm not sure. Is that a problem?"

"I thought you and I could spend some quality time together. Alone. How else can we play baseball?" He wiggled his eyebrows.

"Baseball?" Her face scrunched up, and then her eyes went wide. She blushed. "Oh my. Um, you mean like if we're on a date and going to first base?"

"Exactly. Can you get rid of him? I'm wearing your watch." He lifted his wrist and showed her.

Bree swallowed hard and nodded vigorously. She filled her plate and took a seat on the couch. Mitch followed suit and sat next to her.

"Great pizza, Mitch," Joe said, holding up his plate. "Firefighters know where to get the best food. I'll have to get the menu for the house. So, what movie's playing tonight?"

Mitch stared a hole in Joe. "*Top Hat.*"

Joe snickered. "You're kidding. My mom loved to watch Fred Astaire and Ginger Rogers, but you know what's playing tonight that's even better? The Battle Bots National finals, followed by the world heavyweight MMA championship from Vegas. Those are some great options. What'd ya say?"

"It's Bree's decision." *I shouldn't have thrown her under the bus like that, but what if she'd rather this be a group thing?*

She looked thoughtful. "I'm not much for violence,

but battling robots sounds interesting. We could watch it for a while, but I'd like to see *Top Hat*. Joe, I know you don't want to watch it, but I'd be okay with you leaving me here and picking me up later."

"Great compromise. Battle Bots, it is." Joe grabbed the remote, and within minutes, all three were yelling and rooting for the most dangerous, fire-breathing, hammer and axe-armed killer bot on the stage.

Joe's cell phone buzzed, and he quickly checked his text. "Mitch, Bob needs me to review some security information, so I'll be gone for a few minutes. You're not expecting any other visitors tonight, are you?" Mitch shook his head. "Good. Then lock the door behind me and take care of Bree. I'll be back before midnight."

When the back door clicked, Mitch sidled up to Bree, put his arm around her, and kissed her cheek. "Alone at last. The movie is two hours long, and then we have thirty more minutes before Joe returns. I bet we can hit first base a few times before then." Bree giggled and he said, "Time for Fred and Ginger."

BEING WITH MITCH was a dream come true. Obviously, he was a chick magnet. The epitome of "Tall Dark and Handsome," tall (most men she knew were shorter than she), dark (black hair but not moody dark). From her first encounter with the beach towel, she knew he liked being in the sun, and one day, she'd have to gather up the courage to ask if he was a closet nudist, and handsome (very handsome). She still didn't understand his interest in her, the nerd and introvert, the "fire starter." There were so many beautiful women he could be seeing.

Bree's musings were interrupted by Mitch's toes tapping along with the beat of each dance song. "You get into the spirit of the movie, don't you?"

"How could I not? The story is cute, the music is wonderful, and the dancing is fabulous." He hummed along with the song, and the tapping began again.

"You're right in time with the beat. I bet you're a fabulous dancer."

"I'm not too bad. Do you like to dance?" His face shone with excitement.

Could it be hope?

"Liking and doing are two different things."

Mitch's face turned serious. "Don't say you can't dance."

"I have no experience."

"Then we'll have to change that. This is the best song in the movie. *'Heaven… I'm in heaven.'*" He gently urged Bree up from the couch into a close dancing position and hummed until the last line. "*'When we're out together dancing cheek to cheek.'*"

Bree couldn't keep her eyes off his face. She was in heaven.

"Well, with you it's more like dancing cheek to chest, but it still works." He winked at her.

She snapped out of it. *I'm an idiot. He's just making fun of me.* She tried to pull away from him.

"I didn't step on your toes, did I?" he asked, frowning down at her.

"No. I'd like to see the rest of the movie." She gently released herself, heading back to the couch.

The back doorbell rang in rapid succession before Joe yelled through the door. "Sorry, Mitch, but I must take Bree back home."

Bree was by the door instantly. "What is it?"

"Rambo."

Bree unlocked the door and yanked it open. "Oh my God. Tell me on the way."

Mitch instantly had one shoe on and was putting the other on. "I can stay with Bree until everything's settled."

Joe shook his head as he guided Bree out of the house. "Sorry, Mitch, Bree's going into lockdown mode. She has your phone number and can keep up with you that way."

Joe hurried Bree home and through the mansion's kitchen door, then locked it behind him. "Ten minutes ago, Prissy's security guard saw her go into a nightclub bathroom with a group of women. Somehow, she escaped while he waited outside the door. Her watch shows she's on the move. We have a team going after her now."

Bree's heart rate picked up, fearing the worst. She paced the floor while terrible scenarios flashed through her mind.

Joe's cell phone rang, and he put it on speakerphone. It was one of the security team members. "We have Prissy in our sights. She's with three other women who are entering a large house that's hosting a party. Get this, she's wearing different clothing and a wig. What do you want us to do?"

"Put a man at the front and back of the house. At midnight, bring her home," Joe said.

"I should wring her neck," Bree blurted out. "Pulling a stunt like that is so juvenile. I'll talk to her when she gets home."

"Don't bother." Bob's booming voice resounded behind her. "I'll take care of it. This can't happen again. There's too much at stake. If she can't cooperate, we'll go to Plan B and relocate her to a safe house without friends or places to go. Bree, I'm sorry this broke up your date tonight."

"It wasn't a date, just friends getting together." She tried hard not to look disappointed. "Since you have things under control, I'll head off to bed. I've got an early day tomorrow."

There was no use kidding herself. *Mitch feels sorry for me, that's all. He's a rescuer who thinks I need rescuing from a boring life. My life is fine. I have my work, and the company depends on me, especially now.*

She fell asleep crying.

Chapter 9

BREE LOOKED AT the clock for the umpteenth time; it was seven in the morning, and she had been at work for three hours, had finished two big mugs of coffee, an apple, and two granola bars. She longed to go back to bed but knew sleep wouldn't come. Her eyes stung; they were probably bloodshot. She rubbed them, wishing she had some eye drops.

Prissy knocked on Bree's office door and pushed it open. "Can I come in?"

Bree didn't look up. Maybe if she ignored her, she'd go away. *Fat chance.*

Prissy walked in and shut the door behind her. "I'm sure you know that I was unceremoniously removed from a party last night and then publicly humiliated. I don't know how I'm ever going to live that down. Then, Bob read me the riot act. After considering his ultimatum, I promised to behave and apologize to you. I know you worried about me. My bad. I didn't think about that." She stood in front of Bree's desk, looking unrepentant.

"In my defense, the guard was hovering, and I needed to break loose. You know how I dislike feeling closed in. I'm sorry it ended your evening early, but if you think about it, I did you a favor. Mitch likes to date beautiful women. Being the person you are, it wouldn't have worked. Consider last night a fluke and be grateful you had to leave. I wouldn't want you to get your hopes up and then have him break your heart."

Bree pretended to scan the documents on her desk, her face heating up until she was on the verge of exploding. *I could kill her. Slowly, painfully. Bob would help me bury the body. Joe would too.* The satisfying image was replaced with Gramps' face. His words filled her mind. "Prissy is very different from you—she's younger, was more dependent on her mother than you ever were and is looking for acceptance and direction. She needs your love, and despite what she may say or do, she looks up to you and thinks of you as a sister. Her road will be rocky as she tests her limits and yours."

Bree closed her eyes and breathed in through her nose and out through her mouth. "Not now, Prissy, I'm busy. Please shut the door on the way out."

Prissy stormed out and slammed the door behind her.

Tears welled up but wouldn't fall. *Maybe Prissy is right.* Mitch might not intentionally set out to break her heart, but considering her track record with guys from high school through graduate school and up to now, it was more than possible. Statistically, the odds favored her getting hurt again. Needing to vent her frustrations, she told Bob she would be in the workout room.

"Want some company?" he asked, pushing back his chair and rising.

"Not really. Okay, but only if you have time."

Bree pounded on the treadmill, sweat seeping through her clothes, as she tried not to focus on anything else but the monitor in front of her.

A deep voice broke her concentration. "Nice form. I bet you could easily do a marathon."

She tripped over her feet, but Mitch was there to catch her. "Easy there. Didn't mean to scare you."

She turned off the machine and grabbed a towel to wipe her face. "I'm fine. What are you doing here?"

"Bob thought you might need someone to work out with, so I'm offering my services. Then I thought we could have breakfast together. That is, if you want company." Bree shrugged. He pulled her into a hug she didn't return. "I know you were worried about Prissy, and I couldn't help you. Are you alright?"

"I'm fine." She tried to pull back, but Mitch wouldn't turn her loose.

Eyes full of concern, he said, "Okay, you're fine. For the record, I enjoyed spending time with you last night… I missed you after you left."

Bree's eyebrow rose, and her lips pursed together.

"Whoa. You don't believe me? I did. I didn't even finish watching the movie. I stayed by the door, ready to go if you called, but you didn't. I can't imagine how you felt knowing Prissy was missing. Bob called me a little after midnight to say she'd been found. I was so relieved. I wanted to speak to you, but he said you'd gone to bed. I don't care what time it is. If you ever need me, even to talk, I'm here for you."

Bree didn't want to be curt, but she wasn't in the mood to humor him. "Things worked out, and Prissy is grounded. I hate being the parent in this situation, so Bob dished out the punishment. He told her he'd move her to a secure location far from Wi-Fi, a cell phone tower, or people until things clear up. That seemed to do the trick. Please excuse me, I need some space to clear my head."

"Excellent idea." Mitch pulled Bree off the machine and towed her to Bob's office. "Bree needs to clear her head and relax, and since I'm off today, a little fishing is in order. I've got a buddy with a small skiff in New Bern, and we can head out on the Neuse River. While she changes her clothes, I'll rustle up lunch, the fishing gear, and pick her up in an hour. We should be back about three this afternoon. Sound good?"

"We'll make it work."

"Wait." Bree tried to tug her hand free. "You didn't ask me if I wanted to go fishing—Mitch, stop dragging me down the hall. I know where my bedroom is. Okay, okay. Sheesh, you're bossy. I don't know who's worse, Prissy or—"

"Don't even compare me to her. You'll hurt my feelings." He pulled her up the stairs.

"Fine. But bring sunscreen. I tend to burn and then get freckles."

Mitch let go when she entered the bedroom. He swatted her behind. "See you in an hour."

MITCH RAISED HIS hand to knock, but Joe beat him to open the kitchen door, dressed for a day on the water. "Come in. We're almost ready." Mitch raised one eyebrow. "It's exactly what you're thinking." He leaned in closer. "I'm your chaperone for the day, but I know how to look the other way and pretend I can't hear anything."

Mitch swallowed a groan, but if this were the only way to spend time with Bree, he'd take it. He pointed to a dry bag filled to the brim and then to the large picnic basket. "What's all this?"

"Bree had difficulty deciding what to bring, so she overpacked. Her motto is 'If I don't have it, I'll need it.' The lunch is courtesy of one groveling Prissy."

"What's the holdup?"

"Bree also needed binoculars, sample bags, a notebook, some reference guides, and I'm not sure what else." Joe lifted a large, zippered boat bag to show him. "She might get some ideas, which would kill her if she forgot something to record her thoughts or have reference materials at her fingertips."

Mitch nodded and called out, "Bree, I'm here. We're burning daylight, and we need to make a pit stop before we get to the water."

Joe reached for his phone. "What kind of pit stop? I may need to relay the information."

"We need fishing licenses—holy cow!"

Followed by Bob, Bree stopped inside the doorway, carrying a bulging backpack. Her hat resembled a baseball cap in the front, with a long piece of cloth attached to the back, hanging like a tail. She also wore long pants, a long-sleeved shirt, water shoes, and a small magnifying glass that dangled from a lanyard around her neck.

Mitch stifled a laugh. "Bree, darlin', we're not goin' on safari, we're going fishing. It's almost July, and you could use some sunshine on your long, beautiful, lily-white legs. Go back upstairs and put on a bathing suit, shorts, and a T-shirt. Keep the hat and shoes, they're practical. You've got five minutes. Go." He didn't expect her to acquiesce, but she dropped the backpack and ran up the stairs.

Joe's jaw dropped. "Well, I'll be... not many people can get her to do something like that... that quickly. Mitch, there may be hope for us yet." Bob and Joe high-fived.

Bree's alarm went off as she entered the kitchen.

"Five minutes and on time. I hope I pass inspection. We also need insect spray." She turned in a circle for Mitch's approval, only to get a wolf whistle.

"A woman after my own heart: beautiful, intelligent, and on time. Insect spray, check."

Bob hefted Bree's backpack. "Watches?" Everyone lifted their wrist. "Watch out for gators and don't swim near the yacht basins. Those are nursery areas for bull sharks. Have fun, kids. Joe, give me a sit rep every two hours."

Joe nodded, picking up the dry bag as Mitch picked up the basket and opened the door. They followed Bree to Mitch's truck, and after loading everything in the back, he helped Bree into the cab so she could sit between him and Joe, snug as a bug in a rug.

"I'm surprised Prissy didn't see us off," Mitch said.

"She isn't talking to Bob," Bree told him. "After making our picnic basket, she told Joe she planned to get a mani-pedi, a massage, and her hair done, and then went back to bed. She'll be occupied until late this afternoon, escorted by Chris. I hope she'll be in a better mood by then. She promised to make eggplant parmesan, a caprese salad, and tiramisu for dessert. I'm supplying a vintage Italian red and a dessert wine for dinner. I may not be able to cook, but I studied an online course from the International Sommelier Guild's School Accreditation organization and received my advanced wine certificate. I need to finish some in-person sessions before getting my Sommelier Diploma, but I don't have the time. Prissy loves my pairings. She says she'll hire me at her restaurant for just that." Bree was grinning from ear to ear. Then the smile faded.

"She also told me I wasn't to explain to the customers why the wines pair up gastronomically, or how the vintners could improve the wines. Shame really.

One day, I hope to tour the West Coast wineries and do just that… from a chemistry point of view."

"That's a tour I'd love to do with you," Mitch said. "I have relatives in the Napa Valley area. I'm sure they could arrange some introductions for us. But first, you need to get the company back on track. Have you decided on what to say tomorrow at the staff meeting?"

Joe jumped in. "Bob and I've given this some thought. The best way is to draw the perp out. Make him think we're only concentrating on testing a new product with the help of Station 18. We'll introduce The Chirp and its scope in the world of fire detection. We watch everyone's faces for reactions. We could do this before the Founder's Day Picnic and show the test videos then. Of course, we'll need a warehouse or commercial building to burn down."

"Excellent thinking. We smoke him out… get it? Smoke?" Bree nudged Mitch.

The two men snorted. Mitch patted her hand. "Station 18 gets inquiries about burning down buildings and warehouses more often than you think. Building owners receive tax deductions, allowing fire departments to practice putting out different types of fires under various scenarios, even within a single building. It requires a lot of coordination, especially with outside fire and police units that may need to get involved, and City Hall must approve every aspect of the plan. If you want to present a video on Founder's Day, you need to ask now and hope this can be expedited."

"I'll call Bob now," Joe said.

Chapter 10

DESPITE MITCH'S PLEAS to head to the fishing area, once inside Walmart, Bree found a shopping cart and meandered unhurriedly across the store. First stop was the appliance section. She took out her phone and scanned the QR codes for product recommendations, then found the highest-rated 2-qt and 8-qt crockpots and bought six of each.

Turning to Mitch, she said, "This year I'm entering the chili cookoff at the Firefighter's Day event, and I'd like you to teach me to make chili. Prissy will have a conniption, but I don't care. I have two weeks to do this. Unfortunately, the winner is chosen by popular vote, so my entry must be submitted under an assumed name, since no one will want to try it if my name is on the registration. The winner gets a trophy, bragging rights, and the opportunity to fling a whipped cream pie at a city official. I want to hit Hank in the face. This also means that someone must teach me to do that as well. What do you say, guys?"

"Why, you little devil," Mitch said. "The crockpot is excellent for developing flavors over a long time. If you can master the crockpot, you'll never starve. Might as well buy most of what's needed while we're here and start experimenting tonight. What do you think, Joe?"

"I'm game. A cardboard cutout should work for the practice target. Once we get back, I'll pick up a case of whipped cream, a big bottle of antacids, and a gallon of milk—it's good for diluting poisons." Joe winked at her. Bree rolled her eyes.

Moseying toward the fishing area, Bree perused all the emergency items, especially checking out fire extinguishers, smoke detectors, and CO detectors, then took photos of everything, including the instructions and ingredient labels. Pointing to the rows of equipment, she said, "The safety equipment industry is worth over one hundred billion dollars. I want to keep a piece of that… if I can get things back to normal, so knowing my competitors and their products will help me get there."

After getting licenses, Mitch purchased bloodworms and crickets for bait. Once the group reached the checkout counter, Bree volunteered to the cashier that she was entering a chili-cooking contest and needed the assortment of crockpots for experimentation. Darla, a blue-haired twenty-something woman with multiple piercings in her ears and eyebrow, with sleeve tattoos, didn't find the conversation weird.

"Memaw likes to use coffee in her chili—the kind with chicory, and she says it needs to be cooked in a cast-iron pot over a fire. I prefer using a large pot and simmering the chili for twenty-four hours to intensify the flavors. I also add bits of jalapeño peppers and two kinds of cayenne pepper, along with small red kidney beans, rather than the large ones. Add a cake of cornbread made in a cast-iron skillet, and you have a great dinner." She popped her gum and said, "I won two blue ribbons at the state fair with that recipe. And if you take out the beans, you have hot dog chili for a crowd. Here's my phone number. Text me and I'll give you the recipe. Using the crockpot is a great option."

Bree grinned at her. "That would be lovely. Thank you, Darla."

"You're welcome. That will be $832.59."

Bree looked at Joe, who put the company credit card in the machine. Joe wheeled out one cart, Bree another, and Mitch was relegated to the rear, carrying the live bait far away from the other food.

Joe's phone rang after they started driving down the street. He listened for a minute, hung up, and said to Bree, "Bob wants you to call the mayor, the fire chief, and Hank to get the ball rolling on burning a building. He's writing up a formal request to all the necessary agencies and people. He'll text me the phone numbers and wants you to make the calls while we drive to New Bern. They're expecting your call. We've got about an hour and a half."

Bree took off her hat and ran her fingers through her red hair, combing it down. Then, she sat up straight and assumed the role of SEcure Well President to plead her case.

On the drive, Mitch listened to Bree's chameleon-like change from a focused scientist and beginner cook to the powerful owner of a multi-million-dollar company without batting an eye. He knew no one else who could compartmentalize information, delegate effectively, or execute negotiations as well as she could. Her Gramps should be proud, because he certainly was.

She looked like a wilted flower when she finished her last call. Using the right buzzwords and phrases, adding compliments and passing on her profound thanks in the appropriate measure, she'd been brilliant. Joe took her phone, turned it off, and placed it in his pocket. "The rest of the day is yours to enjoy. Should anything come up, I'll handle it, or Mitch will. We're here."

Leaving the crockpots in the truck, they carried everything to the boat, dropped three ten-pound bags of ice in the live well and cooler. Mitch and Bree found places to sit on the bow, and Joe took the boat out for a nice leisurely ride down the Neuse River.

The weather was perfect. Bree held her face to the sun as the wind blew her hat off her head, but it was kept in place by the chin strap. Mitch couldn't help but drool. She was the most beautiful and remarkable woman he'd ever met, and he would do anything to protect her, including passing her the sunscreen.

Thirty minutes later, Joe dropped the anchor, and Mitch arranged the gear to start fishing. He demonstrated how to unlock and lock the reel, and how to cast the line. Bree practiced several times, and her confidence grew with each cast. She squirmed as he baited the hooks with worms, then cast her line over the edge and slowly reeled it in. In moments, she got a bite. The fish nearly bent the rod in half, and she struggled to stay on her feet. She screamed.

"Pull Back!" Mitch yelled as he and Joe placed their rods in rod holders and ran to her. "You've got it. Now reel it in." She turned the crank repeatedly until she could see the fish's body underneath the surface. Using a net, he lifted the two-pound bass from the water, removed the hook, and let Bree hold it so Joe could take her photo before it was dumped in the live well.

"That one's a keeper," Mitch exclaimed. "Looks like worms are the magic bait today. I'm going to switch my bait next time."

Bree was elated. "It's a shame that a poor worm had to make the ultimate sacrifice."

"Yeah, the ultimate sacrifice for a nice dinner tonight. If Prissy doesn't want to cook, we can grill them at my house."

"I thought we'd make chili tonight." She pouted.

"Sorry, I got caught up in the moment. I'll teach you how to clean and fillet whatever we catch, and I'll grill them tomorrow or Saturday night at our barbecue."

"Deal. That's also something I'd like you to teach me, to cook on a grill."

"Ah, Bree." He chuckled. "Let's not get ahead of ourselves. We'll take it one appliance at a time—first, the crockpot. Not to make you feel bad, but grilling is a guy thing. On Saturday, you can watch me cook hot dogs and burgers."

She turned to face Mitch, and her left eyebrow shot up. If looks could kill.

Joe removed his sunglasses to watch the sweet version of Bree turn into a viper. "This is going to be interesting," he murmured before positioning himself at the ready to throw his body against her in case the fangs appeared, and Mitch's jugular became the target.

Bree stood to her full height and jammed her fists on her hips. "Don't you mean *burn* the meat rather than cook it? Change the authentic food flavor and turn it into some tainted mystery meat?" Her lip curled into almost a sneer.

"Dirk's grill has produced enough smoke residue to stain the house siding a different color. Without proper cleaning and maintenance, old grease and incinerated meat can clog the gas vents, and clogged grease and protein buildup increase the likelihood that Dirk's house will catch fire. Not to mention, a flare-up will singe the facial hair of anyone at the helm. And *you* call yourself a firefighter." She spat the words while looking at him from head to toe. "Fine. But don't be surprised if there's a grill on my patio one of these days, and I'll find someone else to teach me."

The fishing was done for now. She went to the picnic basket, picked up a sandwich and one of Joe's beers, then found a place under the Bimini to eat and pout.

Mitch's mouth hung open as he stared at her and then Joe, who'd faced the other way, his shoulders rising and falling, trying to swallow a laugh.

Joe swiped at his eyes and muttered to Mitch, "This trip was already fun, but she knocked you on your ass with incontrovertible facts. You're about to practice the art of groveling."

Mitch looked to the heavens for inspiration before he knelt in front of Bree. "Sweetie pie, what I said came out all wrong. You're right about everything you said, and I meant to confront Dirk about the grill, but it's his grill, and I don't like stepping on his toes. Darlin', please speak to me."

She sniffed twice. "You're just like other guys, thinking I cannot process such a simple task. Shame on you. No, shame on *me* for thinking you were different and wouldn't placate me. Leave me alone."

"Sweetheart, I didn't mean to say what I did. Please forgive me. Of course, you're smart enough to learn simple tasks and one day, I'm sure you'll master the grill."

Joe stepped in. "You're digging a deeper hole. Say you're sorry and step away. She's been known to throw things, and there are too many things on this boat that she can impale you with."

It was Mitch's turn to pout. He grabbed a beer and resumed fishing.

Joe shook his head. He grabbed a beer and a chicken leg, then sat in the captain's chair to leave them alone.

The anchor hadn't been set well, so the boat drifted under the shade of some scrub oaks and tall pines. With the time of the day and the temperature rising, crickets chirped all around them. Bree's eyes were closed, and in short order, she rested her head on the back of the seat and nodded off to sleep.

Carefully, Mitch picked her up, placed her on the bench seat to keep her from getting a crick in her neck, and kissed her forehead. While she slept, he and Joe ate their lunch and kept fishing.

Mitch lowered his voice. "I'm not sure what I said, but I don't like being out of her good graces. Do you have any advice on how I can return to her good side?"

"If you're not genuinely interested in Bree, it's time to say goodbye. But if you care for her, don't give up. She's stubborn and used to being on the defensive with men. I doubt she understands her feelings for you, so give her time. And if you decide to stick it out, be attentive and protect her. Also, groveling helps." Joe shrugged. "I've been in the doghouse so much, I'm surprised I don't have fleas. So, what will it be?"

He looked at the sleeping woman who occupied his thoughts day and night. "I can't stop thinking about her and want to spend as much time with her as possible. We've only known each other for a little while, but I... I've fallen head over heels for her... I'm a goner."

Bree stirred, and he went to her side. "Hello, sleepy head. Being on the water and in the sunshine has given you time to relax. I hope you feel better. Want to fish some more?"

She narrowed her eyes for a moment and then shrugged. "I suppose so, but let's make it interesting." Bree sat up ramrod straight. "The person who catches the fewest fish in the next two hours must clean, cook, and serve a grand meal to the rest of us."

Joe and Mitch snorted, then nodded in agreement.

"The only thing I need is someone to bait my hook while I tell you about my plan to catch the extinguisher bad guy."

Two hours later, after catching five fish, Bree was glowing. Since Joe and Mitch caught only two fish each, they were both on the hook for dinner. They pulled up the anchor and cruised the river for an hour or so, letting the breeze cool them down as they waved to other boaters going in the opposite direction. They docked at a wildlife ramp so that Joe could contact Bob and reveal her master plan. "Okay, Mitch, you have thirty minutes. Use them wisely."

Mitch didn't waste any time. Nervous and remembering what Joe said, he moved to sit beside Bree. "You're a natural fisherwoman. You must have some secrets you want to pass on."

She eyed him like he was trying to placate her, but wouldn't allow him to get the upper hand. "In the ten minutes I had to research fish behavior from the U.S. Fish and Wildlife Service, two things struck me: fish can see you if you lean over the boat's edge, and as the light gets higher in the sky, the water temperature also heats up, so they want to go deeper and under the shade. I adjusted my casting based on those facts, and with the wiggling worms, the fish had to bite. Simple biology."

"You're amazing," Mitch said as honestly as possible. She was beautiful, intelligent, and a sweetheart. "I'm sorry for saying stupid things. Please forgive me. Things just come out of my mouth. I will always mess up, not because I want to make you mad, but because I'm a guy. What do you say? Can we get back to where we were before I opened my mouth and stuck both feet inside?"

"Apology accepted. I'm sorry too. I became defensive and don't want to jeopardize this... relationship with you."

His smile could have outshone the sun. "I like that word, 'relationship.' Darlin', you've made me so happy." He tentatively leaned into her, wanting her to meet him halfway. She moved in, and they kissed, their lips moving in sync. His tongue pressed into her mouth, and they dueled as a few moans escaped. He pulled her closer, his hands cupping her face, and her arms went around his waist. They separated but pressed their foreheads together to maintain the connection. "Kissing you is my new favorite thing to do. I could spend hours tasting your perfect mouth." Her face flushed as he reached out for both her hands.

"When things settle down, would you consider dating, dating me... for real? Not just for backyard barbecues or breakfasts, although those times are special, but for actual dates like going out for dinner, a movie, and maybe some weekend trips? We could explore Wilmington, Raleigh, Asheville, or other places. Where is up to you. Then, if you still like me in a month or so, I'd like you to meet my sisters. Well, just Kayla, the youngest, because she's the good sister."

Bree smiled. "I don't know what to say. Are you serious?" He nodded vigorously and kissed her again. She blushed from the tip of her head down to her chest. "I've never met anyone's sister, not even a good one. I'll have to think about that, but I'll say yes to dating you. You realize all your station buddies will give you a hard time."

"Let them try. What could be worse than making me dumpster dive in rotten food, fight off vermin, or do the walk of shame? I'm Batman, remember."

"Batman needs to kiss me a lot more before Joe returns."

"My pleasure. You can boss me around for kisses any time."

Chapter 11

BOB MET THE trio in the driveway and helped carry everything from the truck into the house. He laughed at their fishing adventure and listened intently as Bree gushed about catching the most fish, the day they had on the water, and her breakthrough with The Chirp. She also informed him that she'd decided to wait on revealing the Hot Shot and not mention it during tomorrow's meeting. The Chirp needed to be center stage, and she really couldn't spare the time to get two products up and running simultaneously.

"After Mitch and Joe clean and pack the fish in the freezer, Mitch will teach me how to make chili in a crockpot. That's dinner for tonight. And while we eat, I'll work up notes for the meeting. I'll be down shortly." Bree kissed Mitch on the cheek and then headed upstairs.

It was Mitch's turn to blush, starstruck.

Bree yelled from the stairs, "Don't forget to make the cutout of Hank. I'll need to work off some stress this weekend."

Joe slapped him on the back. "These fish won't clean themselves."

WHEN BREE RETURNED, Bob helped her wash the crockpots and place them on towels to dry, so they would be ready to use later. They unpacked all the groceries and lined them up alphabetically—it made more sense to her to do it that way. She found large stirring spoons, measuring spoons and cups, and various-sized mixing bowls, then added those to the island just in time for Joe and Mitch to enter the kitchen smelling like they had worked in a cannery.

"You two stink." She held her nose. "I'll see you both back here in thirty minutes after you've cleaned up. My new blue-haired Walmart friend, Darla, sent me her award-winning chili and cornbread recipes with the instructions. Don't be late, I'm starving."

Later, Bree produced a large, red leather journal, and as Mitch gave her directions, she listened like a captivated audience, taking notes and making diagrams.

"You're the perfect student," he said.

"I approach a task determined to do it correctly, so I don't start more kitchen fires."

While the four were performing different tasks, laughing and teasing each other, Prissy found them. "I don't believe it. What exactly are you trying to make?"

"Chili and cornbread, and I expect you to eat with us," Bree said.

Joe shook the large bottle of Tums.

"Humph. Don't expect me to save you this time. I'm only here to document your demise. Whether I sample your experiment has yet to be determined." She pulled out a tall counter chair and watched in rapt fascination. "Where'd you get that cast-iron pan?"

"It's Dirk's. My mom always uses one for cornbread," Mitch explained, "and Bree's eager to use it." He dropped some oil and butter into the pan and heated it in the oven until it was smoking hot. Bree finished stirring the cornbread batter and when it was time, poured it into the pan, squealing as it popped and sizzled. "Careful now. Looks good." Mitch placed it back into the oven and had Bree set a timer for fifty minutes.

Then he directed her to brown the ground beef slowly in a large stock pot and add the rest of Darla's ingredients, stirring the whole time. About fifteen minutes later, Mitch gave everyone a spoon and said, "Time to test it. Bree first."

She hesitated, looked over her shoulder at her cooking crew, and then took a small spoonful. "Here goes nothing." She tasted it with her eyes closed, and a satisfied smile spread across her face. "It's… It's good. I can't believe it. Mitch, it's *really good.*" She jumped up and down.

There was clapping and cheering, then each person took a bite of the chili, one by one. Prissy stood with her arms crossed.

"This is probably the best chili I've ever eaten," Joe said.

"I agree. Bree, you did it," Bob said excitedly.

Mitch took a large bite. "This is delicious. We'll let this simmer on low heat, and it'll be perfect by the time the cornbread is done."

Bree turned to Prissy. "I'd like your opinion. Will you taste it? Perhaps there's something that you'd add to make it better."

Joe shook the Tums bottle once more.

"Fine." Prissy sampled a tablespoonful. "It'll pass as a mild base recipe. You could add cayenne, peppers, or hot sauce to make it spicy. Then serve it with sour cream or shredded cheese on top, and it will give it another layer of flavor."

Bree rushed forward to hug her. "Thank you. This means a lot to me."

Prissy returned the hug, but in an instant, the mood changed, and she was Prissy once more. "Don't think this means that you can take over the kitchen. This is only temporary until after the cook-off. Now, clean up your prep stations and get ready for dinner." Then she walked out the door.

Bree's smile said it all. Joe and Bob high-fived her before Mitch gave her a big hug. "Thank you. This was a group effort, and I couldn't have done it without all of you. After dinner, I'm going to text Darla about the experiment and invite her to the chili cookoff."

Dinner was excellent, and they ate it all, leaving the Tums bottle unopened. The guys loaded the dishwasher as Bree prepared her notes for the morning meeting. They sat at the dining room table with coffee and chocolate cake that Prissy had made while they went fishing. When the casual conversation ended, Bree got their attention.

"The day I burned Prissy's birthday chicken dinner, I had been listening to crickets chirping in the backyard. As you know, male crickets produce chirps by rubbing their wings together. When the air temperature increases, their chirps become faster and louder. "The Chirp" is modeled after crickets."

Prissy groaned loudly.

Bree didn't flinch. "It's a next-generation heat sensor with nearly unlimited uses. Heat sensors are often paired with smoke detectors, but this design detects rapid temperature changes without smoke, such as in ceilings, wall corners, or where flash fires occur."

Her voice trembled as she spoke faster. "When temperatures rise, the unit will chirp loudly and rapidly, and then fire suppression measures will kick in. Connected to a computer system, firefighters can identify a fire's origin and locate the hottest spots to attack. It can be personalized for firefighter suits or medical alert bracelets. Or customized with voice or text alerts, thermal-color flashing, or even vibrations. Children, pets, and individuals with neurodiversity issues who may be confused or startled by other alarms would have access to early warnings." She took a deep breath and slowed down. "It can be hard-wired or battery-operated and as inexpensive as a home smoke alarm. So our revenue will come from replacing the units or specialized batteries."

Mitch leaned forward, resting his arms on the table. "That's incredible. You got all that from listening to crickets? It's so simple, yet brilliant."

Bree blushed, the color of her hair.

Prissy chimed in, "How soon can we get some prototypes working? What will be the start-up cost, how much time are we looking at before we apply for patents, and when can we start manufacturing?"

Bree glowed. With Prissy's interest, she knew this had merit. "Everything rides on keeping this secret and getting a team working on it ASAP. Perhaps in a few months, because the schematics are finished. That's why I'll use it as bait tomorrow to entice our thief out in the open. What do you think, Bob? Joe?"

Prissy jumped back into the conversation, "What? You plan to use the designs as bait? Absolutely not!"

"Not the *real* designs. I created two realistic-looking designs that will fail every test. I'm hoping that after multiple tests, the thief will conclude that the system won't work because the mechanism is faulty and the math is bad."

"How do you plan for the designs to get taken?" Joe asked.

"Our top suspects are our CEO, David Weisman, and Frank Lassiter, our CFO. I plan to discuss this project with them and emphasize the importance of ensuring its success to maintain the company's financial stability. They will want to see the details and test results before the board votes on it, so I'll give them everything." She held her hand up like a stop sign. "I won't mention the warehouse fire until it's necessary. We'll lock up the actual results and create fake packets to steal from my office during our Founder's Day Picnic, Labor Day weekend.

"Will there be enough time to do this?" Prissy asked.

"Yes, if I can take over our research facility with two other researchers after hours. I've asked two NCSU PhDs to work with me on this. They'll sign an NDA and in return, will receive a SEcure Well grant to further their research. I'll spend a few days in Raleigh getting started, then we'll come back here. They'll stay with us to finish the prototypes, complete the warehouse fire tests, and analyze the data. We have plenty of room. Otherwise, we behave as usual."

Mitch leaned back and rubbed the back of his neck. "I've done some investigating, and we can't rule out someone at the station. We should add Captain Hank Morgan and Steve Chambers to the list."

Prissy and Bree gasped. Joe and Bob eyed each other.

Mitch repeated the information he'd told Dirk. "Dirk's also willing to help out as another set of eyes and ears at the station, and he'll volunteer to help with the testing, as will I."

Bree looked at Prissy, then at Joe and Bob. They all nodded.

"I'll start the background checks on Hank and Steve," Bob said. "We may be barking up the wrong tree, but it won't hurt."

Prissy stood up from the table with a look of determination. "Invite Dirk to go with us to the facility tomorrow. If he can go, he can ask the same questions you do and keep track of other personnel movements. If you'll excuse me, I have an early morning."

Chapter 12

FRIDAY MORNING, MITCH arrived an hour earlier than expected. Prissy screamed when he said his usual "Knock, knock," coming through the kitchen door.

She jumped. "You gave me a heart attack." She wore a silky, short robe that barely covered her backside, fluffy slippers with chicken heads sticking up high over her toes, her hair was in large curlers, and white cream covered her face, leaving her eyes and mouth uncovered.

"Whoa!" He snickered. "You look like my sisters do just before going out on a date, only you have better results." She threw a coffee mug at his head, but he caught it. "Thanks. I'll help myself. I told Bree I'd make lots of coffee this morning because she didn't want to be late leaving for the factory. Oh, and Dirk will be here in about an hour."

Prissy's eyes grew large as she spoke faster, "Since you're here, you can make yourself useful finishing breakfast: scrambled eggs, bacon, and grits. The biscuits are in the oven. Cookies and muffins need another ten minutes—remove them and let them cool on a rack. Then put in the next batch. Don't burn them!" She hustled out of the room before he could reply.

Unfazed, Mitch donned her apron and white fluted chef's hat—he'd never worn one of those, then worked while singing, "Whistle While You Work," the dwarf's tune from *Snow White*.

The long marble top island was lined with all the items for a breakfast buffet: a carafe of juice, plates, cutlery, glassware, mugs, and electric casserole serving dishes. As each item finished, he placed it in the correct dish on warming trays. At the other end, racks with cooled baked goods waited to be put into teal blue boxes for the warehouse visit, so he carefully packed them between cooking, then turned his attention to brewing coffee.

Moments later, Mitch realized Bree was there, dressed in a business suit, her hair swept up in a twisty style held in place with a gold clip, as little ringlets fell from the side of her face and the base of her neck. She sang along with him.

"I imagined you orchestrating the cooking and baking as little bluebird helpers stirred and tied bows on all the dessert boxes, just like in an animated Disney movie," she said.

He laughed in delight, causing her to blush the prettiest rose color—a sight he couldn't get enough of. He picked up another apron, placed it over Bree's head, and gave her a spatula to act as a microphone so they could sing and dance around the kitchen together. He hoped this was enough of a distraction from her complicated reality.

Prissy walked in dressed like a runway model, wearing four-inch heels. "At least you follow directions. Anytime you want a job as a line cook, I'm hiring." She patted her hair in place. "Will Dirk join us for breakfast, or will he drive to the facility alone?"

"He's on the way," Mitch informed her. "He had to give Hank a breakdown of our taskers today. Dirk will shadow me and then sign off on some paperwork, which will also count toward my coursework."

"You look nice today, Prissy. Any… special reason?" He winked at Bree.

"Thank you. One should maintain a professional appearance at a business event."

Bree snorted.

"I'm hungry. Let's eat." Ignoring Bree's reaction, Prissy filled her plate with a small portion of each buffet item, added a biscuit with blackberry jam, and then took it and her juice to the dining room.

It was like an invisible dinner bell had rung. Joe, Bob, six other SEcure Well agents, and Dirk filed in for breakfast. Mitch and Bree discarded their aprons and spatulas, waited to fill their plates, and grabbed coffee mugs to join the others. Although they were the last to arrive at the table, their usual places were reserved.

Bree nodded for Bob to begin. "Today's operation has several layers. This is an official company meeting for all employees and the board, with announcements. Employee packets will be distributed, accompanied by supervisor comments. Prissy will announce the Firefighter's Day festivities, deliver a motivational speech, congratulate the employees of the quarter with a bonus, and distribute a safety questionnaire. She and Joe will gather the surveys and keep people occupied while we upgrade security measures and search for evidence. This will take time, keep the meeting going until I give the 'all clear.'

"Bree will introduce The Chirp. Expect questions, but be intentionally vague. She will introduce Mitch and Dirk and explain what they will be doing. Bree will go to the research area with Daid Weisman and me,

Dirk and Mitch will do their inspection, ask questions, and take photographs."

Joe interjected, "Bob and I will be wearing cameras. Stay alert. If there are no questions, we leave in thirty minutes."

Prissy and Bree rose and went in separate directions—Prissy to the kitchen to pack everything, and Bree to her office. Thirty minutes later, Prissy had plastered on a sweet smile, whereas Bree assumed the persona of the company's stern, unflappable, unfriendly owner—complete opposites. Mitch looked at Dirk, intrigued by their transformations.

Prissy, accompanied by Joe, led the entourage into the facility, carrying a large blue box filled with her cookies. She was greeted by smiling employees. Shortly afterward, Bree arrived with the rest of the security team, and Mitch and Dirk brought up the rear. The executives welcomed the group and moved everyone into a space with tables loaded with food and drinks. The security team slipped out once the speeches began.

Prissy asked for Firefighter's Day volunteers and reminded everyone to bring the whole family. "Don't forget to vote in the chili cookoff. Someone who loves to cook will have some delicious chili to sample." She winked at the crowd. "Before I turn over the floor, I'd like to introduce two hunky firefighters from Station 18, Mitch Strong and Dirk Sullivan."

As if she waved a wand Mitch and Dirk stood ramrod straight, puffed out their chests, and made their torsos even more Hulk-like. "Mitch is working on specialized advanced coursework. He will conduct a standard industrial safety inspection of this facility. Dirk will supervise him while he performs his own inspection for comparison. This will take several hours. If they have any questions, please assist them. We want all our firefighters to be properly trained, and Mr.

Lassiter will be their escort today."

Frank huffed, then approached Prissy. "I need to meet with Bree after the company meeting to—"

She held her index finger over her mouth to quiet-en him. "Not to worry. Bree wants to meet with the research team first, and she'll have time to speak with you before we leave." Prissy flashed her brightest smile, stopping Frank from continuing, then gestured for Bree to speak.

Bree smiled, then faced the crowd. "I'd like to announce the development of SEcure Well's newest fire suppressant safety product, The Chirp. It's a new-generation heat sensor that will revolutionize early fire detection for buildings, machinery, and even human use by converting real-time temperature data into sounds to trigger fire control measures sooner than standard systems.

"We are pursuing patents now, and testing is scheduled to begin in a few weeks, with production after Station 18's testing. The Chirp will be officially introduced at the Founder's Day Picnic. Thank you all for being here today."

The room erupted in applause. Immediately, Prissy and Bree were surrounded by well-wishers and board members, who shook hands and offered congratula-tions. Once the crowd moved away, Frank Lassiter pulled Bree aside for a quiet conversation.

Mitch kept his eye on Frank until he and Dirk were surrounded by fawning females with wandering hands who clearly had a "thing" for firefighters. Never one to ignore female attention, he and Dirk placated their fans, but he didn't miss Bree's raised eyebrow.

Joe shook his head, mumbling, "Doghouse. Again."

FRANK KISSED BREE on the cheek. She flinched. "It's nice to see you, but you look tired... are those worry lines? I know you've been burning the midnight oil. It's obviously taking a toll on you, but you really shouldn't worry your pretty little head." He took her hands in his. "Why don't you let me be your sounding board to help you make overwhelming decisions? Perhaps if you used your research team more effectively, you could relax more and take some time to have fun." He squeezed her hands. "How about I take you to dinner and maybe go dancing?"

What an insufferable, condescending, chauvinistic jackass! She nearly exploded until he mentioned dancing. Dancing! Bree instantly thought about the pizza she and Mitch had shared and their brief dance. It was heaven in his arms. Her face heated.

Frank smirked.

She realized he thought her reaction was to his offer. Frank could very well be the one who stole the secrets or tampered with the canisters, and she needed to use his invitation to uncover the truth. She gathered her composure and smiled. "That sounds lovely. I'm free next Saturday if that's good for you."

"Terrific. I'll call you Tuesday after lunch to confirm." He kissed her cheek again and scurried off.

Bob handed Bree a handkerchief to wipe the spittle off her cheek. "Thanks. It's a good thing I've had all my shots," she said.

David Weisman, the lead researcher, approached Bree, looking around as if he wanted to make sure their conversation wasn't overheard. "I see that Frank moved in as fast as herpes. What do you see in that guy? He's sleazy and has been dating one of our researchers, Angela Smalls, and pulls her around like he's got a ring through her nose. You're not really thinking about going out with him, are you?"

"I beg your pardon!" Bree said, straightening to her full height. "You don't have any say in how I conduct my private life, but yes, he asked me out… and *he's* single."

"I humbly apologize. That was uncalled for."

Bree leaned closer. "I don't like being deceived, and you made me look like a fool. Never again, David."

He lowered his voice. "I completely understand. I hurt you by not telling you I was married, and I'm sorry. I shouldn't have put you in that situation. You had every right to kick me to the curb, but please don't blame me for wanting to spend time with you. You understand me and how I work. When we went out, it was good for both of us…" He forged ahead. "I've been separated for almost a year and will be divorced in two months. I told myself that I'd ask you out once the divorce was finalized, but I'd rather not wait until then. If I show you the papers, would you consider going out with me?"

Bree didn't want to unleash any more ire. She needed to use this opportunity for undercover work. She breathed in and slowly exhaled. "I suppose it wouldn't hurt to combine work and socializing. I have a concept that may interest you, and we can talk about this over dinner, say Sunday night, eight o'clock, at my house?"

"I'll be there and will bring the papers. You won't regret it, Bree." He took both her hands in his and squeezed them. "I'll see you then."

Her mind whirled. Prissy handed her three wet wipes for her hands. "Thanks. Who knows what kind of cooties they passed off on me." Bree headed to the dessert table and picked up a pastry, taking a bite while scanning the crowd.

Prissy always stood out and enjoyed the attention, whereas Bree could become invisible, even as the company's president. Sometimes it was a great gift, allowing her to observe others as if they were under a microscope, and at other times, she wished she could be more like her. But it was her fate to be who she was, and she should be grateful for what she could do. *I wonder if Prissy ever thought about trading places with me? Probably not.*

Everyone seemed to be enjoying themselves, especially Dirk and Mitch. She studied their broad physiques, hugged by tight shirts, and how much Mitch was relishing the attention. Two young women said they planned to attend Firefighter's Day and hoped to spend time with the firefighters, possibly getting a personal tour of the fire station. Bree rolled her eyes when Mitch eagerly agreed to be their guide, then she choked on her pastry as the two women slid papers with what she assumed were their phone numbers into his pants pocket... leaving their hands there a little too long. He laughed at their antics as he removed their wandering fingers. Bree had had enough. The pastry tasted like cement. She threw it in the trash and signaled Bob to join her. "Are we ready to proceed with the inspections?"

"The men have finished searching the employee lockers, the computer stations in the research area, and the executive offices. They've also installed listening devices, so we're ready to proceed."

"Excellent. Let's head to the research building. I'd

like to speak to Angela and David again."

Bree tried to leave, but Mitch caught up to her as they exited the lounge. She refused to look at him or speak. He stepped in, pulling her aside and speaking softly, "I see your social life has gotten interesting. So far, two guys have hit on you. Is there anyone else I need to watch?"

Bree turned to face him, stunned. *Not you too! First, my life was a drought, and now it's raining men.* "I like interesting things… and different people." She turned on a megawatt smile.

"I hope that smile is for me because those two guys are on the suspect list." Her smile didn't fade. "Tell me you're only trying to find out who might be involved in the tampering and not trying to make me jealous… because I am."

Bree's smile faded. "I doubt that… not with those firefighter bunnies chasing after you." She walked away.

He jogged to catch up. "Bree. Honey pie. You're breaking my heart."

"That's unlikely, and pouting isn't a good look on you."

He mumbled under his breath, "I don't trust those guys."

Bree rolled her eyes. "I've got work to do."

MITCH FOUND FRANK waiting for him in the ware-house. "Mr. Lassiter, thank you for taking the time to help me with this inspection. My questions concern various aspects of fire safety, compliance, and procedures within an industrial setting. Although this facility is known for developing innovative safety products, I'm sure you have standard protocols for meeting the state's codes, so this is routine. Here is a map of the facility and a list of standard questions that you can answer with 'yes,' 'no,' or give a brief response."

Frank barely glanced at the clipboard. "Exits marked… biannual drills, yes… expiration dates checked… random testing done… no equipment failures… and the inspection teams initial product tags before items are shipped out."

"Excellent. Thank you."

Dirk followed as they passed two employees loading pallets of other safety equipment: one, a young woman with a nervous twitch in her hands, who avoided Mitch's gaze. *Could she be guilty?*

"So," Mitch asked, keeping his tone light, "any recent accidents or close calls?"

Frank hesitated a beat too long. "Not… recently. We had a forklift mishap last quarter—just an inventory loss. Nothing serious."

Mitch raised a brow. "You log incidents like that?" Frank nodded. "What was the financial loss?"

"Almost twenty thousand dollars."

Mitch whistled. "That's a lot. You weren't concerned with the financial loss?"

Frank shrugged.

"I suppose coming out with The Chirp will help recoup those losses. What do you think?"

Frank's smile was thin. "It's innovative. If anyone can create a successful, profitable product, it's Bree, but I'm worried it will be too expensive in research before it can be produced."

"Perhaps. Temperature-to-frequency conversion like that will be hard to fine-tune."

Frank tilted his head. "You seem to know a lot

about it for someone doing a safety check. Out of curiosity—has Bree shared the specifics with you? Patent details?"

Mitch straightened, registering the question for what it was: bait. "Only generalities, but she's on to something special, and I've volunteered to test it."

A flicker of something passed across Frank's face. They walked on.

Mitch asked one more casual question, "Who signs off on inspections before shipping?"

"COO, Katherine Gates, receives the data from Benny Raye, the floor supervisor, before handling the shipping logistics."

"Has anyone reported defective extinguishers after an inspection?"

"No." Frank stopped to look at him. "Exactly what are you implying?"

"Fire Station 18 received two defective extinguishers from this facility."

"That's impossible. We have strict protocols."

"I'm sure it was an anomaly. Luckily, we were able to replace them." Mitch smiled at Frank. "However, I do need to follow up on this. Have you heard any rumors or complaints about products not working, or maybe employees who are dissatisfied and might have had a chance to tamper with the inventory?"

"That's ridiculous. We have a stellar team of employees, and I can vouch for all of them." He quickly looked toward the security guard area. "Well... if someone had an opportunity to tamper with any products, it would mean having access to restricted zones, especially after hours." He approached Mitch, glancing over one shoulder, then the other. "Does Ms. Kelly know about the faulty canisters?"

"Yes, and it's her priority to make sure that all of the products work properly. Being the CFO of SEcure

Well, you can see how this impacts the company's integrity as well as its financial standing. What would you suggest Ms. Kelly do to ensure this never happens again?"

"I'll speak to her, of course, and with the board's help, we can implement stricter security measures, but I'm not sure what to look for."

Mitch gestured around them. "Have you noticed any equipment or products out of place? Any suspicious activity before, during, or after the workday? Any opportunity for someone to tamper with products?"

"Not that I'm aware of, but we have security cameras and motion sensors throughout the facility. I'd be happy to show you the system, and we could check it right now." Frank's left eye started to twitch.

"That won't be necessary. The video recordings are blank. However, I'd like to perform some random product checks to see if I can spot any anomalies. I assume the boxes are stored in order of the manufacturing date, so I'd like to inspect pallets starting with the oldest products and then move to the more recent ones."

"Okay. This way." Frank's eye twitched again. "Each section is color-coded by year, month, and week of production, so that the oldest products are sent out first. If a product is in high demand the shelves are replenished quickly. However, with larger products, like fire extinguishers, they tend to stay longer in storage."

"Are you saying that extinguishers are more easily available for tampering?"

"Perhaps. But who would do that? Fire extinguishers save lives." He rubbed his left eye.

"Good point." Mitch scanned the area and spotted a pallet with torn cellophane wrapping. "This looks like a good place to start. Dirk, can you take a few photos for me?" He pulled out a folding knife from his pants pocket and cut through the wrapping. Removing a box, he took out a canister. He held it up for Dirk to shine his phone light on the trigger. "Tampered. The inspector is NW. Who is NW?"

"I have no idea, but every inspector must sign the logbook. I must speak to Ms. Kelly immediately. If a random search reveals a faulty canister, I insist that the factory be shut down and every fire extinguisher be inspected. This is a disaster, both for our customers and our company. Gentlemen, this is the end of the inspection." Frank turned and hurried off.

Mitch looked at Dirk. "Is it my imagination, or was he a little too quick in wanting to shut down this facility?"

"As CFO, he should have been upset about lost profits and the wasted time spent checking every box. We're talking about thousands and thousands of dollars, maybe more. My money's on him, but is he working alone or with someone else on the inside?"

"That settles it. When Bree meets Lassiter and Weisman, I'm going on those dates as a bodyguard. Come on. We need to tell Bob and Joe. I think Bree and Prissy are in danger."

EVERYTHING WAS ARRANGED for Operation Friday Night. A crew of security personnel swarmed the SEcure Well facility, removing the faulty canisters and replacing them with new ones that had been confirmed to have originated from another factory. While that was being done, the homes, cars, and phones of Frank Lassiter, David Weisman, and Katherine Gate were tapped, and private investigators were hired to shadow them.

Chapter 13

B Y THE TIME Bree got up Saturday morning, Bob and Joe had the results of Operation Friday Night to share with them. Dozens of sabotaged canisters had been swapped out overnight, and the pallets were rewrapped for shipment.

Personal background checks showed that Katherine was in the midst of a contentious divorce with her ex, but she had been in Bentonville, Arkansas, working out a deal with J.B. Hunt to ship SEcure Well products across the Midwest. That cleared her as a suspect.

David's divorce was amicable. He had no debts, some stock, and had been at a week-long conference at Caltech before going flyfishing in Washington state with some college buddies. With a solid alibi, he was also eliminated from the list of suspects.

That left Frank. Mitch and Dirk agreed that he acted suspiciously and didn't have the company's best interests at heart, especially financially. Mitch added that he didn't like how condescending Frank was to Bree, yet he fawned all over her.

Although Bree agreed with Mitch, the only thing that could be proven was that Frank was guilty of being a jerk.

Frank's bank account showed unusual deposits followed by immediate withdrawals, leaving a modest balance. He had sold all his stock around the time of the first theft, then bought fifty shares three months later. He had dated Angela Smalls and might have convinced her to reveal vital information. Although *her* bank account didn't show a windfall, a possible collusion with Frank couldn't be ignored. After all, love could make a person do crazy things. Bob and Joe decided Frank was their top suspect, with Angela as an accomplice.

"Guardian Systems stands to benefit the most," Joe said. "I want to infiltrate the company, access their security systems, and find out if Frank has been in contact. My gut tells me he's behind it all."

Prissy poured coffee refills for everyone. "We can't *give you* permission to do that—we need plausible deniability. But let's say hypothetically that you *might* do it, how long before we'd know something?"

"Hard to say, maybe a week," Joe said. "Frank thinks we aren't onto him, and I'm hoping he slips up. In the meantime, we need to stick with the plan—work on The Chirp, create some bad prototypes, then when Bree goes out with him, she can explain how much money she needs to get it operational and test the product."

Prissy set the coffee pot back on the table. "What if he gives Bree a hard time about the money? Wouldn't that tell us he's working against us?"

"I'll have a semi-working prototype to show Frank when we meet Saturday night," Bree said. "When I ask him for a lot of money to finish the project, he'll probably make me grovel, hoping to get me to reveal more information. If he gives me a hard time, I'll pretend that I've spoken to the board and asked for his resignation."

"Why? Because we suspect him of being the culprit in all this? We have no proof," Prissy said. She paced around the dining room. "If he denies giving you the funds, then the only thing we can do is to pay for it ourselves and leave the company out of it."

Prissy held up her hand. "No, hear me out, Bree. First, this innovation will benefit our company, and we must implement it. Secondly, I know you've been squirreling away money to help me build my restaurant, but so have I. We should use that money to fund the project and file the patents. Consider it a loan. Once The Chirp is in production, we'll sell it to the company and recoup our investment with a substantial profit. I trust you, Bree, your love for the company… and me. In the meantime, we nail that jerk to the wall and the company that put him up to it. Once that's done, the verdicts in the industrial espionage lawsuits will find in our favor. This is a win-win. What do you say?"

Overwhelmed by her cousin's generosity and faith in her abilities, Bree hugged the stuffing out of Prissy. "Let's do it. Thank you. I'll call Carl Stevens from the bank and have him create a special account for this project and move the money."

Prissy nodded. "He should be able to bring the paperwork to us this afternoon and keep it confidential. In the meantime, we proceed with the plans and try to get Frank to take the bait."

Bree looked around at the others at the table. Heads nodded in agreement. "Alright. Creating bad prototypes is easy, but calibrating the real ones will be difficult and time-consuming until we find the best process. I'll be leaving on Monday, so it's crucial that everyone thinks I'm here and not at NCSU. When I come home on Friday evening, Dr. Anna Murphy and Dr. Scott Leivy will be with me to finish the design.

We'll need to use the research facility after hours under high security until it's finished. I'd also like Mitch and Dirk to see how the prototype works and give me suggestions for improvement."

Bob nodded. "You can ask them tonight at their barbecue."

"KNOCK, KNOCK. I'M coming in." Mitch found Bree at the kitchen island with Joe stirring something inside a five-gallon cooler equipped with a spigot. "What have we here?"

Bree smiled. "Revenge sangria. It should be refreshing for such a warm night, and the fruit has been soaking all afternoon. Now, all we need is plenty of cups."

"Found them," Prissy said.

"Revenge sangria?" Mitch asked.

"I'll explain later. Would you please carry it? It's awfully heavy, and a muscular guy such as yourself should be able to manage it." Bree batted her eyes at Mitch.

"Sure. I can't wait to hear all about it." He made a production of flexing his biceps before lifting the cooler, earning him an eyeroll.

Joe held the door open for Prissy, Bree, and Mitch as they left. "I see you've got your watches on, good. Remember, kids, curfew is midnight."

"Yes, Dad." The trio's unanimous response had Joe smiling.

Before they reached their destination, Bree asked Mitch if he and Dirk would be willing to check The

Chirp prototypes. "I'm sure you can come up with some other uses for smaller models."

"Absolutely. We'll be happy to help. I know Dirk will help, too."

"Thank you. By the way, don't drink the sangria." Bree smiled, her eyes twinkling.

The backyard was filled with lots of people from the station that she recognized. Everyone greeted her and Prissy warmly, then they attacked the container of sangria.

Bree grabbed a beer for herself and Mitch. "Now we wait. In the meantime, would you teach me to play cornhole?"

The sangria was a hit. People asked for the recipe, and Bree gave it out freely. Within an hour, screams came from inside both bathrooms.

"Why the hell is my pee green?"

"Mine's blue!"

An ashen-faced firefighter stumbled out into the backyard holding his pants up with his hands, yelling, "Where are the EMTs? Someone, take my temperature."

Mitch choked on his beer, looking at Bree, "What did you do?"

She casually sipped her beer. "Payback for all the times they called me a 'fire starter' and a few other things. It's just a little industrial food dye. Totally harmless. But when it passes through... voilà. Score one for chemistry and me."

Mitch pulled Bree into a hug and laughed as he spun her around. "You're beautiful and smart. This is our little secret."

"Please," Bree said, eyes twinkling. "If I really wanted crazy revenge, I'd make their urine *iridescent*."

AT NINE O'CLOCK, Brandon made an appearance. Dirk handed him a beer, and Mitch shook his hand. "Good to see you, man. It's been a long time. I understand we may see a lot more of you in the future."

"That's true, just a few more months. So, you're living here with Dirk? Try to keep him out of trouble, will you?"

Dirk punched his brother on the arm. "I think you're the one who always gets into trouble. Heaven help us when you move back in. Now grab a beer and let me introduce you to my station mates. There are a few others you'll recognize and want to speak to."

Uh-huh, thought Mitch. *Brandon's going to look for Bree.* It was inevitable, yet he had to hope that Bree would greet him as a friend and nothing more. Without trying to be a stalker, Mitch moved around the backyard to be within earshot when Brandon spotted her.

"Bree." Brandon gave her a bear hug, lifting her off the ground as she squealed.

"I can't believe you're here. Are you home for good, or do you have more time left in the Marine Corps?"

"Darlin', I have six more months of active duty and then I'm moving here for good. I plan to stay in the reserves for another three years, to get in my twenty years."

"What will you do?"

"I want to get into the security business. Know any firms that are hiring?" He wiggled his eyebrows, and she swatted his arm.

"Of course. The offer still stands. Bob and Joe would love you to interview with SEcure Well. I don't have anything to say about who's hired or for what position, but I think you'd fit in nicely. Why don't you come by tomorrow and talk to Bob?"

"I'll do that. How about I take you to lunch and then I'll talk to Bob afterward?"

"I'd love that, but let's make it a late lunch so Bob can go with us." Bree put on her best poker face.

He didn't miss a trick. "What's going on?"

Bree spoke in a whisper, "I'd rather not spoil the festivities tonight—you'll find out tomorrow."

"You always were good at keeping secrets. Okay, then, why don't we get some food and share a dance or two?"

"Dance? Uh, don't think so, but I could eat a hot dog."

Mitch listened as much as he could while talking to several of Prissy's friends. He tried not to watch the couple, but it was like watching a building on fire. He couldn't help himself. They filled their plates and then moved away from the crowd to talk. Brandon often touched her arm and then put his arm around her, leaning in to speak. She laughed frequently and seemed to be enjoying herself.

It was killing him. *I have to trust her even if I don't trust him.* He needed to look away and try to enjoy the party, so he did the last thing he thought he'd do in this situation: he asked Prissy to dance. It turned out to be more fun than he or she had expected.

During a break in the music, Mitch watched Brandon kiss Bree on the cheek before walking away to take a phone call, then never returned. He casually approached Bree, hoping to be her escort again. "Did you have a nice visit with Brandon?"

Bree sighed. "Yes, it was so good seeing him again. He's leaving the Marine Corps in six months and wants to get into the security business. I think he'd make an excellent addition to SEcure Well."

"I suppose you'll get to spend more time with him—"

"Don't fish for information. If you're asking if I'm interested in dating him, the answer is no. He's like the big brother I never had, but I enjoy his company... when he isn't dating half the county." She laughed.

"I see. Then he isn't my competition?"

"Still fishing?"

"Usually, I'm self-assured, but... I want us to be on the same page."

"Same book, same page, same sentence."

"Whew. Good to know. Let's grab one of Prissy's famous brownies before Steve eats them all."

Their hands linked together, they walked through the backyard. A group of blackbirds began to gather in the treetops, singing to each other. Mitch tilted his head and scanned the area for any movement or signs of danger. As their wings flapped, his heart raced, and he began to hyperventilate. His pace quickened to almost a trot as he looked over his shoulder, watching the birds and pulling Bree along with him. Before they reached the patio, the birds took off from the trees, swooping down close to the ground, then rising into the air, forming a shifting cloud of black shapes. Many of the birds landed on the roof just as Mitch opened the kitchen door. Bree followed behind, and he released her hand.

"I forgot something." He sprinted upstairs, leaving her behind.

BREE WAITED FOR a few minutes, worried that Mitch wasn't coming back. She cocked her head to the side and heard tapping overhead. Tap dancing? Her curiosity got the better of her, and she followed the sound. Mitch wore tap shoes and danced on a large wooden floor in one of the bedrooms. It was both strange and interesting... The room had been turned into a makeshift weight room and dance studio. Dance studio?

On a large TV screen, a YouTube montage of dancers moved to "Uptown Funk" by Bruno Mars, while he danced with his eyes closed. Bree stood, mouth open, amazed by his moves. Once the song ended, he opened his eyes and saw her, so he pulled her onto the floor to join him. At first, she refused, but after showing her two basic steps, he turned the music back on, saying, "Just dance. No worries, no judgments, just move."

She did and couldn't stop smiling at being so free. After several songs had played, and they had both worked up a sweat, she turned off the music and begged Mitch to tell her why he reacted the way he had.

"I had a mental flash of Hitchcock's movie, *The Birds,* and it was unsettling. Tap dancing helps me focus and settle down."

"Uh-huh. Sure, it does." Bree searched his face, hoping for answers.

He stalled. "I don't like birds... okay, I have ornithophobia."

"Wow. I've never met someone fearful of birds. Is it derived from a traumatic experience? A rogue parakeet? Did Big Bird give you nightmares?" A giggle escaped her.

Mitch looked to the ceiling with his hands on his hips.

"I'm sorry for laughing." She snort-laughed. "I don't mean to be insensitive, but I can't help it." She held her hands in front of her mouth, trying to contain it.

Mitch's shoulders slumped. "I've heard all the jokes and been the target of childish teasing growing up. That's why I kept it a secret. But I never thought you'd laugh at me."

As he turned toward the door, Bree realized she had deeply hurt him. She had done to him what others had done to her: laugh. It was an awakening.

"Wait, Mitch." She grabbed his arm. "I apologize for my reaction. I'm not sure why I found it so funny, but once I got started, I couldn't stop. And then the laughter felt good. I suppose I haven't found things funny in a while, so it was cathartic. I shouldn't have laughed at your expense, but I needed it. Please forgive me."

She kissed his cheek and then cleared her throat. "I'm under control now. Let's sit down. Can you tell me about how you came to have ornithophobia?"

He sat down on the workout bench beside her. "When I was a little boy, we went to Burke Park every week. There was a big lake there, and we took bread to 'feed da ducks,' as I used to say. The mean ducks stole food from my hand knocked me down, and pecked me. I refused to go back there ever again.

"At the beach, the seagulls would swarm me for food, flapping their wings and pecking my hands when I covered my face. I can't tell you the number of nightmares I've had." He ran a hand down his face. "Even today, if I go to a drive-in, the pigeons and seagulls come for me—they land on my car, staring through the windshield, demanding food. I hate them so much. So, I avoid places where birds hang out."

His weary sigh broke Bree's heart. "I can see how these events would imprint fear into a little boy. I'm so sorry it affected you that way, but there are ways to handle it."

"Yeah, I started tap dancing to relieve stress. At

first, I imagined I was stomping on them in retaliation. Then I thought the noise would scare them away. I've tried other methods, but tap dancing works best. I dance until I feel better and then rejoin the world."

"It's brilliant, and you're a talented dancer because of it. I envy that… But what if you're in a firefighting situation and there are birds?"

"I've never come across that situation—"

"But if you do, you need to be ready to handle it. You could sing or hum something calming to soothe yourself. What songs do you sing when you go hiking or working out with the other firefighters?"

"Um…" He scratched his head. "'Eye of the Tiger,' or we use a stupid cadence ripped off from the Marine Corps."

"Then picture yourself on a hike with other guys behind you and start a cadence to keep your feet moving and your mind off the birds. Or, how about using a rubber band around your wrist and popping it while focusing on a different sensation to reduce anxiety. Here, take mine and give it a try." She pulled off her black hair band and handed it to him.

It barely fit around his thick wrist. He pulled it back. "Ouch. That hurts."

"Did you think of birds?"

"What birds?"

"Exactly. The next step we should try is desensitization in a controlled setting—using videos and audio, then progressing to real bird encounters. We'll focus on your breathing, muscle relaxation, and associating birds with things that won't harm you. We can also do this while working out. If you panic, you can punch a bag or run on a treadmill."

"I can't let you take your research time to babysit me."

"I don't babysit… I wouldn't offer unless… I didn't

care about you."

"You… care about me?" His sexy smile said it all. He leaned in, giving her a short, sweet kiss. "Tell me more."

Bree was at a crossroads. If she let go, she would be vulnerable to someone who could devastate her if he broke her heart. Or she could take a chance on letting someone into her guarded world. The decision would change her forever. She didn't have to flip a coin or weigh the possible outcomes. This wasn't a mental choice; it was a heart choice. This man tugged at her heart like no one else. If she didn't take the leap now, she never would.

Rising, she slowly straddled his lap with a seductive move that took her by surprise. "Spending time with you helps me more than you'll ever know, and this is the least I can do for you." Mitch wrapped his arms around Bree's waist while she initiated a scorching kiss. Rockets burst, lightning struck, and a marching band played. When they finally parted, they were both breathing heavily.

"Wow. If that's part of the relaxation, I'm all in. Bree, I need more relaxation." He pulled her closer, urging her to take control once more. Biology took over, and the room's temperature rose to a searing level. They needed to be rid of their clothing; they needed more touching—

A voice boomed from the bottom of the staircase, "Bree, Mitch. Bob and another guy dressed in tactical gear are here to walk you home. They said you have two minutes."

"Crap." Bree's voice cracked.

"Crap, crap, and double crap."

She pressed her forehead against his and groaned. "I don't want to leave, Mitch."

"I don't want you to leave either. What if I told

Bob that *I* would take care of you tonight?" A lopsided grin appeared. He moved some hair behind her ear.

She sighed. "I want that more than you realize. I don't want to be Dr. Kelly. I want to be Bree, the woman who wants to fall in love for the first time—with a man who understands me and makes me feel like a woman. I don't know how to do this, Mitch. If you're not serious about us, tell me now before I lose all the dignity I have."

"Falling in love is the easy part. It's what you do afterward that matters. You're not going to lose anything, especially me. Sweetheart, I fell in love with you the first time I saw you in goggles and covered in white dust. I'm in it for the long haul, and I'm right here with you." He pulled her to him for another brief kiss. "Come on. If I don't bring you downstairs, I don't know what they'd do if they find us in a compromising position."

Dirk's voice boomed again, "One minute, kids."

They walked down hand in hand smiling from ear to ear. "No need for the taser, Chris."

Chris's face fell as he put the taser away. "Roger that, Mitch."

Chapter 14

SUNDAY MARKED THE start of Mitch's monthly shift change, working from seven a.m. to seven p.m. It would last for five consecutive days, followed by three days off. The night before, he had followed Bree home with Chris and Bob trailing behind them, and they'd talked until three. Their laughter woke up Prissy, and she insisted he go home. But neither could sleep, and they ended up texting for another hour.

Now, he felt guilty for showing up at Bree's kitchen to pick up his daily thermos of coffee and leaving her a note saying he'd see her at the station to discuss the Firefighter's Day event after lunch. The thermos was waiting on the stoop, so he didn't knock but slipped the note between the door and its casing, hoping she would get it and not Prissy... it had a big heart above his name. Prissy would razz him for it, but he didn't care. He wanted everyone to know how enamored he was with Bree.

Unfortunately, the entire Station 18 crew was severely ill when Bree arrived that afternoon. The cause was Steve's secret chili mac recipe, which included hamburger, chorizo, yellow onions, jalapenos, diced serrano peppers with some seeds, and two drops of something illegal in Texas. From down the street, it smelled incredible, but getting a whiff from over the pot could singe your nose hairs.

With unusual schedules and emergencies occurring at any moment, a three-hour lunchtime starting at ten-thirty was common. The crew often enjoyed spicy food, but they didn't realize the long-lasting effects of Steve's chili would quickly disable them. Three gallons of milk and four cartons of cottage cheese vanished within minutes of eating a bowlful. Men and women rushed to the nearest sinks, sticking their heads under the faucets, hoping to drown their discomfort, but the water didn't help. The EMTs couldn't distribute Imodium, Tums, or Pepto Bismol fast enough to ease their digestive troubles. Steve, however, seemed unfazed even after three helpings. Maybe it was his defective taste buds that fueled his love for hot, spicy food.

Hank ate only a third of his bowl and then tossed it in the sink. Sauce splashed into Steve's eyes, and he yelled like a banshee, running to the eyewash station.

An EMT knocked him to the floor before flushing his eyes with a bottle of saline solution. "I should let you suffer, but my mother always said to take pity on the stupid. Keep flushing your eyes out for the next thirty minutes." He pushed a saline bottle into each of Steve's hands before running to the latrine.

Hank ordered Steve to bury the chili three feet underground in sand and sentenced him to latrine duty for the next twelve hours, with a permanent ban from the kitchen. When it was Steve's next turn to cook, he would have to pay for food to be delivered.

It was fortunate that no emergencies were called into the station that day. Bree had never seen the men and women act like the walking dead—barely going through the motions of cleaning the equipment while groaning or bent over, then sprinting off to the bathrooms, followed by a green cloud. Belching, followed by flatulence, told Bree everything she needed to know; not even noodles or sour cream could stop the burn of Steve's Chernobyl chili mac.

"Joe, have one of the men buy bags of peppermint candies, then call Prissy and ask her to bring three bland chicken and rice casserole dishes by five thirty so the crew has something nourishing but mild in their stomachs."

"Bless you, Bree." Hank was ashen. "I don't know what ingredients Steve used, but it would be perfect as an industrial strength weed killer, because it's killed all my intestinal flora." He doubled over and burped.

Bree waved a hand in front of her face. "Do you feel up to talking about Firefighter's Day, or should we table this discussion?"

"A cup of tea might make me feel better. That's what my wife, Betty, gives me."

"Tea coming up. You relax, and I'll be back in a flash." As she walked away, a car backfired. She stopped and cocked her head. "Nope, not a car."

Mitch was heating water in a 45-cup electric urn and making weak coffee in the 80-cup urn. Bree entered the kitchen, "Hey, looks like you read my mind. I thought some hot tea would soothe the hurt tummies. How are you doing? You look pale."

"I think I lost five pounds. Steve is number one on the station's wanted list, so he's avoiding the crew. Once everyone's better, I can only imagine how they're going to pay him back." Mitch could hardly stand up, and his eyes were bloodshot.

"You're not planning something?"

"No, but he doesn't know that. I'll let him sweat while the others do their worst. He's doled out a lot of crap on me, so he'll assume I'll get inspiration from what the others do and then make it even worse. It'll eat at him, watching my every move while keeping me safe from any more hazing."

"I'm impressed. It's also diabolical. And you're taking the higher road without him even knowing it. Even Prissy would applaud. Do you feel up to meeting with Hank and me about Firefighter's Day?" He nodded. "Then let's take a carafe of tea to his office and get this over with."

As they passed crew members, Mitch told them about the hot tea, and Bree let everyone know Prissy would bring a meal that was gentle on the tummy. Their responses included, "Thank God for Prissy," and "I could kiss her," and "God Bless you, Bree."

Mitch brought a folder with the proposed schedule. It included the children's games and their locations, the pie-eating contest, the pie-in-the-face event, and the chili cookoff.

"Remove the Chernobyl category because Steve is permanently banned from entering. We can't be responsible for overrunning the hospital again this year," Hank said.

Hank liked and approved of everything suggested. Bree said that SEcure Well would supply the prizes, and he promised to get the judges, contact the newspaper, and have a reporter at the event. With less than two weeks to go, Mitch would have the crew create and deliver flyers to the community center, library, and other gathering places. He would also repaint the Firefighter's Day sign and put it out on the lawn as soon as possible. Lastly, Hank decided that Steve would be in the dunk tank's hot seat the whole day, causing Bree and Mitch to laugh.

Hours later, Prissy and Joe entered the station carrying two picnic baskets filled with casseroles, bread, and peach cobbler. The station crew gathered around them, clapping and expressing their thanks. Prissy was in her element. Steve was still quarantined in the latrine until after everyone had eaten and the new crew arrived to replace them. Only then was he allowed to feed off the crumbs before he slunk out of the station, expecting an ambush.

On her way to her car, Bree and Mitch passed by the station's bulletin board. Glossy 8x10 photos of Mitch in his most precarious and accident-prone moments were displayed. She studied them, recalling the stories behind each one, and found herself laughing again. Turning to face Mitch, she blushed as she apologized. "You have to admit that you tend to be in the wrong place at the right time. Even Batman would find it funny."

"Then again, you've laughed a lot. Make it up to me."

She kissed him. Steve appeared to take a photo with his cell phone.

"You tend to be in the right place at the right time," Bree said to Steve. "My lawyers would say you're stalking people with the motivation to defame or blackmail them." She removed the photos from the bulletin board and handed them to Mitch.

"Hey, those are my photographs!"

"No consent. No social media. Last warning."

"You know, Bree, the only things he's interested in are your money and helping his career."

"Not true. Grow up, Steve," Mitch snapped. He walked Bree out and whispered, "I'm highly interested in your cooking and dancing qualities, among other things." He waggled his eyebrows.

She blushed. "I need to ask you something. Would you teach me how to cook spaghetti tonight and then stay for my talk with David? I... I want him to know that I couldn't possibly go out with him now…"

"Because you're my girlfriend?"

She took a deep breath and exhaled. "Yes. And I guess that makes you my boyfriend."

He swooped her up in a big hug, then followed it with a sloppy kiss. "I'm the luckiest accident-prone guy in the world. Come on, I'll race you home."

THE DOORBELL RANG at precisely eight o'clock, and Bree knew it was David Weisman. He was strict about punctuality and discipline in his personal life. As a perfectionist, analytical in his approach, and curious about everything, he embodied the typical scientist.

Joe answered the door and escorted David to the kitchen.

Bree looked up from chopping fresh basil. "Hi, David. I'm learning to make spaghetti, and I thought you'd like to help."

"Prissy isn't cooking for us tonight?" His disappointment, dismay, and confusion were apparent.

She snorted. "Not tonight. Mitch and Joe are trying to improve my cooking skills. You remember Mitch, right?" She gestured to the muscular man wearing an apron. "He's the firefighter who did the warehouse inspection after our company meeting. He also lives next door and is a great cook and teacher."

"Sure. Um. What can I do?" David took off his coat, and Joe handed him an apron.

"Wash first, then you get the honor of chopping onions."

"You're still mad at me, aren't you?"

"This isn't a punishment. Mitch says to soak the onions in cold water for fewer tears."

"That's correct," David said. "It dilutes the enzymes that produce mild sulfuric acid, which stings the eye. Use a sharp knife to cut the cells cleanly, avoid cutting the root bulb, and that should do the trick. Then afterward, wash up with soap, and rubbing the back of a stainless steel spoon over the palms will remove any residual smell."

"I didn't know that," Mitch said. "From now on, every dish I prepare at the firehouse will have onions, and I won't tear up or stink."

Joe snickered.

Mitch wanted Bree to make two kinds of sauce: one using a good store-bought sauce that could be customized, and then a homemade sauce made with San Marzano plum tomatoes, plenty of spices, onion, garlic, and slow cooking. Bree had her red leather journal out and took lots of photos of the process, with the others helping and a few selfies to show Prissy later. While Bree followed Mitch's orders and was under David's watchful supervision, the group settled into a relaxed rhythm and comfortable conversation.

David recommended adding a teaspoon of sugar to the tomato sauce to make it sweeter and help neutralize some of the acidity.

Bree tried it and approved. "This is why you're the head researcher. You seem at home in the kitchen. Do you like cooking?"

"It's always been a hobby that relaxes me. I love trying different foods, and I used to prepare elaborate meals for my wife's dinner parties. She hosted financial clients and loved to show off my skills. But I haven't done that in about three years. I once thought that if I ever left research, I'd open a restaurant."

"Prissy would find that interesting. One day, when

she opens her restaurant, I hope she doesn't whisk you away from SEcure Well."

"She's a true expert. I could learn a lot from watching her."

Everyone got to taste the meat sauce while Joe placed a pot of water on the back burner to boil. Bree added some salt. "This reduces the latent heat for vaporization."

Mitch furrowed his eyebrows at her.

David grinned. "Adding salt reduces the heat needed for the water to boil."

"That's what I said," Bree huffed. "I also vote for garlic toast while the spaghetti cooks. How do we do that?"

"Either rub softened garlic on toast with a little butter, or do it the easy way by buttering the bread and sprinkling garlic powder on top. You choose," David said.

"I'm hungry. Use the garlic powder," Joe said.

Within thirty minutes, the spaghetti was plated with a side salad and garlic bread. Joe opened a nice bottle of wine, and everyone voted to eat in the kitchen. David watched as Mitch took Bree's apron, kissed her cheek, and then held her bar chair. "You two look good together. There was never any chance for me, was there, Bree?"

Bree blushed. "No, David. I'm sorry. I'm spoken for. I guess you think I asked you here to embarrass you, but that's not it. I need to talk to you about what's been happening at SEcure Well and ask for your help. Were you aware that some of our fire extinguishers were tampered with and then sent out? Station 18 received nine faulty ones."

"No, of course not. You mean deliberately? Why would anyone do that?" His mouth hung open.

"To ruin the company," Joe said. "Between the

lawsuits and replacing the faulty canisters, SEcure Well's safety equipment division is in financial trouble. We believe the saboteur will continue until the company is so deeply in debt that it must be sold for pennies on the dollar. To keep this from happening, The Chirp needs to go into production as quickly as possible."

Bree placed her hand on his arm. "David, The Chirp is in the final stages of development. I'd like you to help me prepare it for testing. My plan is for you to pretend to go to a conference in Chicago or elsewhere and work with me and two other researchers at NCSU next week. When we return home, we'll continue to work in the research lab after hours under guard and get the prototypes up and running. Once that's done, we'll have Station 18 test it in a warehouse fire. If everything goes well, we'll make the final adjustments, present it to the board, and request funding for production."

"This sounds all cloak and dagger, but if it'll help you and the company, count me in. I'll pack tonight, talk to the team first thing in the morning, and then meet you in Raleigh by lunch."

"Excellent. I'll text you the information as soon as you're on the road. While we're there, a security team will protect us."

"This is a top-secret project," Joe informed him. "You must not discuss anything related to the research with any team member or anyone within the company while this operation is ongoing, understand? Before you leave tonight, you'll need to sign an NDA, and a security agent will accompany you as a safety measure."

"This sounds dangerous. Bree, are you and Prissy in danger?"

She looked from Joe to Mitch, then to David. "We

have the best security team, and we're all safe with them. Listen to what they say, and everything will be fine. We haven't scared you off, have we?"

"If you're fine with this, then I'll be fine. Alright. I need to pack and get my story straight. Thank you for a wonderful meal and an interesting evening, Bree, and for entrusting me with this project."

Joe presented David with an NDA. He signed it and then was escorted out the door.

Chapter 15

LATE FRIDAY AFTERNOON, Bree returned from Raleigh with her two NCSU researchers. She introduced them to Prissy and Bob before showing them to the bungalow to find a bedroom and freshen up. Once that was done, she returned through her kitchen to find four large pizza boxes, two cold six-packs of beer, and a bouquet of a dozen red roses. The card addressed to her read, "I've missed you. Love Mitch."

Bree's heart raced. She hurried through the house until she found Mitch lying on the sofa, watching the weather channel. He smiled at her. "Hey, Sweetie-peetie. Saturday will be perfect for a barbecue. Got any more sangria or tricks up your sleeve?"

"Not right now, but Prissy might be convinced to use the old X-lax in the brownies trick." She approached the couch, and Mitch winced as she scooted in beside his feet. "Are you okay? You kind of look worse for wear."

"I'm great. Well, I'm good… Make that fair to partly cloudy. It's been a long week at work and a longer week without you."

"That's so sweet. I missed you, too. Thank you for the roses. I've never been given roses, so they're extra special coming from you."

"Never? As in… never?" She shook her head. "That will change, I guarantee it, because if anyone deserves flowers, you do."

Bree blushed.

The kitchen door slammed. The voices of Bob, Joe, and Prissy grew louder as they approached the living room, carrying plates of pizza and beer. Prissy was the first to comment. "Thanks for dinner, Strong man. Bree, I'm so glad you're home. I've never seen a man moon over a woman like he did over you. We're used to him being here when you're around, so I thought we'd get a reprieve while you were away."

"Are you saying I wore out my welcome?" Mitch asked.

"Not really. You provide lots of comic relief for our usual mundane life."

"I resemble that remark," he said.

"What happened while I was gone?" Bree asked.

Bob looked at Prissy before they burst out laughing. Mitch turned red.

"Now, *I'm* curious," Joe said.

Prissy turned to Mitch. "Do you want to give her the week's highlights or should I? Never mind. I want the pleasure."

Mitch winced, getting up from the couch. He hobbled to the kitchen and brought back a pizza box and a six-pack of beer. "Get comfy, Bree. This'll take a while, and I intend to drink during story hour."

Prissy started explaining, "From what I gather, the firefighter's initiation process takes longer than most professions. Since Mitch is the latest newbie, he was chosen to handle some of the more unusual tasks. On Tuesday, he had to rescue a woman who got stuck in her wooden fence." Prissy's voice rose an octave as she squeaked out the story. "She was training her Pitbull-mix dog to walk with a leash, only she was au naturel. A rabbit ran into the yard and out a hole in her fence." Her voice got faster. "The woman thought she could keep the dog from chasing it by holding onto the leash, but the dog took off, and both of them crashed through the fence. The woman's head got stuck, and the dog hasn't been seen since."

Bree held a pillow to her face, laughing into it.

Mitch held up his hands. "It was a shame to ruin her fence, but I had to cut her out of it and then try to bandage her scrapes. I didn't know there were nudist neighborhoods in Carteret County.... Camilla is a sweet grandmother who promised to introduce me to the rest of the neighborhood, but when I declined, she brought a homemade peach pie to the station as a thank-you gift. Steve took photos while I tended to Camilla. And stole my pie." Mitch frowned, and his lower lip poked out. He guzzled his beer and grabbed another bottle.

Prissy was laughing so hard that tears rolled down her face.

It was Bob's turn. "Wednesday wasn't such a bad day for Mitch. The station received a call about a cat stuck in a large tree. Usually, the station doesn't respond to that kind of call, but this was no ordinary feline. A large cat from a traveling circus got loose. Animal control tranquilized it, but it was cradled in three branches, and it was a dangerous situation. If it got down while groggy, it could attack an animal or a person. I'm going to let Mitch tell you what happened next." Bob left the room, but his roaring laughter echoed back to the group.

Mitch sighed. "It was a thirty-foot live oak tree, and Simba was at the top."

"His name was Simba?" Bree asked, biting her lip.

"That's what I called him while I sang him the songs from *The Lion King*. He didn't growl as much, and I figured it would soothe the savage beast. What?"

"Nothing," Bree said, covering her mouth.

"They told me his teeth weren't sharp, and his claws had been trimmed. They lied."

The snickers became snorts.

"Simba must have weighed two hundred pounds, but I managed to flip him over my shoulder and started down the ladder… I never knew lions had dew claws until he left deep marks on my butt, but I kept singing, and he kept kneading. The animal control guys got him on a stretcher. Then he bit my leg. I had to go to the E.R. to get checked out. I ended up with a tetanus shot and a shot of Gamma Globulin in my butt cheek—that hurt more than the bite." Mitch shook his head, trying to imitate John Malkovich from the movie, *Red*. "Of course, Steve was there to take photos… I really hate that guy."

It couldn't be helped; bodies thrashed on the sofa as hands beat the furniture, and riotous laughter erupted. Mitch grimaced, getting off the couch, shuffling to the bathroom. By the time he got back, Bree was asking, "Why is Mitch limping?"

Prissy began the final tale, "Yesterday, Mitch tried to rescue a roofer who had slipped, hit his head, and was hanging by his harness."

"That sounds very dangerous," Bree said, her voice full of concern.

"It shouldn't have been," Mitch said. "I've been on lots of roofs. This house should have been condemned. I went up in a bucket and maneuvered it over a flat area close to where the roofer was lying. I moved the guy into the bucket and was about to get in, when the roof collapsed under my feet."

Bree gasped.

"I guess I fell about ten feet into part of an attic inhabited by a paper wasp nest the size of a watermelon. Wasps flew everywhere. I got stung several times. Have you ever seen hundreds of angry wasps looking for a target? I didn't think I was allergic until my hands and lips started to swell, and my tongue thickened. I suppose I sprained both ankles, and I couldn't stand up or crawl because of the lion bite on my leg, so I called it in. When they realized my speech was slurring, they knew I was in trouble." He gently lowered himself back onto the couch with a grunt.

"I was told to protect myself as best possible and get rid of the wasps using smoke. I pulled a flare from my gear pack and struck it. The smoke either calmed them down or drove them away, but it set the nest on fire. Then the roof caught fire. The next thing I knew, I was being doused with water. Guess who got me out? Steve, holding his camera."

"That sounds awful. Are you okay now?" Bree asked.

"Sure. A couple shots of cortisone, some antihistamines, and ice packs for the rest of the day did the trick. I'm Batman, remember?"

"Why are you smiling?"

"I pretended to break Steve's camera, but instead I took it. He won't get it back until after I'm no longer the newbie. Hank took pity on me with the week I had and gave me today off to rest up. He said I'm accident-prone, and that you and I are meant for each other."

"You poor baby," Bree cooed, taking his hand in hers. "Is there anything I can do for you to feel better?"

"I would love a foot rub, but I'm still tender." His lip poked out once more. "A kiss will do, and then we can watch a Fred Astaire and Ginger Rogers movie.

You also need a large television and possibly tap shoes."

"I can handle all that… and more."

"Yuck!" Prissy protested, then followed Joe and Bob out of the room.

Chapter 16

AN UNGODLY SOUND pierced the quiet, semi-darkness of the early morning. Again, and again. Like clockwork, every minute or so, the sound repeated. What was it? A rooster? Couldn't be. Bree got out of bed, threw open the drapes, and searched the backyard. It was too dark to make out anything, but somehow, it had to be Prissy's doing.

There it was again. The lights in the bungalow flickered on. They had heard it too, so she hadn't imagined it. The back porch light came on, and three distinct voices tried to figure out where the crowing was coming from. A flashlight shone toward the far corner of the property, far enough away to avoid identifying the culprit, until Joe's industrial light cut through three thousand feet of manicured lawn to reveal a large rooster announcing the sunrise.

No way! Prissy had turned the estate into a chicken farm. "I'm going to kill her! It's not enough that I work all hours of the day and night. Now I have a living alarm clock that'll ruin any chance of me sleeping until a decent hour."

Bree threw Prissy's bedroom door open, slamming

it against the wall before flooding the room with light. The melodramatic entrance had no effect. Prissy was wearing a sleeping mask and industrial earplugs. Her mouth was open and quivering while she snored, drool dripping down her chin.

Of all the nerve. Bree filled a large water glass from the bathroom sink, and without any warning, splashed Prissy. She sat upright, flailing and spitting out water as she tried to find her footing. Once she realized she wasn't drowning in a lake, she tore off the mask and scowled at Bree. "Have you lost your mind?"

"No, but you have. How could you possibly think a crowing rooster in the early morning hours would be a welcome idea? Do you have any idea how little sleep I get anyway? How could you be so inconsiderate? And how could you not tell me when I got home that you got a rooster, especially after the exhausting week I've had and what lies before me? You will go outside now and corral that rooster before I do something awful to you and him."

"Keep your boy shorts on. I left a pair of earplugs and a sleep mask on your nightstand with a note explaining about Cluck Norris and his wives."

"Cluck Norris and his wives? Exactly. How. Many. Wives. Does. He. Have?"

"Calm down, Bree. There's only a baker's dozen."

"Out. Now. Before I hurt you."

"Easy. We wouldn't want you to have a heart attack. I'll take care of Cluck and his babes in the morning… I mean, later on. I'll introduce you to my Bresse flock. Until then, put on your mask and earplugs and go back to bed. It's time anyway for me to gather eggs and make brioche for my famous French toast. Set your alarm for nine and then we'll talk. Don't worry about Mitch. I'll fix his thermos. Au revoir."

Bree walked back to her room, took a Tylenol, put

on the mask and earplugs, and fell fast asleep.

THE BACK DOOR stood open, so Mitch stepped inside and froze at the sight of a sea of chickens surrounding an authoritative rooster who'd taken command of the kitchen. "Wh…where did these come from?"

Prissy dropped dry corn kernels on the floor to lead them like the Pied Piper outside. "Humble Bresse Poultry, an organic farm in the Kentucky Bluegrass. Meet Cluck Norris and his wives. I haven't named them yet. Then again, I don't think it's a good idea to name something you might eat. There should be some distance between the dinner source and the chef. Don't you agree?"

"I wouldn't know. I've never played with my food before it lands in the deli section. Um. Why are they in your kitchen?" He cautiously moved to flatten his body against the wall.

"I collected eggs this morning, and I guess I didn't lock the gate properly. The next thing I knew, Cluck and his harem wandered into the kitchen. Rather than spook them, I'm trying to lure them back into the coop. Wanna help me?"

"Sorry. I'm running late. I'll just grab my coffee and go. Thanks for asking. Tell Bree I'll see her tonight. By the way… your dinner just crapped on the floor."

FRANK ARRIVED TEN minutes early that evening. Mitch answered the door dressed in black utility pants, boots, and a SEcure Well polo shirt. He was still unnerved by the rooster incident in the kitchen, so he channeled his feelings into the role of bodyguard and stood stoically waiting for Frank to speak.

"Uh… Mitch, right? I'm here to see Bree."

"Your name?"

"Excuse me? I'm… Frank. Frank Lassiter. We met at the SEcure Well facility, and I helped you perform a safety inspection. You're a firefighter, but you also work security?"

"Please show me some identification."

"Are you insane? I'm SEcure Well's CFO, and Bree and I are going out tonight."

Mitch didn't smile, standing with his legs slightly apart. One hand rested on a large flashlight, and the other touched a taser. His muscular torso and beefy arms looked even more defined in a shirt that was one or two sizes smaller, as if he needed a shoehorn to get into it. Bob thought it made him look tougher, and Bree muttered that he looked like a badass. Mitch was channeling those sentiments to combat the weasel standing at the front door.

Frank shifted from foot to foot, trying to loosen his collar. When Mitch didn't step aside, he reluctantly took out his wallet, pulled out his driver's license and SEcure Well ID, and handed them over.

Mitch studied them carefully, comparing the photos to Frank's face. Satisfied, he returned both and stepped aside to let Frank enter, pointing him to the large room on the left. "Take a seat in the living room. And don't touch anything." Mitch spoke into a walkie-talkie, "Tango in sight."

An unknown voice responded, "Roger that. ETA two minutes."

Mitch resumed his bodyguard stance at the entrance to the living room. While trying to look tough, he softened at the sight of Bree walking toward him, dressed in a vibrant blue dress and three-inch heels that revealed a lot of leg. His lopsided smile told her everything, but she also had a role to play. She walked past Mitch without acknowledging him and extended her hand to greet Frank. "Good evening. I hope I haven't kept you waiting too long."

Frank took her hand and kissed it, gazing at Bree from head to toe as if he were undressing her with his eyes. "The wait was definitely worth it. You look stunning tonight—this is how you should always look, not in a lab coat with your hair in a ponytail or working unrealistic hours fiddling with equipment."

Mitch snarled quietly. Such disrespect. *Would Bree hate him if he punched Frank in the face just once? Or, better yet, twice?*

Bree seemed to channel her inner Prissy, plastering on a sweet smile. "Thank you. I enjoy dressing up for a date with a handsome man."

Frank puffed up. "Shall we go? Our reservation is in twenty minutes, and it'll take us fifteen minutes to get to Belle Mar."

"That's one of my favorite restaurants. Reservations are hard to get."

He beamed, apparently thinking he had finally impressed her. "I know the owner, and I was able to get a quiet corner for tonight." He escorted Bree to his

BMW and flinched as Mitch and three other security personnel paired up, climbing into two black SUVs that were waiting in the driveway.

Mitch snickered as he heard Bree say, "Don't worry about them. I'm so used to having security that I forget they're there. You should, too." She patted Frank's arm in reassurance.

By the time Bree and Frank arrived inside the restaurant, Mitch and another man, dressed similarly, were standing near their table. She chose a seat near Mitch, but Frank seated himself, leaving Bree standing—the jerk.

Mitch pulled Bree's chair out for her. She looked at him and smiled. "Thank you, Mitch." Then she lightly touched her watch to ensure Joe was listening and recording the conversation.

Frank removed his napkin and placed it in his lap, then made eye contact with Bree. "I took the liberty to order a vintage red, an appetizer, and Chef LeBrun's specialty for tonight. I hope you'll enjoy them." A waiter appeared with the wine, warm bread and butter, and a mixed charcuterie of delicate meats, cheeses, and assorted olives. In the background, soft classical music played. He lifted his glass for a toast, "To us."

"To The Chirp's success."

"Ah, yes. Why don't we talk about your design before our main course, and then we can have the rest of the night to talk about us."

Mitch gagged.

"I agree. Let's get the business out of the way. I've run some preliminary numbers for testing different variations of The Chirp and its production. I see an initial expense of $1 million, plus another $2 million before advertising. Production must be set up in a sterile facility, similar to those used for manufacturing computer chips. There's a small facility in North Carolina's Research Triangle available for $3.5 million, and after retrofitting the facility, we can start production in six months. All in all, about $8 million." She removed a mock prototype from her handbag and handed it to Frank.

"This is The Chirp?" He stared at the rectangle in his hand. "I don't get it. It resembles a strip used in air conditioning thermostats, but heavier. I'm sorry, Bree, but do you really want us to invest eight million dollars in something like this, for a project that hasn't been tested or approved by the board? I need to see the schematics for the design and test results. With two lawsuits, tampered fire extinguishers, and low cash reserves, our lenders won't back this. The Chirp should wait. It's more important that we address the extinguisher problem. I propose that we close the warehouse, conduct a comprehensive inventory, and thoroughly inspect all products to ensure everything is safe."

Bree leaned away from the table. "Close down the warehouse? That would set us back in time and money and further deplete our resources. The Chirp *will be* successful and put cash into the company. If we don't march on, the company may be in a position for a takeover, and I can't allow it."

"Now, now. Don't worry your pretty little head about this." He gave her hand a little pat.

Mitch's hands formed fists at his side. *Condescending jerktard.*

"How about you give me all the data and prototypes? I'll review them, and if I think they're worth the risk, I'll present them to the board. I want to help you, but I must insist on closing the facility until all faulty equipment is identified and replaced."

Bree removed her hand and clawed at the napkin in her lap while keeping her voice even. "I don't know. I need to talk to Prissy about this."

"Fine, but don't take too long—the warehouse is our priority."

"I see your point… I'll get back to you. About The Chirp, give me three weeks to gather the information, and we can meet again."

"I'm right, you'll see…" He eyed Mitch and spoke in a hushed voice, "That guy, Mitch, is both a firefighter and a security guard? He's staring daggers at me."

"He moonlights for us when he's not at the station. When he's wearing SEcure Well black, he's as protective and dangerous as our other security agents," Bree said.

Mitch flexed his pecs. Frank's smirk fell.

Dinner might have seemed successful to Frank, but to Mitch, it was as painful as having hot pokers stabbing his eyes. Bree should have won an Academy Award for her spectacular performance. He was convinced she hadn't fallen for Frank's charms because she constantly stabbed her fork into her prime rib whenever he suggested that being together would significantly improve her station in life.

As soon as Frank finished eating and drank the last of the wine, he announced that it was getting late, even though Bree hadn't finished her dinner. He was such a rude, narcissistic man, but Bree didn't rush. Instead, she flagged down the waiter, asked him to box her dinner, and added two slices of carrot cake with cream cheese frosting to take with her. Frank smiled, perhaps thinking Bree would invite him inside for cake and a nightcap… and then for something else. Unfortunately for Frank, Mitch opened the front door and stepped over the threshold, holding the door open to wait for

Bree to enter. Before Frank could kiss Bree goodnight, her phone conveniently rang. It was Mitch.

Bree stepped out of Frank's reach. "I'm sorry, but I must take this call. Thank you for a lovely dinner. I'll contact you soon." He was left standing on the stoop as Mitch not so gently closed the door in his face.

Mitch took Bree's doggie bag and draped his arm around her shoulder as they strolled into the kitchen. "Did you enjoy your dinner, sweetheart?"

She rolled her eyes. "Just as much as you did. What a pompous ass! It looks like we'll go with Plan B. But I'm still hungry, so if you fix some iced tea, we can share the rest of my prime rib and a piece of cake."

TWENTY MINUTES AFTER leaving Bree's neighborhood, Frank messaged his real bosses. "I've seen the initial Chirp prototype. It doesn't look like an innovation, more like a modified thermal strip used in a thermostat control box. Bree is convinced it works. Assuming that I need to review the real version and schematics before recommending spending money on it, she will provide them to me in three weeks. When I deliver it to you, I'm through."

He waited for thirty minutes, but there was no reply.

Sweat formed on Frank's forehead. He loosened his tie and unbuttoned his shirt collar, then slammed his fist on the steering wheel. *It's time for an exit strategy... they're going to make me take the fall.*

Back home, he opened a hidden wall safe, then fingered three different passports and a large stash of cash in various currencies. It was time to start liquidating his stock portfolio online and transferring his cryptocurrencies into a Bahamian bank account under his real name, Frank Wainwright. Then he looked at villa properties in the Maldives, where there was no extradition. There was time to develop his plan, make The Chirp drop, and disappear. Forever.

Chapter 17

I T WAS NEARLY eleven o'clock in the morning when Mitch introduced himself to Dr. Anna Murphy and Dr. Scott Leivy while they relaxed by the pool. Anna removed her sunglasses and licked her lips. Scott shook hands with Mitch and asked, "Are you and Bree an item?"

Mitch grinned. "Yep. We're in a relationship."

"A pity," Anna said. "I was looking for some fun. Oh well."

"We've got fun planned. Tonight, we'll have cornhole, horseshoes, a fire pit for s'mores, and we'll be showing some of the July Fourth celebrations on an outdoor screen. Plus, hot dogs, hamburgers, lots of sides, and homemade ice cream. Don't forget sparklers and bottle rockets for later. Everyone from the station who isn't working will be there. Seven o'clock."

"Now you're talking. Bree said she needs your help with chili, whatever that means," Anna said, then replaced her sunglasses and picked up a Hollywood magazine.

Scott turned his head and continued to listen to something with his earbuds.

Mitch looked out over the pool. Now he saw it. The pool was shaped like a fire extinguisher. How clever. The top of the canister was a hot tub, the hose part was a lap pool, and the main pool part was the body. *I'd love to see Bree in a bathing suit.* He was determined to make that happen.

"Knock, knock." He walked into the kitchen. "Did you need help with chili?" Mitch gathered Bree in his arms and kissed her like he needed the practice.

"Do that again, please," she requested, her eyes sparkling.

Mitch's lopsided grin morphed into another stellar kiss. "Hey, beautiful. Why are you in the kitchen working on chili when you could be out by the pool, playing with me?"

"When you say it like that, I'd love to play with you, but only after I fill the crockpots with different spice variations. I just have one more week to perfect them before the competition. We cook, then we can play."

"Then let's get going, woman. Chop, chop. I want to see you in a bikini."

Once the crockpots had started cooking, Mitch gave Bree ten minutes to put on her bathing suit. When she reached the kitchen, he scooped her up and carried her to the pool. She squealed, but it didn't affect his stride. He walked into the water, step by step, until it was over his knees.

"What are you planning to do? You're not going to drop me, are you?" She squirmed, trying to get out of his arms.

"Would I do something like that? Okay, beg me not to."

"Mitch. Babe. Don't drop me…" Her voice rose an octave. "Don't do it, Mitch… I'll—"

Too late. He dropped her with a big splash. She

came up sputtering. "I'll get you for that."

Mitch dove underwater and surfaced beneath her. He scooped her up again and let her float on top of him while he performed a backward scoop stroke. She didn't hesitate, finding every ticklish spot on his torso. He flailed in the water, trying to escape her grasp as quickly as possible. By the time he reached the end of the pool, she was at his feet. She pulled him underwater.

It was a battle. Mitch thought he had the advantage because of his muscles, but she had the edge of being slender and quick, like a shark. If she didn't pull him under, she was on top, pushing him down. Within minutes, he realized she had the upper hand and called a truce. "I yield, my little Sharknado."

Bree laughed. It felt good to act like a teenager. She got the chance to play, and she loved him for it. "Fine. Feel like doing a few laps? I'll race you." She swam to the side of the pool that opened into the lap area, and Mitch followed.

"How many laps can you do?" he asked.

"I don't know, I swim by minutes. I usually do twenty to thirty minutes, take a break, and repeat."

"Then let's see how we do."

After thirty minutes, Bree and Mitch had matched each other stroke for stroke, Scott said, "You both completed twenty laps. Quite impressive."

"Now, I'm hungry," Mitch said.

She clapped her hands. "Oh, good. Bob bought me a new panini maker, and we can make sandwiches for everyone. What do you say?"

"I think you need to carry me to the kitchen," he said, faking exhaustion.

"Fat chance." Bree took off at a run, giggling. Mitch was right behind her, and both stopped short in front of Prissy, holding out beach towels.

"Dry off. You're going to break your neck otherwise. The deli meats, cheeses, and condiments are on the island and I just made a pitcher of lemonade. When you're finished, clean up, and by that time, the patio tables will be ready." She carried the lemonade, chips, a plate of her brownies, tablecloths, glasses, and napkins to the patio.

Mitch snickered. "She acts like a mother hen."

"I heard that."

It was Bree's turn to snicker.

LATER IN THE afternoon, Bree called everyone in for the chili tasting. Out of the six crockpots, two were clearly the best; those would be the recipes she used for the cook-off. "I can't seem to get the third heat level right. What am I doing wrong?" Bree looked from one person to another. No one had any suggestions, not even Prissy.

Dirk chose that moment to announce himself at the kitchen door. "Mitch, I need some help setting up. What smells so good?"

Mitch indicated the crockpots behind him. "We're taste testing some chili recipes for the cook-off. See what you think. Bree thinks there should be something different."

"My pleasure." Dirk tasted each one and agreed with the two winners. He examined the ingredients and snapped his fingers. "You need a different kind of chili. Not one with beef, but chicken. White chicken chili like my grandmother makes."

Comments flew back and forth before Bree asked,

"What's in it?"

"Chicken, two or three different kinds of white beans, corn, and spices, in a creamy white sauce."

"That sounds yummy. Could you get the recipe for me?"

"Sure. I've got her cookbook. Give me a few minutes."

While he was gone, Bree said, "That could be the overall winner because no one ever does that type of chili. I've got four days to get it right." She rubbed her hands together.

"We've created a culinary monster." Prissy shook her head. "I'm going to take a bubble bath and get ready for the celebration. Tell Dirk I made Rice Krispies treats in three variations, four gallons of tea are in the fridge, and there's a large cooler at the back door for ice. If he's nice to me, I'll help him serve dinner. I sure hope he's using the thick paper plates instead of those dollar store ones." She walked away mumbling under her breath.

Once the backyard was set up, Dirk and Prissy took care of the guests, serving up food and drinks as if they were a couple entertaining friends. Bree donated a few crockpots of chili, which Prissy accepted compliments for, and Mitch got the screen to show four different television shows at the same time. When people weren't watching the screen, they played games, danced to the musical entertainment, or headed to the food tables to fill up.

Off in the distance, the clouds gathered, and thunder boomed, signaling a storm out at sea. Living in Morehead City, North Carolina, like everywhere along the coast, when the waters got rough, the seagulls flew inland. Mitch stopped to watch the laughing gulls flying overhead, calling out to each other with a laughing cry, the reason for their name. Some of the guests tossed them pieces of hot dog buns. The more the gulls were fed, the more they cried, and even more birds showed up in the backyard. They fought for pieces on the ground, swarming each morsel before scaring each other into flight, and moving to different areas across the yard.

Mitch stood still. His eyes dilated and sweat formed over his lip. His breathing became erratic, and his hands rubbed up and down his thighs. He took a step backward, then another, and another before turning to run toward the house. He sidestepped one of his buddies and ran up the stairs to his bathroom, then slammed the door. Bree followed him without a word. With all the bathroom breaks, no one suspected the reason for his retreat.

The door was closed, and she called over the sound of running water, "Mitch, it's Bree."

"Go away. You can't see me like this."

"I-I thought… You were leaving me…" She tried to make her voice small and helpless. "There are so many people out there I don't know… I didn't want to be alone."

"Prissy's downstairs, stay with her."

"I'd rather stay with you… I can wait outside the door if that's okay. I'll just talk." She rested her head against the door and made her voice loud enough to be heard. "Sometimes when I get scared, I try to remember what Bob told me. He said to count my breaths. It might help me… would you count with me?"

"Fine. Tell me what to do."

"I'll count to ten slowly, and you can say it with me. Ready? One. Two. Three. Four. Five. Six. Seven. Eight. Nine. Ten… That's better. I… I'd like to come in. May I?"

The doorknob slowly turned. Bree pushed the door open, shut it, and leaned against it. Mitch's face and the front of his shirt were soaked. His head hung over the basin, his eyes closed, his hands gripping tightly to the sides of the sink. She kept her voice soft and gentle, "Why don't you sit down?" She carefully guided him to the closed toilet lid. "I'll stand. There's another exercise I do, but it's challenging and requires more concentration. Will you do it with me?"

"Sure."

"I'll say breathe in, and count to two silently, then we blow out, counting to two, silently. Then I increase the numbers by one until I get to ten. Ready?" He nodded, and she said, "Breathe in… blow out." She held up two fingers. Then she repeated the phrase, holding up three fingers. "Breathe in…" She continued to hold up fingers until they reached ten. And on her final exhale, she started giggling. "That was hard."

Mitch smiled. "That wasn't too bad. Do you feel better now?"

"Much better, thanks. Um, how do you feel? Correct me if I'm wrong, but you had a panic attack. Can you tell me what caused it?"

He narrowed his eyes. "You did the breathing exercises for me, didn't you? That was sneaky."

"I suppose so, but what I said was true. I don't like being in crowds with people I don't know, and Bob taught me to use breathing exercises when I get scared or overwhelmed. I hoped it would help you, too."

"It was the birds." He gave her a fleeting glance before staring at the floor. "They were screeching and flying all around, getting closer and closer. I knew they were going to swarm me, dive at me, claw me, and peck me. I had to get out of there… I need to get out of here. I need air. Air. Air."

Mitch was panicking again. Bree grabbed his hand and pushed him against the door. Without thinking, she did the only thing she could do—she kissed him.

Her arms slid up around his neck, and she over-whelmed his senses. Mitch tried to resist, but eventually, he let go of the panic and responded as she wanted him to. He returned her kiss with skill and finesse.

The distraction turned into something else. Personal. Intimate. It stirred her inside. He pulled her close and chased after her. She needed air. She pulled away from him, noticing his eyes glazed over for a different reason, and she was breathless.

"Sometimes, a distraction is needed to take away anxiety."

"Promise to kiss me whenever I freak out?" His lopsided grin could have melted an iceberg.

"That… was emergency medicine."

"The best mouth-to-mouth resuscitation I've ever gotten." He pulled her to him again and went another round. "Wow. You may be a beginner cook in the kitchen, but when you kiss, you really cook."

"Now you're embarrassing me. We've been in this bathroom for so long, and I don't want ugly rumors to start about us. It's getting late. Walk me home?"

"Of course, sweetheart. I've already had my fire-works tonight. But I'm going to need a few more sparks once you're home." She blushed.

Once out of the house, Bree checked the sky and the backyard. "All clear, but I felt a drop of rain." Mitch took her hand and they sprinted to her kitchen.

They were laughing and holding hands when Joe opened the door. "Give us a second, will ya, Joe?" Mitch asked.

Joe backed away, hiding a grin.

"Thanks, Bree. I was spiraling out of control. I don't know what I would have done without you there."

"Keep working on your exercises. You'll get there,

and I'll be right there with you." Her hands wrapped around his neck, and she pressed her lips to his, conveying more emotion than she ever had before. She slowly pulled away. "Night, Mitch. I'm going to dream of you." Who was this Bree? She was starting to like her a lot.

Mitch's eyes crinkled at the corners. "Me, too, babe."

Chapter 18

BREE STARTED THE morning meeting after Mitch left for work. "Things are running smoothly with The Chirp's development, and I couldn't be more pleased with Anna and Scott's work. They'll come for lunch before their evening shift begins. They certainly enjoyed the Fourth of July celebration, and I'd like to make sure they're happy here. They might want to attend the Firefighter's Day event. In the meantime, I need to perfect my white chicken chili recipe, and Mitch mentioned a movie night on Wednesday or Thursday evening, so that will give me time to get some taste testers. Bob, you're up."

"Good news. Our intelligence revealed that Guardian Systems made substantial payments to Frank Lassiter before the industrial thefts. Beneath their research and patent documentation, our techs uncovered the special encrypted watermarks used in all Secure Well's research—Guardian never removed them. It's proof that they stole the company's property. Patents were filed quickly, suggesting that favors were exchanged, so we're investigating that. Unfortunately, we obtained that information illegally, so we must continue and catch Frank in the act. Joe and I will reach out to some contacts to see if we can interest the authorities in Mark Stokes and James Fuller."

He flipped a page in his notebook. "One of their researchers will retire at the end of this month and is willing to cooperate with us if we protect him. We'll relocate him to a secure location. And if we stay on schedule, the warehouse fire can happen next Saturday. This gives us a few days before you hand over The Chirp schematics and prototypes to Frank. The local authorities have been notified and will be monitoring his movements. Otherwise, we will proceed with our current plan."

Prissy spoke next, "I contacted our lawyer to draw up the LLC agreement. The name of the company is Two Chicks Ventures." She smiled broadly. "I thought it was a great play on words. And he placed a bid on the factory complex in Raleigh. We should have an update by the end of the week."

Bree gave her an enthusiastic nod. "Excellent, and clever name."

LATER IN THE afternoon, Mitch helped Dirk carry two giant watermelons into Prissy's kitchen.

Surprise was written all over her face. "What's this?"

"Dirk had a brilliant idea to spike some watermelon for a movie night on Wednesday. We thought you might think of some other fruity things we could make with a dozen watermelons."

"I haven't done that in ages. How did you get

twelve?"

"My uncle is a Boy Scout leader, and his troop is raising money for new camping equipment," Dirk said. "He persuaded me to buy twelve Bogue watermelons. I thought they would be small, five-pounders, but no. They must weigh ten or twelve pounds each. I can't eat that much, and I'd rather not take them to the station. They're sitting in the back of my truck. So, Mitch thought we could put 'em to good use."

Bree walked into the kitchen, wearing a lab coat and goggles around her neck. "What's going on? Watermelon? Can we cut one? I love watermelon."

Prissy pulled out a butcher's knife and sliced a watermelon with expert precision, then arranged the slices on a platter. She also grabbed two saltshakers. Everyone took a piece.

Mitch said, "I need salt. See, watermelon is everyone's favorite. Add an outdoor movie with popcorn and a pig pick'n, and we've got a great party. Besides, there are three guys at the station having birthdays this month, and they said that if they could have a birthday party at our place, they would buy all the food and beer."

Prissy's eyes narrowed. "What's the catch? You're overselling this because there's something you're not saying."

"The Redneck BBQ Lab is supplying the barbecue, sides, hush puppies, and banana pudding. Can't beat the menu, and Steve dropped a few C notes—"

"Steve's coming?" Prissy raised an eyebrow. "I thought he was the bane of your existence."

Mitch shrugged. "Yeah, well, he's kind of turned over a new leaf, and this might be a good way to see if that's true. Besides, he's going to crash the party anyway. Wild horses won't keep him away. So if he's coming, why not make him pay for the food and beer since he never does?"

"What else?" Prissy asked.

Dirk coughed. "He… um requested that you invite all your girlfriends."

"The nerve." She threw a towel at him. "And you… You know what he did to me at my birthday party."

"It was cruel, but he's had this huge crush on you forever," Dirk said. "If you invite some of your friends, it'll keep him busy, and if that doesn't work, I'll keep him away from you. What do you say? I know it's a lot to ask, but I've got all these watermelons, and the barbecue is coming."

"You'll owe me a big, big favor."

"Done. Where do you want the watermelons? I'll drop off the vodka later."

Prissy pointed to a corner in the room.

Out of nowhere, a white six-rotor drone buzzed into the kitchen and hovered.

Prissy screeched. "What the heck is that and who's maneuvering it?"

"Um… probably Steve," Mitch replied. "He splurged on a birthday toy. Everyone, say 'hello' to Steve." Dirk and Mitch turned to face the camera lens and waved.

Bree grabbed a stool, stood on it, and examined the drone's design. She muttered words and phrases befitting an engineer. Then gave Steve a thumbs up.

Prissy, on the other hand, reached into a drawer and grabbed metal measuring cups, spoons, and anything else she could throw at the drone. The first two objects hit their target, but Steve anticipated the throws and adjusted the drone's position before any damage could occur. His laughter echoed from next door.

Prissy opened another drawer and pulled out a

two-and-a-half-foot French pastry roller. Instead of throwing it, she was determined to bat it out of the sky. Again, Steve laughed. That was the breaking point. Prissy opened a cabinet, pulled out a large container, and removed the lid. She then backed toward the hovering drone, keeping the container out of sight. When close enough, she turned and threw five pounds of flour onto the drone. The flour had the desired effect: it clogged the spinning blades, coated the lens, and weighed down the drone. It fell with a loud thud.

Seconds later, Steve ran into the kitchen. "You killed Drone Solo."

Prissy assumed her famous stance, one hip cocked and both hands on her hips. "You're lucky I didn't throw knives. I could work in a circus act with my accuracy, but they dull easily, and you don't make enough money to sharpen them."

Bree picked up the drone and blew the flour off. "This is a high-end drone, and I'm sure it cost a pretty penny. When did you learn to fly one? How difficult is it to maneuver? What kind of weather can it with-stand? How about excessive heat? Would you be interested in helping me test some prototypes in a fire?"

Steve grinned. "Top of the line. Three years ago. Tricky, but I'm a joystick junkie, so it's easy. Never flown it in lightning, but it works well in moderately high winds. Never played in heat or fire, but it could be modified. So, count me in."

"Excellent." Bree handed off the drone and dusted her hands. "Let this be a lesson to you, Steve. Mess with Prissy and she'll hurt you. Give her a reason to pull out kitchen paraphernalia and use it on you, then you deserve it. So, what did you learn from this little trick of yours? And what do you say?"

"Not to mess with Prissy. I'm sorry, Prissy. I won't do that again. Bree, you sound like my mom...

Cheech."

"Good. Clean up your drone and then Prissy's kitchen. When you're finished, find me, and we'll talk, okay?"

"Yes, Mom."

A LARGE OUTDOOR movie screen was set up in front of a table holding a computer and a projector. Mitch picked the films and was in charge of playing them once the sun set. Large bags of movie popcorn and bowls were ready as camp chairs and blankets were spread out in front of the giant screen.

"What are we watching tonight?" Bree asked.

"The first one is a Bruce Willis fan favorite, *Red*, and then my favorite Mark Wahlberg detective movie, *The Other Guys*. There's action, adventure, chaos, and lots of laughs. Just the kind of movies firefighters love to watch. Come on, I need popcorn and beer before it starts."

"I see people are starting to pair off. Dirk placed a chair next to his for Prissy. I hope they get along tonight."

"It's possible. If I fall asleep, please wake me to start the second movie. I have to be at work at seven tomorrow, and I promised Dirk I'd help him clean up."

"Don't worry, we'll all help. Bob and Joe just dragged their chairs in, and they're helping themselves to food. Hmm. I guess they're tired of chili."

The movie started with a theme song playing. In the background, a rooster crowed repeatedly. Fifteen minutes later, Cluck Norris was perched on the fence, crowing loudly. Beer bottles were thrown to quiet him down, but instead, he hopped down and gobbled up the spilled popcorn. Prissy nearly had a fit.

"Leave Cluck Norris alone. Here, Cluck, Cluck. Dirk, Mitch, Bree, help me."

In the background, Steve was showing off his drone and using Drone Solo to make a video about Cluck's escape and backyard travels.

Bree burst out laughing as she watched Prissy bend over, shooing Cluck toward the backyard, his wings flapping wildly while zigzagging between human hands reaching out to catch him. She looked at Mitch, standing in his chair, frozen in fear. "Oh no."

Cluck moved as if chased by a pack of hungry dogs, charging straight toward Mitch with all eyes on him. Bree had to act. She grabbed a blanket, stood in her chair, and held one end out to Mitch.

"Listen, Mitch. When I say throw, then throw it over the rooster. This way, we keep your secret and get rid of the bird. Nod if you understand." He nodded. "Good. Just look at me and do as I say... ready? Throw."

It worked. Cluck Norris was trapped. Prissy was relieved, and the crowd cheered. Bree touched his hand. "Good call, Mitch. Cluck will live to see another day."

Mitch blinked a few times. "Thanks, sweetheart."

Prissy and Dirk grabbed the blanket and carried Cluck back to the coop. "Thanks for helping me, Dirk. He's an escape artist, and I don't know how he keeps getting out."

"I'll look at the latch. In the meantime, I'll zip tie it."

The movie continued to play despite the chaos, and now stories were swirling about the elusive Cluck

Norris. Mitch held Bree's hand tightly, and the artery in his neck pounded rapidly. There was no other option. Bree carefully sat on Mitch's lap to try to distract him. Faster than a stampeding rooster, Mitch calmed down. He wrapped his hands around Bree's waist, and he kissed the top of her head. "Smooth move, Baby-waby."

Bree rested her head on his shoulder. Soon after, his head leaned on hers; his pulse slowed, and gentle snoring began. It gave Bree time to think about what she needed to do because of Prissy's chickens.

DURING LUNCH ON Thursday, Bree got everyone's attention. "I'm getting used to Cluck Norris and his harem living on the property, and the eggs are spectacular. But he's got lock-picking skills to be envied by our agents. The chickens can't be wandering the neighborhood and upsetting every dog and cat. Once the pullets arrive, we're going to need a special helper—a border collie." She raised her hand. "Don't say anything. Officially, the dog will belong to Mitch, but while he's at work, the dog will be here, learning how to herd chickens."

Joe snickered, and Chris snorted coffee out his nose. "Son of a... sorry, Bree."

"When he's off duty, he can be our shadow—a guard dog or companion, so to speak. I've already checked with the local shelter, and they have a nine-month-old border collie mix that should be perfect. Prissy, I expect you to get a handle on this, or your brood will need to find another home. No arguments. The company that trains our security dogs is willing to come for the next two weeks after Mitch gets off work, and the two of you will work together on this starting tomorrow."

"Do Mitch and Dirk know about the dog?" Prissy asked.

"Not yet. I'll drop by the station after lunch. If Dirk has a problem with it, then the dog will need to board with us. However, they both had dogs growing up, and I think they'll be open to this. We'll pick up the dog this evening, so I'll let you know.

Bree arrived at the station to find Steve showing Dirk and Mitch the footage from Cluck Norris's escapade the previous night. "You sure know how to throw a party, Dirk, but from what I saw, Mitch has a major problem… he's afraid of roosters! You and Bree can't cover for him anymore. So, what do you think our crew will say about working with a 'big chicken?'" His laughter turned sinister. "What will it take to keep this quiet?"

Mitch rubbed his hand across his face. Dirk got to his feet and fisted Steve's T-shirt. "You're the one with major problems. You're better suited as a gossip columnist than a firefighter, and what you're proposing is blackmail. It's illegal. Normally, you act like a juvenile, but now, you're just stupid. If this gets around the station, no one will trust you. No one will want to work with you, fearing they may be videoed and blackmailed, like what you've done to Mitch since he's been here. But now, you've crossed the line. You'll be branded a traitor. More likely, the crew will demand that you be transferred or thrown out. You have five seconds to rethink this." He paused before counting. "Five. Four. Three. Two. One. What's it going to be?"

Steve swallowed hard. "You're right. I thought this was a game, but I took it too far. I'm sorry, Mitch. Look, I'm deleting the video. Are we good? You're not going to report this, are you?"

"For now, neither Dirk nor I will report this, unless

something similar happens to any crew member in the future, understood?"

"Yeah."

"My mother would say that you do these things because you're insecure and are looking for attention any way you can get it," Mitch said. "Personally, I think you're trying too hard to make friends. I'm sure underneath it all, you have some redeeming qualities."

Dirk snorted.

"Why don't you make an appointment to see the county therapist and get some advice. If you do, then Dirk and I will be here to help."

"You'd do that for me after all the crap I've done to you?"

He shrugged. "Sure. Making friends can be hard, and I'm a softie for second chances. Don't blow it."

"I won't… thanks. I have a phone call to make."

Once Steve left the room, Dirk turned to Mitch. "Are you really afraid of roosters?"

Mitch looked up at the ceiling and sighed. "Roosters, chickens, and all birds. It's paralyzing, but I'm trying to work through it."

Bree stepped forward. "I have a proposal to help with that." Mitch looked from her to Dirk and back. "It may kill two birds with one bark, so to speak. I'd like Mitch to get a dog, specifically a border collie mix that can shoo away any birds, especially Prissy's chickens, and give him comfort. The dog will stay with Mitch while he's at home and then with me while he's at work, providing another layer of security for Prissy and me. In the process, Mitch will continue using therapies to alleviate his phobia. If you two agree, I've found the perfect candidate, and we can pick up Chewbarka at the shelter after work. What do you think?"

"Chewbarka? Oh yeah," Mitch said.

Dirk nodded. "Promise me you'll housebreak him and keep him from eating the baseboards. And my food. And stay off my bed. And the couch."

Mitch looked from Dirk to Bree and back. "Done."

"Okay. I'll buy what we need and meet you at the shelter at seven tonight. Puppy training starts tomorrow night."

BY SEVEN O'CLOCK, the shelter was packed with people: Joe, Prissy, Bree, Mitch, and Dirk. They were led out back to a fenced-in area to meet Chewbarka. The curly-haired black and white border collie mix was huge for a nine-month-old.

One look at Mitch, and it was love at first sight. Large paws landed on his chest, knocking him over, followed by furious face licking and love barks. "Down, boy… I mean, down girl?"

Bree looked at Chewie's belly. "Of course, Chewbarka would be a female. I haven't seen a girl yet that wasn't attracted to Mitch."

Prissy laughed. "Bree, you've got competition."

"No way. Bree is number one in my heart, but Chewbarka is a close second. Aren't you, girl? Yes, you are. Yes, you are, my pretty girl."

Mitch rolled to his side, and Chewie took off. She ran around the entire enclosure to her right and then reversed before jumping into Dirk's arms. He laughed, then gently set her down. She ran circles around Bree and then Prissy before lying down and rolling onto her back, looking for belly rubs. Her tongue lolled out the side of her mouth, and everyone rushed to pet her.

Joe pulled a dog whistle out of his pocket and blew into it. Chewbarka immediately stood up, ran over to him, and then sat in front, waiting for a command. He handed her a treat and gently patted her head. "She's smart and trainable. Good. She's a keeper in my opinion. Mitch, are you ready to sign the papers?"

As Mitch approached Joe, Chewie turned her head toward him and lifted a paw. Mitch took it and said, "We've got a deal, sweetheart. Officially, you belong to me, but unofficially, you've got a big family. Come on, girl, let's get you home."

THE SUN HAD long set before Chewie's welcome home party ended. She had sniffed every inch of both backyards, herded Cluck Norris and his harem inside the coop several times, and then jumped into the swimming pool to fetch a toy. Everyone got into the fun and ended up in the pool under the lights. By ten o'clock, exhaustion took over, and Mitch took Chewie home to an extra-large chew-resistant dog bed at the end of his bed. However, he woke up to the smell of dog breath and the sound of her whimpering, as she needed to go outside. He laughed. "Okay, Chewie. I need to get up anyway."

As prearranged, Mitch and Dirk escorted Chewbarka to Prissy's kitchen, where breakfast bags and thermoses of coffee were exchanged for the dog. Chewie took five minutes to sniff the entire house, locating Bree in bed, and then she returned to the kitchen to find her bed near the laundry room, where she curled up. Mitch patted the dog's head before saying he'd be back at the end of his shift and exited.

Chapter 19

THE REST OF the week was an interesting but chaotic time. Prissy saw Mitch and Dirk every morning, made them breakfast, and welcomed Chewbarka as company while Bree caught up on sleep in preparation for her long night of work. When Bree woke up, she played with Chewie for about an hour after lunch while Prissy returned to bed, and she only saw Mitch if she stopped by the station.

Friday morning, Bree was the one who met the guys and Chewbarka for breakfast. Mitch wrapped her in a big bear hug and bombarded her with questions, "You're up. Why aren't you in bed? Are you okay? Is your work finished? Why aren't you answering me?"

Laughter echoed around them. "I'm tired and will go to bed in a few minutes, but I wanted you all to know that The Chirp is ready for warehouse testing. It performs exactly as it should, and while we had the time, we also created prototypes for other tasks that also worked perfectly. We've made about 30 of each type, including wristbands for you to wear during the test, scheduled for next Saturday.

"Anna, Scott, and David will prepare the warehouse next week while Prissy and I handle the business side. I'll go to Raleigh on Monday to retrofit the factory, meet with the production director, and return Thursday afternoon without anyone knowing. Here's the tricky part: I'll call a board meeting for Friday morning, and Prissy and I will present all this to the board. They'll be invited to witness the warehouse test, review the information, and decide whether to purchase The Chirp from us. Regardless, The Chirp will start production in less than six months. Frank will oppose it. So, we need to be careful that he doesn't do anything to sabotage the testing. That's what I'm most worried about—your safety."

Mitch took her hand and squeezed it. "We train for this, and we have each other's backs," he said. Dirk nodded.

"Security will be tight during the test," Bob said. "Frank needs to be present so he can report the results to Guardian Systems. When the tests are considered successful, we need him to try to steal the prototypes and schematics, but we must catch him in the act. Therefore, the company's annual picnic has been rescheduled for the following Saturday here. Bree and I will talk with Hank this afternoon about releasing you two from duty so you can attend the picnic. Additionally, everyone not working at the station will be asked to attend as extra security."

Prissy handed out the breakfast bags. "We're sticking to our usual routine. Firefighter's Day is tomorrow. I've got cookies to bake. Bree has crockpots of chili to prepare after her nap. And you two need to get moving if you don't want to be late for work. Come on, Chewbarka, I've got a treat waiting for you upstairs." She and the dog left the kitchen amid everyone's watchful eyes. Who was this Prissy?

LATE IN THE afternoon, Frank called. Bree looked at the screen and gagged. "I know he wants to see if we're going to close our warehouse. What should I do?"

Prissy huffed. "Let it go to voicemail. We should see what he has to say."

They listened closely. "Bree, it's Frank. I'm sure you're playing with your experiments, but I need to know what you and Prissy have decided about closing the warehouse. We can't afford for anything else to go wrong with our fire extinguishers. Call me back. If I don't hear from you, I'll see you at the fire station. Otherwise, I'll be forced to notify the board myself."

"What a douche bag," Prissy said once the voicemail ended. "Does he really think he can intimidate us? Bring him to my kitchen, and I'll show him how I can fillet him with the best Japanese Deba knife on the market."

"That's my Rambo girl," Joe said.

Everyone laughed.

"Prissy's right. He's an insufferable toad," Bree said. A toad that could cause problems.

"Ghost him for a while. It'll drive him crazy and show him you have the power. No. Let *me* return his call." Prissy smiled like a great white shark ready to go in for the kill. "I want to have some fun. Scratch that. I'll be diplomatic."

Joe's brows furrowed. Bree nodded.

Prissy dialed his number, but it went to voicemail. "Hi, Frank, Bree's tied up now and asked me to return your call. We discussed your recommendation and thought it could be better handled without closing the warehouse, so we've had a team working on it after hours. No need to worry, the warehouse has been purged. Thanks for your help. See you soon."

Bree took her phone back and said, "Nice job. He's going to show up at the station to embarrass me."

"Then let's gather the board together there. I'll invite them to lunch next Friday at our home to announce something extraordinary, and they won't want to miss it. I'll stick to you like glue and knee Frank in the balls if he gets froggy."

"Thanks, Rambo girl."

SATURDAY MORNING WAS hectic at the station; it took three hours to set up for the Firefighter's Day event. All the shiny fire trucks and emergency vehicles were parked outside, beckoning visitors to climb aboard and talk with the crew. Inside the empty bay areas and outside along the building's perimeter, activities were set up for children and adults.

There was a table with fire safety information, a large bouncy house, a ball pit for young children, and a rock wall with harnesses and ropes. Sparky the fire dog walked around, having his photo taken with the kids as popcorn and cotton candy were handed out.

Since this was also a community event, all proceeds went to the hospital's children's wing. Tickets were sold both beforehand and at the event for admission, as well as for participation in the pie-eating contest, the dunking booth, the pie-in-the-face event, and the chili-eating contest. Individual and corporate sponsors had already pledged nearly $2 million, and for every dollar raised at the event, a silent donor would match it.

Mitch stood with Bree, helping to sell event tickets at the door, with Chewbarka keeping them company. Darla, the blue-haired young Walmart cashier, approached wearing all black, including black motorcycle boots, even in the ninety-five-degree weather. Bree hugged her. "Thanks for coming. There are a variety of activities, so check the board to my left for event times and locations, and feel free to explore. I'm really looking forward to you tasting the chili entries. It's because of your recipe that I was inspired to create several variations, and I'm hooked on learning to cook. I'm keeping my fingers crossed and would love to hear your thoughts. Since I invited you, I've saved some tickets for you—once you vote, I'll tell you which ones were mine. Have fun."

Mitch volunteered, "Let me show you around. All the emergency vehicles are out here, so most of the activities are taking place out of the hot sun—we wouldn't want the kids to get sunstroke in this heat today. If you need anything, look for one of the crew dressed in a black T-shirt with the Station 18 logo, pointing to his own shirt. He showed her where the chili tasting contest would take place and how to vote by placing a ticket in the jar next to the crockpots.

He and Darla moved over to the Dunk Tank. A muscular guy in short bathing trunks and a black Station 18 firefighter's shirt climbed up the stairs and tested the seat for sturdiness. "This is one of my favorite events," Mitch said. "Our volunteer," he used air quotes, "was relegated to man this station as his debt for trying to kill his station mates. Don't ask, it's a long story, but his punishment is less than he deserves, and we hope to cash in on it by getting him dunked at least a thousand times."

"Now I'm curious to learn more. He reminds me of a younger version of Nathan Fillion."

"You think so? Hmm. Never thought about it. Hey, Steve. Darla here thinks you look like Nathan Fillion. Are you related?"

Steve searched for Mitch's voice and smiled. Laugh

lines formed at the corners of his eyes as everyone laughed at the comparison. "Hey, Darla. Thanks for the flattery, but I don't think we're related."

Darla's pink blush complemented her hair color.

Once seated correctly, Steve began to taunt the crowd, and insults flew back and forth. He boasted that he would raise more money than the others through his sacrifice.

"We're going to help you keep that promise," Mitch said. "Excuse me, Darla, I need to help Dirk with a task." He and Dirk uncovered a wheelbarrow filled with 100 pounds of ice, and bag by bag, they dumped it into the tank.

Steve pleaded with them. "Aww… Mitch, do you have to do that?"

"Yep. You deserve it." Dirk and Mitch high-fived. Everyone cheered.

By that time, a large crowd had gathered around. Even though Steve repeatedly landed in ice water, he was determined to fulfill his commitment and interact with the crowd to encourage them to spend more. It was evident that he loved being the center of attention, and no doubt, he would use this sacrifice to get himself out of whatever doghouse he was in.

Tickets were sold for $5 each or three for $10, and Mitch was the first to spend $50. He flexed his left hand and threw two balls, but missed.

Steve yelled, "You're an arthritic has-been."

Mitch smiled like a gator fixin' to eat an unsuspecting gazelle. "Not at all. That was my catching hand. I'm a right-handed pitcher." Mitch rolled his right shoulder a few times and dropped Steve into the tank with each throw, as Steve yelled about falling into the freezing water. Crowds surrounded Mitch. Payback. Once he hit the target ten times, he decided it was time for others to try their luck. Instead, people started giving their tickets to Mitch, including other firefighters. Even Hank handed him his three tickets.

The chants motivated him to continue. "Dunk him. Dunk him. Dunk him."

Mitch asked Dirk, "Do you think he's had enough?"

"I don't think so, but why don't we ask him. Steve, will you ever poison your fellow station mates in the future?"

"It wasn't my intention to do that—" At Dirk's nod, Mitch hid the target again. Steve plunged to the bottom, then popped up instantly, eager to get out of the water.

"Want to rethink your answer?"

Steve nodded like a bobblehead. "Absolutely. Never again." He quickly climbed out of the water to sit on the bench seat and wiped his face with a towel hanging on the cage.

Hank said, "I think he has a short memory." He pointed at Mitch. Mitch hit the target.

Steve came up shivering. "I said I was sorry. I promise never again to hurt my station mates, but I really don't understand how it could have happened."

Mitch hit the target once more. "I think he's telling the truth. Perhaps he should take an hour-long class on this subject. Would you be willing to do this?"

"Yes," Steve said through chattering teeth. "Yes. I promise. I'm freezing."

Mitch looked around. "I'm out of tickets, Dirk. So, I'm giving him a reprieve. It's someone else's turn."

Steve yelled, "Thanks, Mitch."

Mitch and Darla continued to walk around for a few more minutes before he excused himself. "I've got to keep things on schedule, so I'll catch up with you again at the chili event."

BREE FINISHED HER volunteer shift and waited for Prissy to join her. As expected, the board members of SEcure Well met them at the entrance, with Frank arriving last. Bree greeted them warmly. "I'm so glad you all could make it today. Prissy and I are committed to upholding our grandfather's vision of maintaining and enhancing this station's fire safety and overall security. We chose today, in this setting, to announce a significant breakthrough in fire safety with the launch of a new product called The Chirp. We'd like to invite you to our home next Friday at noon for lunch and a brief presentation, during which everything will be thoroughly explained. You won't want to miss it. Until then, please enjoy the day's activities, and definitely try the chili."

Prissy and Bree shook everyone's hands. The board members were excited to meet them on Friday, except for Frank. He pulled on Bree's arm and led her away to talk privately. Chewie growled and positioned herself between her and him. Frank stepped back, but then leaned in with a low, threatening voice. Chewie kept a close eye on him, growling every few seconds.

"What do you think you're doing?" He snarled. "You've ignored my insistence on closing the ware-house, and you've gone against your word to have me review the schematics and prototypes of The Chirp for my assessment before going to the board. In *my opinion*, this suggests that you may not truly prioritize the company's reputation or financial stability. Your grandfather would be very disappointed with your flagrant lack of foresight and inability to manage this company effectively. Surely, you don't want me to ask the board for your resignation… I need to review this information by Friday."

Bree's mouth dropped open. Had he just threatened her?

Frank ran his fingers through his gelled hair. When he finally looked at Bree, his hostility was under control. "Look, I know you've been under a lot of stress lately, and I really should have helped you more than I have. I want to support you, and maybe it's my fault that you've managed to get yourself into this predicament. So, why don't I come to your house for dinner tomorrow? Prissy can whip us up something, and you and I will go over everything you plan to discuss with the board. What do you say? I'll bring a nice bottle of wine and meet you there at seven."

He took her catatonic stare to mean she agreed.

"Good. I'll see you then. And lose the dog. She's a mutt." He left the station without speaking to any of the other board members.

Bree knelt to pet Chewbarka, tears brimming in her eyes. The dog snuggled close, showering her face and neck with kisses and licks. Bree was ready to vomit. Frank was dangerous, and this had to be handled carefully. She tapped her watch and said, "Xena needs help."

Within thirty seconds, Joe, Bob, and Prissy found Bree sitting on the floor in the corner of the bay with Chewie in her lap. Prissy sat down beside her and wrapped her arm around her shoulder. "What's wrong? Who do I need to kill?"

Bree sniffed. "Frank yelled at me, then threatened to ask the board for my resignation, before demanding Prissy feed him dinner tomorrow night while I show him everything about The Chirp. He scares me. But you know what was the worst part? He told me to lose the dog because she was a mutt." Bree cried with full force.

Prissy pulled her closer. "He's pure evil. Let's get through Firefighter's Day, and tonight we'll come up with a plan. We're in this together, cousin. Now wipe your eyes. You have a chili contest to win, and some of the board members are still hanging around. We must stay strong."

Prissy had helped set up the EMTs' pie-eating contest earlier in the day. As part of a month-long fundraiser, people bought tickets to guess which of the six volunteers would win. Each EMT walked around the area, wearing a number on their shirt, proclaiming they would win and encouraging people to vote by dropping their ticket into the jar they were holding. From the winner's jar, a ticket was drawn for a gift certificate and a dinner with that EMT. Local companies and donors sponsored individuals, raising tens of thousands of dollars.

Each contestant sat behind long tables covered with plastic, their favorite pie placed before them. Hair out of their faces and hands behind their backs, they leaned just over the surface of the pie, waiting for the signal to start eating. The newspaper and television station covered the contest as if it were a major sporting event, announcing play-by-play coverage while men and women yelled, urging each contestant on.

In the end, Glenda Smythe beat the others by thirty seconds, and even with blackberry filling all over her face, James Greyson, a county emergency dispatcher, won a date with Glenda to the only five-star restaurant, Starfish in Pine Knoll Shores, fifteen miles away on the island of Bogue Banks. From James's expression, he hadn't added his ticket to Glenda's jar; yet her jar had been stuffed with tickets that had his name written on them in an effort to get them to hook up.

When James's name was called, both he and Glenda blushed. He was encouraged to accept the gift certificate and then asked Glenda out on a date. He politely offered her his handkerchief to wipe her face, then kissed her cheek, and they posed for the cameras, both smiling widely.

A gong signaled the end of the chili cookoff voting. Hank's voice resounded over a speaker. "Please join us in ten minutes for the announcement of our chili contest winners."

It had been tricky getting Bree's crockpots into the station without attracting attention to her. Most people assumed it would be Prissy entering her chili variations, but if Bree had carried in a crockpot, it probably wouldn't have received any tastings, much less votes. So, while Prissy and Bree helped in other areas, Mitch, Dirk, and Joe each carried in a crockpot without revealing who they belonged to—they were just extra help. The lids already had numbers and letters corresponding to the correct category, so the two volunteers helping with the event knew where to place them without asking questions about the entrant.

Three eight-foot tables, covered in plastic, were arranged in front of a wall, with extension cords to keep the crockpots warm. Red ribbons divided the five category spaces based on the number of entries. Beside each crockpot was a tall restaurant-style card holder for the entrant's number and a ticket jar. Small ladles with spoon rests made it easy for people to serve samples and helped keep the tables clean. At both ends, two small tables held cups, plastic spoons, and napkins, with large garbage cans nearby for disposal. Since this was a community favorite, two volunteers sold extra tickets as curious tasters wanted more samples.

Prissy met Bree off to the side of the tasting area while Dirk and Mitch stood behind them. Bree's whole body shook, and she was wringing her hands. *Why am I so nervous? This isn't the prestigious Blakely award I won in physics, nor is it the Vince R. Gorman award for innovative inventions in engineering. Keep breathing. It's only a chili contest. I haven't poisoned anyone, nor set the house on fire in the process, so I've already won. Yeah, I've already won.*

Mitch squeezed her shoulders and then gave them a light rub. "You've won in my book, Snookums. As long as you don't pull a revenge Sangria trick, it'll all be fine."

Bree turned to face him and laughed. "You're right. Thanks, babe." She pressed into his chest and felt his warmth radiate through her.

Darla had joined the group and spoke to Bree, "I purchased extra tickets and tasted all the entries, but you're going to be the favorite today."

"What makes you think that?"

"I recognized the crockpots you bought, and when I picked up the lids to smell the chili, I detected my family's secret ingredient. Your chilis were excellent, especially the last category. Perhaps you'll share the recipe with me."

Bree wrapped her arm around Darla's shoulder, pleased with her feedback. "It would be my honor to share it with you, but it's Dirk's recipe that I added a little of this and that to. Let me introduce you to everyone."

"Do you like cooking home-style foods?" Prissy asked.

"Yes, if they're family recipes. But I prefer collecting historical, obscure ones and then modernizing them without compromising the original flavors.

Perhaps one day I'll publish a collection of receipts."

"How interesting. You and I should get together and compare notes."

Darla shyly looked down. "That would be fun. Thank you."

Bree was suddenly proud of Prissy and knew her circle of friends had increased.

Hank grabbed the microphone. "Ladies and gentlemen, if you'll gather around. The judges have finished counting the tickets, so thank you for voting."

A large group assembled in front of the mobile podium, and Hank picked up the microphone once more. "We've had the best chili entries this year, and my stomach would like to thank every participant. So much so that I would love to invite our chili experts to drop off their culinary creations anytime." The station crew yelled louder than the audience in agreement.

"There were five categories this year, from mildest to hottest: Bathtub Warm Chili, Hot Tub Chili, Forest Fire Chili, Lava Flow, and The Most Unexpected. Since this was a blind taste-testing contest, each contestant's name was hidden so that neither the judges nor the counters knew who submitted them. Each winner will receive $100, bragging rights, and an invitation to compete again next year. In the category 'Bathtub Warm Chili,' the winner is number 12." He turned over the card and stuttered, "Dr. Brianna Kelly. Bree? This must be a mistake. Surely, the winner is Prissy."

"It's Bree, alright," yelled Prissy. "She's been honing her culinary skills, and I'm so proud of her."

Bree didn't move. She couldn't speak and couldn't breathe. Prissy nudged her. "Please don't make me get a bag for you to breathe in. Come on, you should be used to accolades by now." She pulled Bree by the hand over to Hank's side.

Hank cleared his throat. "Then, congratulations are definitely in order, Bree. What are you going to do with your winnings?"

Bree looked up at Hank and then at the audience. In a small voice, she said, "Th… thank you. I'm donating it to the hospital fund."

Everyone clapped. Bree left the stage with her blue ribbon, stunned but grinning from ear to ear, with Prissy following behind her.

Darla high-fived Bree. "See? Now wait."

"I think it was a fluke."

The next winner in the 'Hot Tub Chili' category is… number 12. Bree Kelly again? Amazing."

Bree blinked several times, "Me?"

"Yes, you. You did it again, cousin." Prissy nodded toward Hank and pushed Bree toward the podium. "I'll hold your ribbon, so go get your prize."

Bree walked toward the podium a little faster, face flushed and grinning. "I can't believe it. Thanks. And the winnings go toward the hospital fund." Hank shook her hand and then handed Bree another blue ribbon.

She couldn't have been happier and nearly skipped back to the group, where congratulations came from Mitch and Dirk. This time, Darla hugged her.

"Okay, let's see if anyone else won the chili contest today." The audience laughed at Hank's comments. "The 'Forest Fire Chili' winner is number 5, Nancy Brown. Come on down, Nancy."

After Nancy received her money and a blue ribbon, Hank said, "The next category is the hottest one, the 'Lava Flow.' And the winner is number 11, Tabatha Jones. Congratulations, Tabatha."

After handing Tabatha her blue ribbon, Hank said to the crowd, "The crew at Station 18 loves to eat, and chili is one of our main staples. The last category, 'Most Unexpected Chili,' had some very creative entries. I'm told that some ingredients included coffee and chocolate, and one was cooked in a Dutch oven over a fire. At least there wasn't an old sock added." The crowd laughed. "The winner for White Chicken Chili is number 12... again? Well, that's what it says, folks, Bree Kelly."

Bree handed her ribbons to Prissy and then nearly danced to Hank's side. "Ms. Kelly, with three wins today, looks like you should open a chili stand. And let me be the first to say, your cooking," he coughed, "your crockpot chili is welcome at the station any time."

"Thank you, Hank. That means a lot to me, but I think I'll let Prissy handle the cooking, if you don't mind."

"Thank goodness—I mean, what a shame." He cleared his throat. "Audience, in case you're interested, the chili contest raised fifteen hundred dollars for the children's wing, so thank you all. Winners, if you'll gather round, the newspaper would like to take your photograph."

Prissy carried Bree's two other ribbons to her and then hung one on her shirt while Bree held the other two in her hands. Bree stood next to Hank with a smile that lit up the room. After the photos were taken, she shook hands with the other winners.

Mitch hugged the stuffing out of her, followed by Joe, Bob, Dirk, and then Prissy. "This is another feather in your cap, cousin. If I'm not careful, you'll take over my kitchen."

"Never. This was a mental challenge, but I don't have the determination... or their stomachs to keep going." She pointed to the others in the group. "I only need a few basics to keep from starving, and I'm good."

Steve joined the group, wearing the station's standard uniform, with wet hair, and used his fingers to dry it out. Mitch looked at him wearily. "Who let you out?"

"Hank did. He said I was turning blue and was afraid he'd have to use the defibrillator on me. Besides, I didn't want to miss the chili-eating contest. I may not have been able to enter this year, but I wanted to know who won." He goggled at the ribbons Bree carried and said, "Butter my butt and call me a biscuit. You won three categories! Who would have guessed that you could cook something edible? I didn't, but then again, when you put your mind to something, great things tend to happen. So, congratulations, Bree. Just between us, I think the white chicken chili needed some jalapenos and lots of hot sauce."

Everyone burst out laughing.

"I'll take that under advisement. Steve, I'd like you to meet Darla. She helped me with the initial chili recipe, and I invited her to come today."

Steve didn't even blink at Darla's appearance and shook her hand. "Nice to meet you. My Chernobyl chili is the best, but the last batch was a little too hot for the crew, and Hank wouldn't let me enter it." His lower lip extended slightly.

"That's an understatement," Dirk said. "He'll have to explain that catastrophic incident while Mitch and I get ready for the last event. We'll see everyone later."

"Chernobyl chili? Remarkable. Why don't we get some lemonade? I'd love to hear all about it," Darla said.

Talking a mile a minute, Steve led Darla away while the rest of the group watched with curiosity. "Maybe there's more to Steve that we haven't figured out," Bree mused.

A gong rang, followed by a male voice over the loudspeaker. "It's time for the pie in the eye event.

Three of our local celebrities have volunteered to be the recipients of a whipped cream pie in the eye for a meager donation of $25 each. Step up, buy your tickets, and let's make a huge donation to the children's wing at the hospital… all without retaliation on our victim's part."

There was whooping and hollering followed by laughter and commentary from the newspaper and TV crew.

Despite the high-ticket price, long lines formed as people vied for the chance to smush whipped cream on the faces of the mayor, the chief of police, and Hank, the station's captain. Each man was cloaked in a black garbage bag and stood behind a wall covered by a large blue tarp that extended over the concrete to catch most of the whipped cream. After each pie hit their face, a helper wiped off most of the cream before the next person took their turn.

When the lines died down, it was announced that the winners of the chili cookoff could smash a pie in the face of one of the city officials.

Bree jumped up and down. "I won three times, and now I get three pies to throw. I think this may be the ultimate prize. Come on. Prissy, I need to borrow your apron so I can get up close and personal."

Only three winners stood in front of three city officials. Each official begged them not to get hit in the face, causing the crowd to burst into laughter. Bree grabbed a pie and then walked back and forth in front of the men, dragging out her choice. On her second pass, she went straight to Hank and aimed carefully. The crowd applauded.

Bree returned to the table and grabbed the second pie. "Now, who should I hit this time?" She walked her usual path, and halfway through, she slapped Hank with the second pie. She did a little happy dance as she headed back to the table.

"Excellent shot, Bree," Mitch yelled. Behind Mitch, other firefighters whistled and clapped.

The next two winners took their revenge on the mayor, while the chief of police laughed. The crowd was lively, shouting and clapping. All in good fun.

Bree was the last person throwing pies. She turned to the crowd and asked, "I have a pie left. Who should get the pie in the face?"

Someone started a chant, "Hank. Hank. Hank."

"The audience has spoken." Bree turned and walked straight toward Hank without hesitation. *Splat!* The crowd erupted in applause. Bree strutted back to the group without looking back. "Boy, that felt good."

Firefighters took the opportunity to speak to Bree and congratulate her on her wins, and to do to Hank what they all wished they had the guts to do: smash a pie in his face. Bree found it difficult to accept the praise but smiled brightly and said, "Thank you."

After twenty minutes, all the pies had been sold and thrown. The announcer said, "Ladies and gentlemen, the pie in the face event raised $2,500 for the hospital's children's wing. Thank you for your participation. Don't forget, we have one last event we've all been waiting for, the relay race. Gather around back, and it will begin in thirty minutes."

The final event of the afternoon gave spectators a chance to cheer for their favorite firefighter relay teams. Five teams of four members each, randomly selected, competed in various tasks: carrying a dummy, rolling and unrolling a fire hose before connecting it to a makeshift fire hydrant, running fifty yards before doing ten pull-ups, and climbing up and down a three-story staircase in full gear. The winning team earned an extra day off, providing a strong incentive to win. Although every firefighter could perform all the tasks, each person excelled in one or more areas. However, the leader of each event gave the next competitor a time advantage, so in the end, the winner might not be the fastest but rather the one who performed most consistently at a proficient rate.

Mitch and Dirk were on competing teams and had been given the stair-climbing event. Dirk slapped Mitch on the back. "You know I'm faster than you at this, but let's make it a little more interesting. If I win, you clean the house from top to bottom and cut the yard for a month. If you win… nah, you won't. Okay, you're dreaming, but if you win, I'll clean the house from top to bottom and cut the yard for a month. What do you say?"

"You're on." They shook hands. "Not to be a downer here, but Max is on your side to complete the fifty-yard dash and ten pull-ups. He's slower than Tony on my team and does half the number of pull-ups in the same time, so good luck with that."

"Son of a… I think I need to motivate the others." He pointed at Mitch. "Don't go anywhere or start without me. And you'd better be in your full gear." Dirk headed toward the rest of his teammates, drawing laughter from the crowd. Hank was overheard making bets with the mayor and the chief of police, not in Mitch's or Dirk's favor.

Mitch snickered. Oh, how he loved to get Superman riled up.

Eighteen men and two women were divided into five teams of four for the relay heats. To start and end each relay, a firefighter had to tag the person immediately before or after them. Both Dirk and Mitch had a woman on their team; not a bad thing, nor a deficiency, because they were trained professionals meeting the same standards as the men. And they were the fastest at rolling perfect firehose coils. So, they were paired against each other in the starting heat, the firehose roll, giving Dirk and Mitch the advantage over the other three teams.

First, they had to quickly gear up, grab the firehose from the truck, unroll it, attach it to a makeshift fire hydrant, disconnect it, roll it back up, and finally carry it back to the waiting fire truck.

The second heat involved running with full gear to pick up a 125-pound dummy off the ground, roll it onto their back, carry it fifty yards, drop it, and then sprint to the next person.

The third heat involved running a fifty-yard dash in full gear to the pull-up bars, doing ten pull-ups, and then sprinting back for the final heat.

The final heat was the most nerve-racking and challenging to complete: a fifty-yard dash with a three-story climb up and down, followed by another fifty-yard dash to the finish in full gear. However, as Mitch pointed out to Dirk, the heats could add or subtract time with a small mistake, an incomplete task, or a slower pace. These firefighters were experts in every task. At a fire, it was second nature to them. Yet, in a contest, the noise, the optics, and the ticking clock increased the pressure—and the desire for bragging rights. The losing team would be given extra chores, while the winners earned an extra day off. There was a lot at stake.

Dirk's and Mitch's teams were tied going into the third heat, and as expected, the pull-ups took longer for Dirk's team, so Mitch had about a thirty-second lead. Mitch sprinted ahead to the stairs, but by the second floor, Dirk was right behind him. When Mitch reached the third floor and turned around, Dirk was coming up behind, but Mitch's toe hit a screw that had popped up from one of the boards, causing him to stumble forward. Dirk caught him.

Mitch said, "Thanks, buddy," before scrambling down the stairs two at a time, with Dirk breathing down his neck. Dirk jumped the last two steps, they looked at each other, then ran as fast as they could toward the finish line. Together. The television crew replayed the finish, and it was confirmed that they both crossed the line at the same time.

Hank grumbled, "Now I have to give eight people an extra day off... but not on the same day, by George."

Dirk and Mitch leaned over, hands on their thighs, trying to catch their breath. After removing their masks, they patted each other on the shoulder in congratulations.

"I would have beaten you, you know," Dirk huffed.

Mitch snorted. "Yeah. Sure, you could have, but you didn't."

"Looks like Hank bet against us. We get a day off, and he lost two bets. Serves him right."

"Agreed. Let's get cleaned up. We've got to put the station back together. How about we take the ladies out for spaghetti?"

"Can't. I promised Brandon we'd go out tonight."

Mitch nodded, "Okay, see you later."

Mitch caught up with Bree, Prissy, Darla, and Steve. They congratulated him on the win. "Dirk's got something he's got to do, but I think we should celebrate with a nice Italian dinner. What do you say?"

Steve was excited. "Yeah. I'll go. Darla, want to?"

"Sounds good to me."

"After such a long day, I definitely don't want to cook... or eat chili," Prissy said.

"Italian it is. I'll talk to Joe," Bree said, giggling.

Chapter 20

MITCH WHISTLED, WALKING up the pathway to Bree's kitchen door, before going to work. He knocked once and then peeked inside. He was surprised to see Bree and Prissy looking over a portfolio of fancy desserts. "Good morning, ladies. What's going on? I'm surprised to see you both up so early."

"I'm hosting a baby shower for a college buddy tonight, and I need to make a cake, cheese straws, some heavy hors d'oeuvres, and a virgin party punch," Prissy said. "Bree's helping me with the options. She's been promoted to baby sous chef to help prep and then pack up everything before her dinner date with Frank."

"Excuse me? What did you say?" He whipped his head around to stare at Bree. "A date with Frank? Where's this taking place, and why wasn't I told about it?"

Bree stopped drinking her coffee before speaking as calmly and slowly as possible, "It's going to be here. I'm going to grill some steaks, make salt-covered baked potatoes, and a salad. But I won't have dessert because I doubt he'll stay that late."

"You don't have a grill."

"I've ordered one, and I'll pick it up after lunch." Her smile didn't reach her eyes.

There were so many things wrong with this idea that he felt his head was about to explode. "But you don't know how to use a grill. Cooking on a grill is a tricky business. And I don't get off shift until seven. Why not ask Dirk to cook for you?"

"I already did," she said even slower and quieter, "but he had an appointment out of town and won't be back in time, so Joe will supervise."

"You mean Joe's going to cook for you?"

Bree gritted her teeth. "No, I'm going to cook everything after I assemble the grill. Then, during our conversation, I'll give Frank a false prototype and schematics before I kick him out."

"You're going to put a grill together, attempt to cook dinner, entertain that creep, and do some spy stuff? That's not safe. I don't trust him, and I won't allow you to do it."

"Excuse me?" She sat up straight and gave him the evil eye.

Uh oh.

"Whoa. Down girl," Prissy said.

Mitch paced in front of Bree with his arms flung out to the side and moving like a windmill. "Look, I just don't want you to singe your eyebrows off or create five-foot flames that set the backyard on fire. I love your eyebrows… they perfectly frame your beautiful face. And we live so close—Dirk would be angry if the trees caught on fire, and think of Hank—"

It was Bree's turn to stand and stare. "Are you trying to play the macho protector with me? You've just crossed the line, buddy boy. Listen up, Mitchel Strong." She drilled a finger into his chest. "I'm a grown woman, and I don't need your permission to do anything, so back off… And in case you don't remember, I'm a fast learner, and I have security. Prissy, I'm heading to the gym for a while. Call me if you need me."

As she turned around to storm out, Mitch tried to follow her, but Joe appeared in the doorway, arms across his chest and legs spread apart in a "don't mess with me" stance. "You really like being in the doghouse, don't you?"

Mitch pointed toward the patio and raised his voice. "She's going to get burned using the grill, and that jerk will try to take advantage of her. Can't you talk her out of it?" This was too much. He needed to be with her when she met with Frank. "Maybe I can take a day off, or call in sick?"

"That won't be necessary. For her, building a grill is like playing with Legos, and I'll write down the cooking directions. Bree has handled much more dangerous things than a grill, and she'll be outside, away from the trees. I'll even make sure there's a fire extinguisher handy."

Joe placed a hand on Mitch's shoulder. "I hate to point this out to you, but you hit a major nerve. Prepare to do some serious groveling. And like she said, she has security. What she's planning to do will be stressful enough without thinking that you're going to barge in like some knight in shining armor to save her from Frank. She'll be wearing her watch, and we'll be listening. I suggest staying away until I call you. But wear your watch tonight, just in case."

BREE BOUGHT THE most expensive, top-of-the-line stainless steel Weber Grill, complete with every bell, whistle, and gadget available. She liked its sleek, modern appearance and appreciated the sturdy construction. It also gave her a new perspective on another piece of machinery that required integrated fire protection.

Mitch was right. She hmphed. Even though he'd been rude to her this morning, he did have a point that grilling can be dangerous. Maybe after all this was over, they could brainstorm safety features for both novice and experienced grillers. For now, she'd focus solely on assembling the grill, piece by piece, while entering her Zen mode.

She sorted the nuts and bolts by size and type, then arranged the parts on the patio's concrete in the order they would be used. She looked at the images on the box and knew the order to start building, so she left the instructions folded inside. Opening her toolbox, she pulled out a three-quarter-inch socket wrench, a Phillips screwdriver, and a flat-head screwdriver to begin.

Two and a half hours later, with three screws and two bolts left over, Bree checked and double-checked the connections, making sure everything fit together securely. She pressed the start button. Nothing happened. She opened the lid, then closed it. She crawled on the ground to look underneath. Everything looked as it should. *So, why wouldn't it work?*

It was after five thirty. Frank would arrive at seven. The food was prepped, but she needed to shower, change her clothes, and get The Chirp ready. There was only a short time to figure out why the grill wasn't working. Should she call Joe, or worse, contact Mitch to come to her rescue? This was maddening. Then it hit her; her palm hit her forehead as if the lightbulb finally went off. It needed a source of heat, and the clock was ticking. Duh.

Behind her, Mitch whistled. "She's a beauty. Dirk's going to be jealous. This grill will cook enough food for an army—nice job putting it together. Then again, you are the genius Dr. Brianna Kelly, and the love of my life." He opened the gate and walked toward her, holding a propane tank in one hand and a spray bottle of grape seed oil in the other. "Joe called and said you'd bought a gas grill but forgot to buy the gas. So, I'm bringing these as a peace offering for your... 'date' tonight."

Mitch looked like a puppy that had been spanked with a newspaper. "I'm sorry, Bree, for being a jerk this morning. You were absolutely right, and I will do my best to refrain from telling you what to do in the future. Forgive me?"

How could she not forgive him with an apology like that? "Of course. I'm sorry too for not telling you that Frank was coming over tonight. I'm nervous about baiting him. If this doesn't work..."

"Hey, don't talk like that. I've seen you in action, and you'll do just fine." He handed her the spray bottle and placed the gas cylinder on the ground by the grill.

"Speaking of work, why aren't you at the station?"

"I told Hank that you were putting together a gas grill and planned to try it out before I finished my shift. He told me to get over here ASAP so the fire station wouldn't have to come later." He shrugged. "I'm at your disposal."

"Would that also include a hug and kiss for the tired Dr. Kelly?"

"Definitely." He wrapped her in his arms and gave her a make-up kiss that knocked her world silly. "Wow. That was spectacular. Here's what I'll do: while you get ready, I'll hook up the propane, test it, and burn off the manufacturer's coating before spraying the grill with grape seed oil to lubricate it. Then you'll be all set. I think Bob can provide us with com links, and I can give you pointers as you grill. Creepo won't know the difference. I'll stay out of your way unless you need me, and once Creepo leaves, we can relax, and I'll even rub your feet. What do you say?"

"That would be amazing. Thank you, Mitch."

Frank arrived on time and was led by Bob, who'd answered the door, to the backyard.

The patio was decorated with hanging white lights, and the large wrought-iron table was covered with a tablecloth, two place settings, cutlery, folded napkins, and crystal glasses. An ice bucket holding a bottle of French sparkling lemonade was within reach. A silver breadbasket containing dinner rolls, crystal salt and pepper shakers, and a butter dish with a butter knife and pats of butter was set in front of the dinner plates.

A covered platter of filet mignons waited on the grill's shelf while foil-covered potatoes stayed warm inside the grill. Bowls of salad, sitting on the dinner plates, were covered with napkins and would be eaten while the steaks were cooking. Off to the side of the grill lay a chef's apron, mitts, a thermometer, and tongs. Chewbarka roamed the yard until she heard Frank's voice, then hurried to sit at Bree's feet, watching Frank intently.

Bree had opted for stylish navy capris, a lightweight navy and white boatneck sweater, and flats. Her hair was arranged in a French twist, and she had diamond hoop earrings, a matching necklace, and a ring as her only jewelry. Frank looked around the patio to find Bree at the grill, checking some potatoes before closing the lid. "You look pretty enough to eat."

Mitch gagged in Bree's com link. Chewie growled.

"I suppose that's a compliment. Why don't you

open the wine?"

"What's that sound?" Frank looked around. "Are you cooking crickets?"

Bree laughed. "The grill has reached the optimum temperature to cook the steaks, according to The Chirp. How do you like your steak cooked? Medium? Good. I'll set a timer to turn them, and in the meantime, we can start with our salad."

He pointed to a rectangular metal piece attached to the lid. "That's The Chirp? So, you've modified it for grilling. Interesting little byproduct. Does that mean we're going into the grilling business, too? When did you learn to grill?"

Mitch growled in her earpiece. "That pompous ass. He wouldn't know an innovative idea if it bit him on his tiny—"

Bree coughed. "This afternoon, after I put the grill together." Frank's eyebrows shot up. "Just like Legos, really. By understanding the laws of thermodynamics and some basic skills, I think grilling will become one of my favorite hobbies. And The Chirp has unlimited applications."

"I look forward to finally seeing the schematics and your prototype… after dinner."

MITCH WATCHED THROUGH binoculars, giving Bree instructions, as she finished cooking the steaks, placed them on the plates, and added a baked potato, then passed the plate to Frank. "Everything looks perfect. Well done, Bree. Now, turn off the grill, remove The Chirp, and leave it close enough for Frank to grab it."

"You're not going to remove the foil on my potato?" Creepo asked.

"Are you saying that you can't remove your own foil? Really, Frank. I assembled a grill and cooked a perfect dinner. Do you want me to cut your meat as well?"

Mitch laughed in her ear. "Good one, babe."

Frank sniffed. "A perfect hostess, like Prissy, would pamper her guest, even removing the foil around a potato. Perhaps you should take some lessons from her."

"This is not a date, and you're not my guest. This is a business dinner *you* demanded. I'm friendly enough to humor you, but if you keep insulting me in my own home, then Chewbarka will get your steak for dinner, and you can leave by the back door."

"Bree, Bree, Bree." Frank patted her hand. "I can tell you need a long rest away from work. I should blame Prissy for not cooking tonight, but you might be right in finding a hobby of your own. Have some wine and let's eat."

Mitch said, "Say the word, Bree, and I'll throw him in the pool and hold him down until he learns some manners. By the way, he slipped The Chirp into his pocket. Now, all he needs is a bad schematic. Just say the word, and Bob will bring out the one with a big coffee stain on the edge."

Bree phoned Bob. "Would you bring the paperwork for The Chirp, please… Oh my. Well, it will have to do. Frank doesn't need the full design. Just wipe it off."

Looking apologetic, Bob delivered a stack of papers, heavily smudged with a coffee stain. "Sorry, Bree. The coffee pot overflowed, and this soaked most of it up before I could react."

Frank grabbed the papers. "The most essential

information is beyond recognition. This is ruined." He pointed at Bob. "You're lucky you still have a—"

"That's enough!" Bree snapped. "This was an accident. Accidents happen all the time, and I won't tolerate your snide remarks. Take the papers and The Chirp prototype you pocketed and leave. I doubt you'll understand anything anyway, but mark my words, I will be presenting this to the board, and they will be eager to see the other variations."

Bree stood and crossed her arms. "I dare you to say anything negative to the board. In fact, I dare you to show your face at all! Perhaps you should consider your position on the board and whether you're a good fit for SEcure Well now. Bob will walk you out. And take that cheap bottle of wine with you."

"Well, I never!" Frank shoved his chair back and stomped away, followed closely by Bob, who was trying not to laugh.

Mitch laughed in Bree's ear. "Way to go, girl. You're my hero. If he didn't drool over his steak, I'm heading your way. I'm starving after watching your magnificent performance."

By the time Mitch reached the backyard, Bob was holding a sobbing Bree. Coming closer, Mitch raised his hand to rub her back, but stopped, unsure what to do as another man comforted her. As Bree's tears slowed, Bob turned Bree over to Mitch and walked away. Mitch picked her up and cradled her in his arms before sitting down in a lounge chair. "What do you need from me, babe? Whatever it is, you got it." His hand gently rubbed circles on her back.

"Just hold me." The wobble in her voice tore at his heart. "I'm not cut out for this cloak-and-dagger stuff. I'm not sure what he'll do when he learns that the papers don't match the prototype, and that the prototype was made to work only once. Bob has someone following him, and once Frank takes it to Guardian Systems headquarters, any researcher will see the problem in a day or two. I only hope there's enough time between now and Friday to finish things properly for the warehouse fire on Saturday. Promise me that you and Dirk will be extra careful, because Frank will be desperate by then and is liable to do anything."

"Don't worry, sweetheart. We can handle ourselves, and Bob and Joe will look after you and Prissy. So, are you hungry? Can you eat? What if I feed you? You can pretend to be my princess, and I'll take care of you."

"Oooh. Role play. I could get used to that."
"Done."

BY THE TIME Frank reached his car, he was grinning. Bree handed over the information more easily than expected. The little tart had yelled at him and treated him like a subservient. Bah. She wasn't worthy of cleaning his shoes, much less running a company. Fingering the prototype, he snickered. In less than three weeks, she would be wishing she had paid more attention to him. But it was too late; she would see her end, just like so many other women had before, when he ruined their reputations or took their money. Perhaps she could earn her living assembling grills at Home Depot. She had a knack for that, but not much for anything else. He laughed. He was so funny. Perhaps he should have set his sights on Prissy instead. At least he would have gotten some great meals from her. Oh well.

Before handing anything over to Mark Stokes or James Fuller, he would meet with Angela. Then check if his bid for the house in the Maldives had been accepted. It was early evening, so he decided to pack more boxes for the move.

Chapter 21

THE WEEK BEGAN with the station being notified of a potential gas leak in the backyard of an elderly couple. The fire truck arrived, and Mitch looked at Steve. "I gather it's my turn, again, to assess the situation. Did you bring your cell phone to make another video?"

Steve took out his phone and handed it to Mitch. "I'm taking your place today, and as far as the crew and I are concerned, your initiation is over. You've been a good sport, and I've learned a lot from you. You also have my permission to video me if I do something heroic."

Mitch slapped Steve on the back. "There's hope for you yet. Let's go. I'm on your six."

Jogging into the backyard, Steve immediately found the leak. He slipped and fell into a sinkhole created by an overflowing septic system. Covered from head to toe, he waded up to his chest in stinky poop, trying to get out.

Mitch stopped short and gagged from the smell. "Steve… uh, are you alright?" He turned his head away to catch his breath.

"Yeah, man." Steve wiped his eyes and blinked. "Just another day on the job… Mitch, did I tell you how sorry I am about you getting into all kinds of smelly stuff, and me laughing at it? Well, if I didn't, I understand how you felt now. Sorry, man."

"Good to know. Can you tread in the poop, or are you sinking?"

"Surprisingly enough, I'm buoyant, but I'd really like to get out of here." He coughed a few times.

"Copy that. I'll get some rope, and we'll pull you out." He hurried back to the rig, taking several fresh breaths along the way.

A large crowd had gathered on the other side of the property, laughing at Steve's predicament. In less than two minutes, Mitch created a loop on one end of the rope and threw it over Steve's head in the first try. Steve secured it under his arms and wrapped it around one arm to help leverage his body out. When he was ready, he yelled, "Good to go."

Two firefighters lined up behind Mitch, pulling in tandem. Steve rocked back and forth, but the poop wouldn't relent. They tried again, but no matter how hard they pulled, the suction held Steve in place.

"Sorry, Steve. I think you're going to be there for a while… unless we hear you sing, 'Splish Splash,' by Bobby Darin."

"That's harsh, Mitch. I thought we were good."

"Oh, we're good. It's just that Derick and Brady still have bad dreams about your chili. And they want to hear you sing. So, start singing."

"I only know one verse." He spat out a mouthful of goop.

"That'll work. Oh, I also need to tell you that once you're out of the hole, you'll be walking back to the station. *They* don't want you to stink up the truck. That's three miles, and it's ninety degrees."

"They hate me that much?"

"Yep. I'll also give you two water bottles, one to wash off your face and the other to drink. Don't want you to dehydrate."

"That's generous of you."

"By the way, Brady has your phone." One firefighter held a cell phone aloft while the other hauled the rope back to the waiting fire truck and tied the end to the winch.

The motor whirred, and within seconds, the line yanked Steve out, towing him like he was on a stinky, gooey brown water slide, moving him across the yard to the only dry spot, in front of Darla.

Steve got to his knees and tried to stand. He slipped once, twice, and when sludge spewed from his bunker pants, he fell again.

Mitch threw his hand out. "Need some help there, buddy?"

"Nope. I'm good. It's like trying to ice skate for the first time, only on brown, stinky stuff." Despite his predicament, he laughed along with the audience. His eyes focused on Darla, who watched the show without commenting. "Hey, Darla. What brings you out today?"

"I live down the street, or should I say, downwind. I wasn't sure what died, so I rode my bike up here. Seems you like getting dunked, even in sludge, but I think this time you would have preferred ice water." She backed up a few feet.

Steve chuckled. "Good one. While the city and the homeowner figure out how to handle this, my work is done." He moved closer to her as she stepped back. "Want a hug?"

"No thanks. Later, Steve." She climbed onto her bicycle and headed home.

"That was nice of her to drop by," he said as Mitch

came closer. "I think I'll call her to hang out with me sometime."

Mitch shook his head. "You do that. She seems to be a nice person. Let's roll."

Steve headed toward the truck but was blocked by the two burly forms of Derick and Brady. He hung his head. "Splish, splash, I was taking a bath…" He repeated the verse until the fire engine turned the corner, leaving him alone, sloshing brown stuff behind him.

By the time Steve arrived at the station, Hank was waiting on the sidewalk. "Stand against the brick." At Hank's signal, the fire hose was turned on him.

Steve howled as the water hit him, forcing him against the brick wall. "Crap, that hurts."

The water stopped. "Turn around." The water hit him again. "Strip down to your shorts and get in." Hank pointed to a dish soap soap-filled kiddie pool, with a toilet brush propped up on the side. "Hit the shower when you're disinfected, and make sure your gear is pristine for tomorrow's shift."

Mitch walked to the pool and set a two-gallon watering can and a hand towel within Steve's reach. "Thanks, buddy." Steve sighed. "Do you think that's the last of the chili retaliation?"

Mitch shrugged. "Hard to say. Has Jason, Case, or Dirk done anything to you?" Steve shook his head. "Then you have your answer. To take your mind off things, Wednesday night is *Star Wars* movie night at Bree's house. Ask Darla, and you two can join us. Bring pizza and the good beer."

Steve scrubbed off the lingering goop with a smile on his face.

FOR ONCE, SINCE Mitch had known Bree, *he* wasn't the target of a station prank. He couldn't wait to tell Bree and Prissy the story. He was sure that his firsthand blow-by-blow account would elevate his status in their eyes. Sadly, he hadn't taken any photos, but someone else had, and perhaps they were now on the internet. He'd ask Dirk.

"Knock, knock." Mitch opened the door to the kitchen to find Bree and Prissy staring daggers at him. "Hey. Did I do something wrong?"

"You tell us," Prissy said. "Was turnabout, really fair play?"

"I don't know what you mean."

"We heard that poor Steve fell into a stinky sink-hole, and when you pulled him out, you humiliated him by making him walk back to the station singing some bath song. Do you deny that?" Prissy narrowed her eyes at him.

"It was really funny."

"Bree, he's your boyfriend. Do something."

"Prissy is right. I can't imagine you, of all people, doing that to him. You're the most kind-hearted, forgiving person I've ever known. You told me you wouldn't retaliate against Steve for what he did to you, but now you've broken your word. I'm sure Steve was mortified, poor baby." Bree shook her head, looking disappointed.

"Poor baby, my foot! How did you hear about it?"

"Darla called me. She was upset that you were in charge and took advantage of it."

"Sure, Darla rode her bike there from her house to see what caused the big stink, but I think that she was feeling empathy for Steve and missed the rest of the story. You know, like not seeing the forest for the trees."

"Are you saying that Darla skewed the truth?"

"Not totally," Mitch replied. "Why don't you let me tell you the story and you decide for yourself?"

"Fine," Bree snipped. "Dirk, Steve, and Darla are coming over. You can tell it then."

"Fine," Mitch snipped back. "Then I'm calling Derrick and Brady to vouch for me. While we wait, can I ask what's for dinner?"

Prissy and Bree stormed out of the kitchen and Joe appeared in their wake. "I've tried to teach you about being in the doghouse. Perhaps I should build you one and then point at it for you to go there for a time out." He shook his head.

What's wrong with everybody? "I didn't do anything. Fine. I'll order Chinese food for everyone."

Within an hour, the kitchen was crowded with people talking over one another, trying to explain what had happened. Steve was the only one not speaking. His smile lit up the room.

Prissy asked him, "Why are you so happy? Didn't you fall into a poop hole and then have to walk back to the station in the heat, singing some stupid song?"

"Yep. You also forgot that I got flushed by a fire hose, then had to wash in a kiddie pool with dish soap and a toilet brush. It was great."

"Huh?"

"See, this is what I've learned," Steve said. "Derrick and Brady could have really done something bad to me for destroying their intestines, but Mitch was there to ensure it didn't happen. He supervised them to have a little fun. Sure, it was at my expense, but I deserved it. Now we're even and we're okay. And the best part was that I got to see Darla again." His smile grew bigger as he stared at the woman sitting beside him.

Vindicated, Mitch stood with his arms crossed, smirking as Dirk, Derrick, and Brady continued to eat. Prissy and Bree stared with their mouths open. Steve looked like he was a happy camper, no worse for wear, and Darla had stars in her eyes.

What was it about Darla tonight? Mitch looked long and hard. She had removed all the goth makeup and was wearing a pink short-sleeved T-shirt and blue jeans. The black motorcycle boots remained, as did her blue hair.

Apparently, Bree and Prissy would hold him accountable for his actions and support the little guy, even if it was *Steve*. He had to hand it to the guy; Steve was resilient, enjoyed being the center of attention in a positive way, was learning how to make friends, and might even have found a girlfriend. He was like an onion, with many layers that needed peeling to reach the center—stinky all the same.

Prissy didn't apologize to Mitch, but Bree did, "There are three sides to every coin, yet I only saw one side. I'm sorry. I didn't let you explain, and I'm sure your story would have been funny too. Maybe one day you'll tell me. Forgive me?"

He slipped an arm around Bree's waist and squeezed her. "Certainly, buttercup. It's a funny story, but I'll tell it when the time is right. For now, you should know that I've invited Steve and Darla to come over on Wednesday night to watch *Star Wars*, but you'll need a bigger TV. If you and Joe can meet me at Appliance Depot at noon, we can pick one out, and I'll help you set it up after work."

"Fine, but I'll handle the setup if you bring sub

sandwiches and chips for dinner. Prissy can make tea, and the others can bring whatever."

"Perfect." He whistled for everyone's attention. "Wednesday night, seven-thirty, here. Bring snacks and beer; a date is optional. *Star Wars* will be playing."

"Which one?" Steve and Darla asked together, then she blushed. He grinned.

"The first one that was renamed but shouldn't have been," he said.

Chapter 22

MITCH WAS RUNNING late for work. He barely had time to say hello to Prissy, who was working on a fancy dessert. "Morning sunshine. Is Bree up?"

"Not yet. But she's stoked about the movie. I don't know why, but she is. She said to tell you that she's already done research on several televisions and has narrowed it down to three. She'll meet you at the store at noon." She looked up from piping little roses on the side of a cake. "Now that I've done my good deed for the day, your coffee and breakfast are on the counter. So, go."

Mitch snickered. "I can take a hint. Thanks, Prissy," then ran out the door.

Several hours later, Mitch phoned Bree to tell her he couldn't get away to meet her. "By any chance, did you measure the wall space?"

Bree hit the speaker, but Joe snorted into the phone. "Are you kidding. Measure twice, cut once? Nope. She measured every inch of the wall, from floor to ceiling, and drew a blueprint. Bree researched the optimal TV size for the living room, studied different models, their country of origin, pixel count, color tone, and screen size, checked Consumer Reports and five other online sources, and then made a mockup on butcher paper to stick on the wall. Then she walked around checking to see if everyone could see the screen. And moved the furniture around for an hour."

"That's my girl."

Bree said, "Considering everything, I'm going with a sixty-five-inch TV. The salesman said if I didn't like it, I could return it. So, let's test it tonight."

"Sounds good. Gotta run. See you tonight."

BREE PURCHASED A "smart" TV that had every new feature on the market. The options sounded interesting, but she didn't have the time to experiment. For the time being, she thought Mitch and the other guys should take charge, and at a later date, she could ask him to give her a tutorial. Then it hit her. *If I give the guys free rein, I may never regain control of my own TV.* Oh well. *What's the worst thing that could happen?*

She never suspected that her living room would become TV central for every sporting event known to mankind. Joe told Bob, and Mitch told Dirk. By the end of the night, they had watched sports highlights, WWE wrestling, and MMA fights. Neither Bree nor Prissy had ever seen Joe and Bob so enthusiastic or laugh at the sight of blood while men were thrown around, punched, and kicked into concussive submission.

Bree and Prissy flinched, ducked, and hid to avoid the gory parts. Two hours later, the ladies went to bed with earplugs as the sportsfest continued until midnight. Bree reevaluated her decision to buy a television with acoustic surface technology, where she not only heard the sound but also felt the vibrations in her bones. Still, she reached the same conclusion. She liked having people and chaos in her home. The TV was probably the best decision she had made in a long time. She told no one.

In the past, Bree would have been happy spending twelve hours in her office or doing research without talking to anyone except Bob or Joe. Usually, she and Prissy were like ships passing in the night. When they saw each other, it was only to handle a business matter. Prissy had an exciting social life, but Bree didn't. It was the way things worked.

Now, things had changed. Bree and Prissy communicated more often, and their bond grew stronger. They started to feel more like sisters. Prissy became more settled, while Bree spread her wings. Their group of friends also grew, mostly with firefighters. They enjoyed feeding them, doting on them, and spending quality time with them—even if they acted like juvenile boys, but that was also part of the social experience, and it was becoming the highlight of their days. Movie night would be another milestone, and she and Prissy wanted it to be perfect.

So, they cleaned the house from top to bottom. Prissy flew through the house like a whirling dervish, using a Swiffer in one hand and leather furniture wipes or fabric spray in the other. Bree set four automatic vacuums in motion downstairs, then cleaned the two downstairs bathrooms in her white coat, goggles, and yellow dishwashing gloves, armed with a portable carrier filled with various disinfectants. The kitchen was already pristine, so they didn't need to touch it.

Bob called Joe to watch the security feeds within the mansion. Neither dared to watch in person, much less comment and risk getting an earful.

"Should we help?" Joe asked, watching Prissy on one of the screens, wiping down the dining room table.

"And get vacuumed or dusted? This appears to be cathartic, and Prissy hasn't complained once. No. Why don't you head home for a few hours, and I'll hold down the fort? If I have to throw someone to the wolves, it'll be Chris." Bob snickered. "In fact, take the rest of the day off, and I'll make Chris join the festivities. He might even have some fun."

"Roger that. Might hide his taser."

MITCH ARRIVED LOADED down with several grocery bags and two big boxes of assorted sub sandwiches. He handed them over to Prissy, then led Bree out of the kitchen. "Honey pie, you seem nervous." Mitch took her to the living room, where he pulled her down to sit on his lap in *his* favorite leather chair.

"I've never hosted something like this," she confessed. "Business meetings, yes, but not social functions."

"It's just like our cookouts. You seem fine at those."

"I can always talk to whomever I want to, and leave when I want to…" She shrugged.

"Same here. Guys can be dense. If you're uncomfortable, find me. When you want everyone to leave, give me a sign, and I'll herd them out. No problem. Don't worry, guys generally don't take offense. They know they can wear out their welcome." The front doorbell rang, and he kissed her reassuringly. "Showtime."

Prissy answered the door to greet Steve, dressed as Luke Skywalker, wielding a lightsaber, and the blue-haired Darla, dressed as Princess Leia.

She darted a swift glance at Bree before smiling brightly. "Hi… Luke and Leia? Don't you two look cute." Steve and Darla beamed. "Come in. Everyone congregates in the kitchen, so go on back. You can drop off your food there." She pointed toward the area. "From now on, use the back door. Only guests use the front door. Oh, and don't mind us, Bree and I are running late. We'll be down after we change."

Steve and Darla strutted to the kitchen. "We do look cute," he said. Darla nodded.

Bree and Prissy studied the happy couple. Mitch snickered. Bree punched him on the arm and gave him the death stare as the couple walked by. She whispered to Prissy, "I think the guys told them to dress up for movie night. Another prank."

Mitch held his hands up. "I had nothing to do with this, I swear."

Bree pushed Prissy toward the stairs. "We need to derail this before their feelings get hurt. To the attic, Padme. Mitch, go entertain."

Fifteen minutes later, two costumed Padme Amidalas greeted their guests. The other firefighters' faces said it all. They had been caught trying to ambush Steve and Darla, and there was no way Bree and Prissy would allow them to be collateral damage.

Bree entered the kitchen and hugged Darla. "I'm so glad you came tonight. You both look fabulous." Darla blushed, and Steve stood taller, grinning. Bree made sure the others heard as well. "I love a dress-up movie night. Mitch just got here and didn't have time to change, and it looks like the others forgot."

Mitch cleared his throat. "I'll just run next door. Be right back."

Prissy raised an eyebrow, staring at Dirk.

"Um… I should go change, too."

Faster than a Land Speeder, Mitch returned wearing all black, a black Darth Vader cap, and a pull-down mask, carrying a green lightsaber. Dirk followed behind, wearing a Han Solo outfit and a long-handle taser strapped to his thigh.

The kitchen exploded into laughter and applause. Now, it was a party.

Padme Bree nuzzled up to Darth. "You just earned big brownie points."

Padme Prissy winked at Bree. "I think a Halloween costume party is in our future."

More whooping and hollering. "Done," Bree said.

Chapter 23

DURING THE MONDAY morning meeting, Bree confirmed that the warehouse fire was scheduled for Saturday. The usual security team members, including Bree, Prissy, Dirk, and Mitch, were present. Dr. Anna Murphy and Dr. Scott Leivy spread out a blueprint of the building that would be burned. The blueprint showed color-coded areas indicating the type of The Chirp prototype being used and its location. They set up redundancies in case one failed, so that one was on the left side and the right side of the building's zones. Thermal imaging sensors and high-resolution cameras had also been installed.

Each board member would be invited to tour the warehouse facility before the fires started and then answer questions before being escorted to a tent about a football field away from the fire. There, the board could watch the fires being set, hear comments from the firefighters, and see all the information on a large screen through real-time video footage streamed directly to a computer.

"Mitch and Dirk will wear full gear, including body cams and communication devices, and test the personal Chirp prototypes on their wrists and air tanks," Bob stated. "If the fires aren't electrically started, they will independently start fires at the far end of the building, wait for confirmation and video feeds, and move away. As an extra layer of safety and information, Steve will fly a drone equipped with sensors and communication links to guide Dirk and Mitch, and relay information to the VIP tent command center. The drone is being outfitted and tested today."

Dirk cleared his throat. "I suggest that each area have a color-coded sign with a number hanging down from the rafters to identify each zone. After the mission is completed, the firefighting crews will extinguish the fire. When it's safe to enter, Bree's crew can recover anything left. I think it will take about five days before that can happen."

It was Mitch's turn. "Two fire trucks and two EMT vehicles will be on standby, as well as a contingency from the fire station, sheriff's department, and city police department on site to oversee the event. However, they won't receive the physical location until one hour before the walkthrough to keep this secret. Once the fire crews move in, the location will be released to the public."

Joe told everyone that the warehouse had been under security surveillance since Anna and Scott placed the prototypes. It would be guarded until after the recovery was completed. "If word leaks out, there will be lots of activity around the building from 'lookie-loos' to journalists, and even our competitors. So, we have arranged for the board members to be picked up at our warehouse facility and driven to the site at eight a.m. They will leave their personal belongings, including cell phones, in the warehouse's lockers. If everything goes according to plan, they will return to the warehouse before eleven to a catered lunch in the lounge. The board will have an opportunity to ask questions before the fire and in the tent during the fire."

Bree nodded. "Excellent work, everyone. Thank you, Anna and Scott, for making all this possible. At the luncheon tomorrow, I will provide as much information as possible and show a dummy prototype. I'd hate for the real one to walk out. As you know, Frank has a spent unit that worked once on the grill, along with a defective schematic sheet. I thought if he'd gotten a working model, he wouldn't have shown up for work this week, but he did. There's no doubt he will be at the luncheon tomorrow." She sighed. She wasn't looking forward to seeing him.

"I imagine Frank will denigrate me in front of the board. However, he will discover that The Chirp belongs to Two Chicks, LLC, and when it's successful, Prissy and I will offer to sell it to the company. I also believe he will try to acquire a real prototype tomorrow or at the warehouse fire."

Prissy cleared her throat. "I know I speak for Bree and myself when I say, Dirk and Mitch must use every precaution in this fire because their safety is our utmost concern."

"What's to worry about? I'm Batman, and he's Superman. And we both have a sidekick." Mitch looked at everyone. "Steve. Although I'm not sure which superhero he is. He'll have our backs, too."

Bob snorted. "Then, let's take a tour of the warehouse."

Dirk and Mitch took detailed photographs and made extensive notes, including the types of fires to be set, a practical timetable between fires, and the kinds of problems to expect. They also noted that the most dangerous situation would be the last fires set and then outlined a plan to exit the warehouse safely. When they finished, Dirk and Mitch spoke softly away from the others.

Prissy nudged Bree, concern on her face as she studied the two men. "Spit it out, Dirk. Are you backing out? Because if you are, I need to find someone else to help wrangle Cluck Norris."

Dirk shook his head. "The first two fires to set are the easiest. The third one will be challenging due to the narrow spaces we need to navigate through. But that's doable."

Bree said, "Go on."

"The fifth and sixth fires will be the most danger-ous because of the mixture of combustible materials, possible pockets of hazardous gases forming there, and from the other fires set while we move toward Zone 6. The temperatures will be exceptionally high. Unless a rescue were needed, firefighters wouldn't enter a building containing these materials, especially if the building had been condemned. We feel that either Zone 5 or 6 shouldn't be set."

"I'd also like Hank to confirm our findings before this is done," Mitch added.

"Do we have any other options?" Prissy asked.

Mitch and Dirk shook their heads.

Bree called Anna and Scott to join the group. "How many prototypes have been positioned in the warehouse? And how many different ones were used in areas 1 through 4?"

Anna said, "Total of sixty units. There are forty units in Zones 1 through 3."

"Okay. If you had to leave out Zone 4, 5, or 6, which would you omit?"

Anna and Scott pulled out the blueprint and stud-ied it. Scott said, "Dirk and Mitch could go to the middle of Zone 5 and watch number 4 ignite. Then move to Zone 6 and watch 5 go up. Zone 6 can be left out. Is that what you want to do?"

Mitch and Dirk looked at each other, nodding. "That would be the safest," Dirk said. "But to be on the safe side, I'd still like Hank to approve it."

Bree nodded. "Absolutely. We'd feel better knowing that we aren't putting you two into a more dangerous situation. Would you call Hank? We can wait."

As expected, Hank agreed with the firefighter's assessment and expressed gratitude for their due diligence in the research. Being forewarned, he was able to plan how to handle the warehouse fires after Mitch and Dirk exited the building.

THE HOUSE WAS too quiet, and Bree was restless. She was exhausted, and although it was only ten o'clock, her mind wouldn't shut off. She wandered into the kitchen, finding only the vent light over the stove illuminating a small section of the kitchen island where Prissy was gently stirring a pan of milk. She added a dash of nutmeg and cinnamon before turning off the burner. "I guess you couldn't sleep either. Would you mind fixing me some, too?"

"Sure thing."

Bree's phone rang. It was Angela Smalls. She turned the phone so Prissy could see. "Should I let this go to voicemail?"

"No, put it on speaker phone."

"Hello Angela, what can I do for you?"

"Dr. Kelly, I feel like the biggest fool. Two days

ago, Frank Lassiter brought me a burned-out heat sensor with a document that didn't match. He asked me to find out all about it and give him a report by tomorrow morning. It didn't take long to recognize that it was your design, simple but brilliant. With modifications, it has endless uses. I don't know how he got it, but whatever he's planning, it can't be good for the company or you." She cleared her throat.

"You see, we've gone out a few times, and he stops by the lab to see what's being developed.... I stupidly thought he was there to see me, but with the questions he asked and the last two company thefts, I've tried to avoid him. I don't want to accuse anyone of espionage, but I believe he's been trying to use me to get to the research. What do I do?"

"Angela, you did the right thing by calling me. It's okay to tell Frank what you've found. He got the prototype and the document from me, but your instincts are correct: Frank has been difficult to work with lately, and he's trying to keep the board from investing in this design. It's a long story, but don't worry, we've got it covered. Send him an email with your findings and BCC me. I will handle Frank. I'm sorry he put you in this situation. Why don't you take a few days off, and when you get back, hopefully, he won't bother you. But if he does, let me know."

"Thank you, Dr. Kelly, I'll do exactly what you've asked. Goodbye."

Prissy shook her head. "That was interesting. Do you think Frank used Angela to get the other research, and she doesn't remember?"

"I think that's exactly what happened, and now she's scared. I'll tell Bob tomorrow."

Chapter 24

TODAY, BREE WOULD present The Chirp to the board, so she'd called in the big guns for support: Mrs. Ketchum. Although she stood only five feet tall in her stocking feet, with gray hair and having been a widow for decades, the sixty-five-year-old woman was the equivalent of a fairy godmother, possessing incredible skills and abilities that bordered on the ninja scale.

Prissy squealed, opening the kitchen door. "Mrs. Ketchum. I'm so glad to see you. Come in. It's been too long." She pulled her into a big hug and rested her head on her shoulder.

Bree also rushed to see the dear woman. "Mrs. Ketchum. Thank you for coming. We're over our heads and could really use your help." She also wrapped her arms around the older woman, and together, they sandwiched her.

"Really, my dears. I'm just glad to see that you're well and that Joe and Bob have kept you safe. While you work your magic in the kitchen, I'll spruce up downstairs, set the table, and then head upstairs to do my magic. When your guests arrive, I'll serve you so you can focus on your board meeting. Now, who is this good-looking gentleman?"

Bree grinned and pulled Mitch by the hand to meet her. "Mrs. Ketchum, this is my boyfriend, Mitchel Strong. He's a firefighter in Station 18 and lives next door."

Mitch held out his hand but Mrs. Ketchum pulled him into a bear hug. "Mitchel, my dear, if you're Bree's boyfriend, then you're family. But I will tell you the same as her grandfather would say, 'treat her right, or you may be wearing cement overshoes.'"

He blinked several times and swallowed hard. "Yes, ma'am. Good to know."

The three women laughed at the stricken look on Mitch's face.

"Uh, Bree, I think I'll head into work now. Good luck with the meeting, and I'll see you tonight." He picked up his thermos and a breakfast sandwich, nodded to Mrs. Ketchum, and then hurriedly kissed Bree on the cheek, whispering, "It's best not to tempt fate."

MRS. KETCHUM HURRIED through her chores as if she used a fairy godmother's wand. With everything that had happened over the past nine months, Bree and Prissy decided she would be safer staying away from them. One look at her and they knew how much they had sacrificed being on their own without her guidance and love.

The house looked beautiful. Fresh flower arrangements adorned most flat surfaces, from the foyer to the living room, and low crystal bowls featuring late-summer flowers graced the dining room. Bree was most proud of the lovely vase of red roses from Mitch that sat on the kitchen island. She would finger the card inside her pantsuit pocket whenever she was nervous.

The antique grandfather clock struck twelve as the front doorbell rang with the first three board members standing on the porch. Prissy ushered them into the living room, offering a tempting selection of tiny tea sandwiches, cheese straws, and tea or coffee while they waited for the other board members to arrive. The last person to arrive, fifteen minutes late, was Frank. He spoke to the others jovially, acting more like the cat who ate the canary than in anticipation of a secret board meeting.

Mrs. Ketchum announced, "Luncheon is served family style today. Ladies and gentlemen, please follow me to the dining room."

The evidence of work or weekly meetings had vanished from the dining room. The banquet-sized mahogany table was dressed in antique Irish lace placemats, fine china, sterling silver, and crystal glassware. Name cards directed each person to their designated seat; Prissy, Bree, and Bob, as Chief Security Advisor, assumed their usual places, while Frank, as CFO, was seated away from Bree and Prissy, between members at large, Milton Hendricks, and Stacy Abraham. COO Katherine Gates sat between the two other members at large, Casey Wiggins and Laurel Miles. That left Head Researcher David Weisman to sit next to Prissy.

Mrs. Ketchum arranged platters of individual quiche Lorraine pies, bowls of cucumber caprese salad, and large bowls of squash with zucchini and green beans, topped with garlic and parmesan, on either end of the table. She added soft yeast rolls with butter, then filled water and iced tea glasses. "Please help yourself."

When lunch was over, she collected the plates,

removed the serving dishes, and then served individual plates of warm cinnamon apple crisp with vanilla bean ice cream and coffee. While the others finished dessert, Bree stood next to an easel stacked with large cue cards. Prissy rose to welcome the board members and introduce the reason for the meeting.

"Thank you all for coming," she said. "I hope you enjoyed your lunch. It was our pleasure to treat you. Thank you for attending Firefighter's Day. Of course, if you stayed to see the chili cookoff, you saw Bree take three blue ribbons. I was so proud of her tenacity in learning how to cook chili and excel, as she always does. Speaking of excelling, Bree has done it again. Inspired to fill a gap in the fire safety products niche, we'd like to introduce her latest invention." Prissy pointed to the unit on the cue car.

"Meet The Chirp." Bree passed around a prototype. "This is a next-generation heat sensor with nearly unlimited applications for detecting rapid temperature increases where smoke or flames are not visible. As the temperature changes, chirping increases, enabling quick deployment of fire suppression measures. Firefighters will be able to detect a fire's origin and locate the hottest spots to target." Bree changed the card as Prissy passed out the presentation handouts.

"The Chirp can be customized with voice alerts, mobile alerts, thermal color flashing, and even vibrations when worn on the body. The beauty is in its small design. And it chirps before a smoke detector goes off. It can also be hard-wired or battery-operated and as inexpensive as a home smoke alarm, so our revenue will be derived from replacing the units or the specialized batteries."

Casey Wiggins raised his hand. "Is this theoretical, or do you have data to prove that it works as you say?"

Frank folded his napkin and tossed it on the table.

"I've seen the prototype work on a grill, then it stopped. It had a one-time lifespan, as verified by our researcher, Angela Smalls, and the accompanying schematics were bogus. I seriously doubt Dr. Kelly has invented something that does all that she says. In fact, she wants the board to bankroll this folly to the tune of $8 million, which is a waste of money. In my opinion, she's trying to salvage her reputation, and that of the company, and I won't vote to give her the funds."

He stood and walked around the table. "Did any of you realize that defective fire extinguishers were sent to customers, including our own Station 18? Some were also discovered during a spot visit inside the warehouse. I brought this to Bree's attention and asked her to close the warehouse until every product had been examined and to retrieve and replace those that had been sent out. Do you know what she said? She would think about it."

There were gasps and murmurs. Board members looked at each other, then whispered. They looked at Bree with disappointment.

Milton Hendricks raised his hand. "If that's so, what happened to them, and why weren't we notified?"

Prissy said, "Frank is partially correct. We collected and replaced the defective cannisters at the station. We also did a thorough search of the warehouse after hours, found more tampered canisters, and replaced them. Shutting down the warehouse would have cost us tens of thousands of dollars. Working after hours, using SEcure Well agents, it only costs a few thousand dollars. It was swiftly handled in-house, but we intended to address this at our regular board meeting."

Katherine Gates asked, "What do you mean by tampered canisters?"

"Someone got into the warehouse to sabotage our

fire extinguishers, and they were sent out," Bree said. She waited for the chatter to stop. "This is currently under investigation. We have video of the perpetrator tampering with many fire extinguishers over a long weekend when the warehouse was closed." Frank couldn't hide his surprise. "Rather than go into the details now, just know that the authorities have been notified and we're determined to find the perpetrators involved."

Frank refused to keep quiet. "I must say that I'm disappointed in the way you've handled recent incidents in the company, Bree. I think you're overworked, you don't rely on your board to do their jobs, and you've lost sight of how to act as president. So, at the next board meeting, I will make a motion that you be removed from your position and suspend Prissy's position because of your direct influence."

Bob stood. "Please take your seat, Frank. Don't forget where you are and who you're insulting. As the Chief of Security, I can assure each of you that Dr. Kelly and Ms. Matthews have been proactive in implementing extraordinary measures to ensure this company's reputation remains solid and its financial position remains solvent. These women are extremely capable of running this company, and with the innovative inventions Dr. Kelly has inspired and created, this company will continue to thrive well into the future."

"Thank you, Bob." Bree smiled at him, then turned to address the others. "Frank's lack of confidence has spurred Prissy and me to form our own company, Two Chicks, LLC, to develop The Chirp and other products in the works." The cacophony of questions from the board forced her to raise her hand.

When they settled down, she continued. "As you know, our company is facing financial difficulties due to two lawsuits and the challenge of keeping the business afloat. Until these issues are resolved, Two Chicks, LLC will assume all risks and responsibilities for completing the research, development, and manufacturing of The Chirp and related products. However, we are highly confident in their efficacy. After the final testing, we will offer them to SEcure Well, making it the leading safety product company in the U.S."

"What?" Frank looked thunderstruck. "When is the last phase of testing?"

"I'm glad you asked," Bree said, grinning. "Tomorrow, we'll test different prototype models in a warehouse fire under a variety of situations. The two firefighters you met at the company meeting a few weeks ago will monitor how well The Chirp works. And they will also be wearing personal units. Prissy and I would like you all to see The Chirp in action. After the data has been collected, we will pass it along, and at the next board meeting, we will request a vote."

She looked at each board member. "Because of security measures, the location is not being disclosed. Meet us at the warehouse at seven a.m., and we will transport you to the area where you'll have the opportunity to tour the warehouse setup before the fire and observe the event in real time. Please wear casual slacks and closed-toe walking shoes."

Prissy ended the meeting. "Thank you for coming today, and we look forward to seeing you tomorrow. Let me show you out."

Frank stormed out of the room. Bree looked at Bob and frowned.

IT HAD BEEN a long day and tomorrow would be

longer. A great deal was riding on the prototypes being tested. Were they placed in the right areas? Would the charges be enough to set the fires, or would Mitch and Dirk need to do it? Bree and Prissy were sending both men into a man-made, experimental hellhole. What if something happened to them?

Bree and Prissy studied each other. Concern and fear of the unknown were telepathically sent until Mitch and Dirk came through the kitchen door laughing and making jokes about something. The women shook off their fog and pasted on cheerful faces.

"Who's up for some spaghetti tonight?" Prissy asked, pulling out containers of frozen sauce, and then filled a large pot with water to boil.

"I am," resounded throughout the kitchen. Like a well-oiled machine, Bree found the pasta, and Dirk and Mitch washed their hands. Magically, a loaf of Italian bread with butter and garlic powder was prepped for the oven, a salad was tossed, and dishes were set out around the island. Bob and Joe debated Chianti versus red wine, but when Chianti was chosen, the others opted for iced tea, and that became the drink of choice for everyone—no need to have a hangover for the big day.

There was small talk, and then there was even smaller talk. Dirk discussed mowing the backyard and needing Mitch to help him carry away some fallen branches. Prissy and Bree asked whether she should wear capris or pants tomorrow. Bree picked at a hangnail, then asked to borrow her clippers. Bob eyed Joe.

"I think I'm going to fix some warm milk and head to bed," Joe said. "Anyone else want some?"

One by one, they all accepted his offer, and while that was being done, Bree found some mugs, and

Prissy warmed some cinnamon rolls. Joe yawned while raising his arms high over his head. "Well, good night. I'll see you all for breakfast."

The cue was given, and "good night" was offered as the guys put their dishes in the dishwasher. Mitch kissed Bree on the forehead, and they all went to bed early. Sleep was something else.

Chapter 25

EVERY MEMBER OF the board arrived at SEcure Well's warehouse early enough to change into white, sterile jumpsuits, leaving their belongings in a locker, including cell phones. Stacy Abraham complained that her husband was undergoing tests and needed to be available for the doctor's results. The receptionist was instructed to hold onto Stacy's phone, take a message, and if it were crucial to speak with the doctor, a driver would pick her up and return her to the warehouse. The other person who objected was Frank, who said it was unnecessary and that he didn't want to be treated like a criminal. Bob gave him the option of remaining at the warehouse or giving up his phone. He reluctantly placed his phone in the locker while Bob watched. Once everyone was ready, they got into two stretch limos and headed to the fire site.

Bree and Prissy led the group inside the warehouse, followed by Bob, Joe, Mitch, and Dirk. "Please follow me to the back of the building," Bree said. "The warehouse is divided into Zones. The fires in each Zone will mimic fire behavior patterns, target areas with rapid heat buildup, and demonstrate the effectiveness of The Chirp under different conditions and increasing hazards."

She pointed out the numbered signs. "Zone 1 is designated for testing the least hazardous fires, specifically those involving paper and electricity, like in office fires, laptops and microwaves, as well as storage and break rooms containing cardboard boxes, shelving, and wall insulation. Consider shipping and receiving areas where forklifts move boxes, and damaged items could ignite a fire. The Chirps have been placed on the ceiling, in wall corners, near electrical panels and fuse boxes, and at the top of doors. The Chirp isn't a replacement for fire alarms, but an additional security measure."

Prissy interjected, "One firefighter will be stationed on the left side of each Zone, and another one on the right. They will move in tandem from Zone 1 through 6, staying in contact via their comm units, and everyone in the VIP tent will be able to see what's going on through cameras positioned throughout the area and the firefighters' video equipment. They will be holding thermal monitoring units and identify when The Chirp chirps."

Bree walked them into Zone 2. "The fires will either be remotely started or lit by the firefighters for a controlled burn. This Zone simulates grease fires from stoves, overhead vent hoods, mechanical grease, and other oily substances, such as soaked rags from vehicle oil changes. Imagine the number of kitchen or grilling fires that happen each year... I know from experience." Everyone laughed.

Prissy led the group to Zone 3. "Have you ever seen a boat fire? When they go up, it's fast, producing high heat and toxic fumes. They contain several fire-prone items, such as fuel, oil, electronics, and carbon monoxide from the engine exhaust. With multiple compartments, heat and gases are trapped. The Chirp would be great at marinas, and trailered boats like this small one."

Bree spoke as they moved into Zone 4. "I'm sure you smell the flammable substances in this area. So, let's move to Zone 5 to talk." When they got there, she turned to face everyone. "Zone 4 is more dangerous because it contains cleaning chemicals, degreasers, paints, solvents, and paint thinners—just like what was found in this warehouse before we staged the areas. Not only are the chemicals inside containers, but they're already in the air. Since fires will be raging in Zones 1-3, the firefighters will move to Zone 5, and then Zone 4 will be triggered to ignite. Our instruments will register the results."

"Zone 5," Prissy said, "might be considered a typical residential garage, which often stores gasoline or diesel-powered machinery, such as cars, as well as lawnmowers that use both gasoline and oil. There may also be fertilizer, paint cans, insect spray, and storage boxes with old clothes or Christmas decorations. Does this space remind you of your garage or a maintenance shop?" Heads nodded in agreement.

"Let's finish with Zone 6," Bree said. "This is the most dangerous area because there will be combination fires having multiple hot spots that produce toxic gases. Some things ignite quickly, like hay. Crates have been stacked to mimic a storage facility with paper and excelsior. A refrigerator has been plugged in. There's an outdated electrical panel with knob and tube electrical wires, rolls of insulation, and PVC linoleum flooring, golf cart batteries, partially used propane tanks, empty oil drums, and an acetylene tank. There are also rat and bird nests, but without the animals."

Prissy led everyone outside. "Observations in each Zone are handled carefully. Besides the cameras inside and live video feeds from the firefighters, each Chirp is wired to register the temperature when it starts chirping and when it stops. Additionally, we will have a drone flying into each Zone as the fires begin, providing a real-time 360-degree view. It will be flown by Steve, another firefighter located outside the warehouse, and he will direct when the fires are set. You'll also hear the firefighters' comments as they move through the Zones. This should be a fabulous show. Now let's move to the VIP tent so we can begin. If you have any questions, you can ask them there."

In the tent, Bree put on a headset and spoke to Mitch and Dirk, "We're monitoring everything you're doing and saying. Be careful, please."

"Copy that. See you in a few." Mitch said.

"Ditto. We'll be careful," said Dirk as both men entered the warehouse to Zone 1, followed by the drone Steve was handling.

"Before we get started, I want to check a vent." Mitch climbed onto a large metal box for a peek. "Looks like there's a draft that will blow the fire toward us. I'll try to close it… got it. Now we're good to light it up."

Things caught fire immediately. At first, it sounded like a backyard fire with crackling noises. Then there was a large Whoosh, and everything was ablaze. Mitch shielded his face with his hand turning slightly before Dirk did. They monitored the number of chirps and the intensity each prototype emitted as the temperature increased, watching their personal wrist bands respond as expected.

"Drone Solo is working great," Steve said. "The carbon monoxide levels just hit the red line but are holding."

"You've got to be kidding me. Drone Solo?" Dirk groaned.

"DS is my fifth drone. She reminds me of the *Star Wars* fighter ships that fought the Fifth, so I had to name her Drone Solo."

"It's *not* the Fifth, it's the Sith," Mitch said.

"Po-tay-toe, po-*tah*-to."

After ten minutes, Dirk said, "Looks good. Mitch, you ready to move on?"

"Zone 1 good. Ready. Move on, Steve."

They moved through Zone 2 and toward Zone 3 to avoid being caught, as the fires had been set. When the drone was in position, they both said, "Go."

Steve repeated the command "Go."

There was hissing and popping as the grease fires flashed, and the area burst into flames. A flaming glob of grease dropped onto Mitch's sleeve, which immediately caught fire, but he easily smothered it.

There was a collective gasp in the tent. Bree grabbed Prissy's arm for support.

Steve's voice came through. "This looks like the time Dirk's grill caught fire, melting his plastic spatula, and then singed the wood trim." Steve giggled.

"Shut up, Steve," Mitch and Dirk said together.

"It's time to go to Zone 3, Dirk."

"Roger that, Mitch."

Steve spoke. "Have you guys ever seen a boat fire? The fiberglass melts, then burns, before emitting noxious fumes. They get nasty really fast. I'd stand back to throw in the flares, if I were you, and then run like hell. I'm heading to Zone 4. Meet you there."

Was Steve right? Bree held her breath, staring intently at the video feed.

Mitch and Dirk were about ten feet away from each other on the port and starboard sides of the boat, staring at each other. A flare was taped down on top of each gunwale out of the way. They pulled off the tape and got ready to strike the top.

"All set here," Mitch said when he lifted a flare, ready to ignite it.

"Good to go," Dirk replied. He fingered the other flare. "Give us a count of three, Steve."

"Three. Two. One. Hit it."

Mitch and Dirk struck their flares and threw them into the boat. They turned and ran to the edge of Zone 4 like demons were chasing them. The sparks caught some cushions on fire. There was hissing, and then a roar. Items in the galley caught fire before progressing toward the electronics. The electronics sparked, followed by the oil in the engine, then the batteries. When the fiberglass melted, the cabin with noxious gases, and the prototypes were set off in sequence almost immediately. Black, grey, and white smoke billowed around the boat, and the area was consumed in flames and thick smoke.

"We can't see anything now. Leaving now, guys. Heading through Zone 4," Dirk yelled over the deafening sounds.

"I'm right behind you. The drone has moved out," Mitch said.

It took about eight minutes for them to move through Zones 4 and 5 and reach a safe area at the front of Zone 6. When Zone 4 was triggered, consecutive explosions and fireballs occurred. Bree imagined that the heat, smoke, and flames would have been unbearable to work in if this fire hadn't been staged. Then again, firefighters would have been dousing the building with water and or foam, hoping the explosions inside would be minimal.

The drone zipped from one side of Zone 6 to the other. "I'm in position and I'll give you a count of three. Mitch, Dirk, are you good?"

Both men responded, "Good to go."

"We're good to go in three. Two. One. Now," Steve shouted.

Zone 4 exploded. Mitch and Dirk raised their arms across their faces to block out the light, heat, and flames. Balls of fire shot out like bottle rockets, and they ducked. From the safety of the tent, it sounded like a dull boom. In the warehouse, the explosion must have been deafening. Concussive shock waves knocked Dirk to his knees and Mitch to the ground. Even the drone dipped and struggled to maintain an optimum altitude. It took a few seconds for both men to rise. Bree sighed with relief when Mitch wobbled a bit but moved out of the area.

Steve laughed. "Drone Solo indicates an exponential rise in temperature. Flash fire is expected. Gas rising too. Get to the next Zone pronto."

"Roger that," Dirk and Mitch said together. They ran to the next Zone.

"It's still going. Wow, that looked like something from a *Mission Impossible* movie," Steve declared. "Makes me glad I'm outside."

Dirk yelled, "That was insane. I'm glad I didn't have to go in there to rescue someone."

"It took my breath away," Mitch choked out. "Let's move back." He coughed two or three times. "The fumes are killer here."

The drone was positioned in the back of Zone 6 near the rafters, and Steve adjusted the cameras for long shots. "Give me a thumbs-up when you're ready."

Dirk reached his safe spot about two minutes before Mitch.

Steve cried out, "Mitch, your body temp is spiking. Your hands are trembling. You okay?"

On the video feed, it was obvious that Mitch's steps were more difficult than the ones before. He bent over, gloved hands on his knees. "Give me a second. Feels like an elephant sat on my lungs." His ragged breath came out in spurts. He took a deep breath. "Okay, I'm good."

Steve said, "Roger. If you're ready, I'll give you a count. Three. Two. One. Go."

Two electrical sparks ignited at opposite corners of Zone 5, triggering a series of cascading explosions seconds apart. Dirk and Mitch turned away from the flash of fire and light. The monitors indicated that the heat was climbing to that of a smelting furnace, and both men moved back deeper into Zone 6.

"My face feels like a cooked lobster," Dirk said. "I'm moving farther back."

Mitch wheezed. He covered his face mask with his hands, but he didn't move.

There was no laughter in Steve's voice as it resonated over the comm unit. "Mitch, talk to me."

"Lightheaded. My tank can't be empty. Let me check." Mitch seemed to struggle with the dial. He swayed.

The drone focused on Mitch and the regulator dial. "Mitch, you've got a problem—time to get out. I don't think you've got air left. Can you hear me?"

Mitch didn't respond. He fell forward with a thud.

Steve yelled, "Dirk, Mitch is down. I repeat, firefighter down. Need a stretcher and oxygen, Stat! I'm coming in."

BREE RAN AS hard as she could to Hank's side. "Tell me about Mitch," she demanded, watching the ambulance lights fade in the distance.

Hank's face fell. "I'm sorry, Bree. It looks like he inhaled bad fumes and passed out. Luckily, Dirk and Steve got him out before the rest of the building went up. He's breathing on his own now, but I don't know anything else. Why don't you head over to the hospital, and we'll join you there once we get this fire contained."

Prissy, Bob, and Joe appeared at Bree's side. "Mitch is breathing on his own, thank God. He's… he's… breathing." Her brain was shutting down.

Prissy hugged her. "Bob and I will take care of the board members. Go to the hospital with Joe, and we'll meet you there." She pulled Bree into another hug. "You need to be strong for Mitch. Now go."

Joe helped the stunned Bree into the front seat. She didn't move. Joe reached over and fastened her seatbelt. "Bree, lean back and close your eyes. I'll get us there in a few minutes."

Her mind was spinning. She saw everything happening again in slow motion. She felt the heat and heard the ungodly sounds of things being consumed by fire. She flinched, and her hand reflexively moved across her face. She felt the burning grease on Mitch's sleeve and his coughing. Her bronchial passageways were closing. She felt his wheezing and lost her breath. She moaned. Her head hurt when he fell, and she thought she'd died before being brought outside. She whimpered. The images were imprinted on her brain, and she would relive them repeatedly as a hellish movie she could never unsee or undo, ever.

It was her fault.

She whimpered. Why hadn't she thought more about putting those men in harm's way? Why hadn't she more carefully monitored the warehouse setup to reduce potential dangers? How could she consider herself a safety product expert without ensuring the safety of Dirk and Mitch?

It was *all* her fault.

What if Mitch didn't come out of it? What would

she do? She had just found him. He had become part of her life and her whole heart. Her crying turned into sobs and then into something primal, guttural. She was dying because she felt that he was.

"Bree. Bree! Snap out of it," Joe demanded. "Don't do this to yourself. We don't know anything yet, so don't jump to conclusions. I know he means the world to you, but you are his world too, and you must help him get better, no matter what. Open your eyes and tell me you'll go into the hospital and be there for him, because he'd be there for you."

Her eyes fluttered open. "You're right. I pray for the strength to get me through this and for Mitch's recovery. It may be the only thing I can do at this time, but it's what I will do. I'm ready, let's go." She wiped tears from her face. "Thank you, Joe."

BREE HAD WORN a hole in the waiting room carpet. She'd counted 395 steps to the nurse's station. One thousand six-hundred and seventy-two steps to Mitch's door. She'd consumed four bottles of water and made two trips to the ladies' room and back in less than eight minutes each time, with her phone ready to read a text or get a phone call.

Five hours later, still dressed in their bunker suits, sooty and stinky, Hank arrived at the hospital with Steve in tow. Hank hesitated, but folded Bree into his arms and then gently released her. "What have you heard?"

Her face was splotchy, but there were no more tears left. "They won't let me see him because I'm not family." She twisted tissues in her hand. "Dirk was allowed to stay with him because he's listed as an emergency contact. He comes out occasionally to tell me something, and the nurses have kept us informed of any changes. The blood work was bad. They're trying to flush the gas poisons out of his system, but it's been touch-and-go. They're doing all they can to stabilize him, and I'm scared. Really scared. This was all my fault. If I hadn't pushed to test The Chirp in a warehouse fire, he'd be fine right now."

"You can't blame yourself for what's happened." Hank looked up at the ceiling as if seeking divine intervention. "I'm sorry to do this now, but you all need to know something very important." Prissy, Joe, and Bob gathered closer to Bree. "Mitch's regulator hose was cut." Prissy gasped, and Bree covered her mouth with both hands. "Steve told me that his gear was good to go when we arrived this morning. That means it was intentionally cut before he went inside the warehouse. The chief of police was notified, and it's now an attempted murder investigation."

Bree swayed. Steve caught her before she landed on the floor in a dead faint.

Chapter 26

IT WAS AFTER midnight when a nurse entered the waiting room. Bree jumped up. "Is there any news about Mitchel Strong?"

"Mr. Strong was a very lucky man," she said. "He breathed in a lot of nasty gases that will take time to leave his system. Right now, his vitals look better, and I just gave him something to help him sleep, so it should take effect in about ten minutes. He's awake for now and asking for someone named 'Be'?"

"I'm Bree, his girlfriend. Can I go in to see him?"

"Only for five minutes. Let him rest tonight. The doctor will be in to check on him in the morning, and you can come back then."

Bree entered Mitch's hospital room and quickly moved to his side. "Hey, babe. They don't want me to stay long, but they say you're doing better and they'll know more tomorrow. I'm going to let you sleep and be back here when you wake up. So, we'll talk then. I love you, Mitch." She squeezed his hand and was comforted when he tried to squeeze it back.

She watched him sleep for a few minutes. His chest was struggling to rise and fall. It broke her heart all over again, but she looked at the monitors and found encouragement in the steady beeping and the sounds of the blood pressure cuff expanding and deflating. He was hooked up to a drip bag, an O2 monitor, and wire leads attached to his chest. But *he* was alive.

She looked around at his small, single-bed, windowless home. A light box hung over his bed with only ambient light. The walls were painted mint green. Except for a recliner and one chair, the room was bare. His sheets were expertly wrapped around his body, and Bree detected the unmistakable odor of hospital soap. Nothing about this room personified Mitch, so she vowed to add a few colorful drawings on the wall and fill the room with whimsical balloons—anything to keep his spirits up. Hope filled her heart. The doctors would do what was necessary for Mitch, and in turn, she would do her part, starting tomorrow.

Once Bree returned to the waiting room to share information about how Mitch looked and that she was hopeful for his recovery, Prissy took over. "Let's get you home. Some warm milk and sleep will help."

"Sure. But I want you all to know something. If I hadn't developed The Chirp, Mitch wouldn't have gotten hurt." She held her hand up. "However, in retrospect, I know we did everything to make the situation as safe as possible, and both Mitch and Dirk are professionals. They didn't do anything wrong. In fact, their actions were superlative within a dynamically challenging situation. So, who do I blame? That's what I want to find out."

"What? Now you want to play Jessica Fletcher?" Prissy asked incredulously.

"I'm quite a bit younger than her, but if we can lend the police a hand then we should do it," Bree snarked. "If you all want to help me, then I'll see you for breakfast."

"Well, since you put it that way, I'm in. Come on, Jessica," Prissy bossed.

BREE SLEPT VERY little, and it seemed that Prissy hadn't either, because she was preparing breakfast when Bree entered the kitchen. Soon after, Bob, Joe, Chris, Dirk, Steve, and even Hank appeared. While they ate and drank coffee, Hank directed his question to no one in particular. "What can we do to figure out who did this to Mitch?"

"I've been thinking about that," Bob said. "Steve practiced recording video around the area after the fire trucks arrived. He was playing around, taunting the EMTs, and teasing every female there."

"And your point?" Steve asked.

Bob caught Bree's eye. "That early video will let us know who was there and if they were close to Mitch's equipment. Did you also take a video of the board members arriving and moving to the VIP tent?"

"Sure. I needed to get a feel for all the extra weight put on Drone Solo before it went into the warehouse."

Dirk rolled his eyes.

Bree got excited. "Let's go through all the video as soon as you can bring it back, Steve. Additionally, we need to see if anyone was on their phone taking photos before the fire started. Lastly, were there any people there who shouldn't have been there? Let's ask around."

Steve raised his hand. "I talked to Darla and introduced her to Drone Solo." Everyone turned toward him. "She was cool. I asked her why she was there. She had to take her grandmother to a dental appointment and was running late. So, she took a shortcut through the warehouse district and saw the trucks. After dropping her grandmother off, she came back to see if everything was okay. I spoke with her for about fifteen minutes. She was with me the whole time… but she took some photos of me with the drone, just before Mitch and Dirk went inside the warehouse. Maybe she saw or photographed something."

"Good. We'll check it out. Maybe you could go with me to ask her," Joe said.

"Sure thing. She promised to bring me lunch today at the station."

Hank looked up from his coffee cup. "As far as Mitch goes, he's been put on a medical furlough. Once we know something, his schedule will be adjusted to allow for rehab."

Even though Mitch had only been in town for a short time, it was because of him that Bree had gotten to know the people around the island. They were friends coming together under severe circumstances, with a plan to find the culprit.

"Please take me to the hospital, Joe. Unless we get kicked out, that will be our war room," Bree avowed.

BREE PACED BACK and forth in the waiting room, clutching papers with The Chirp data. She had read the same page several times, but it was no use; she couldn't concentrate. Recognizing a doctor coming out of Mitch's room, she hurried down the hallway to confront him.

"Excuse me, doctor, I'm Bree Kelly. Mitchel Strong is my boyfriend. Could you tell me how he's doing this morning?"

The doctor took pity on her. "Mr. Strong's vital signs are getting better. I'm hopeful that he will recover, but it will take time. He's a strong and previously healthy man, so that plays in his favor. Every day will tell us more." He patted her arm and walked away.

Bree rushed into Mitch's room and didn't come out.

Joe asked the charge nurse about Mitch. "He's still sedated, but his vitals are steadily improving, and the doctor hopes he will be conscious in a day or two." Joe texted Bob and Dirk the information.

Joe didn't interrupt Bree's time with Mitch, but when lunch was being delivered to the other patients, he popped into Mitch's room to find Bree curled up next to him on the bed, asleep. Without making a sound, he took a photo, sent it to Prissy, and then pulled out his laptop to help analyze the drone video.

Several hours later, Bree found Joe working in the waiting room. "Mitch's heavily medicated. I'd like to go home for a while and see what Anna and Scott have come up with. I assume that you and Bob have a plan to find out who did this to Mitch, so I won't get in your way. Just keep me informed. I'm sure Prissy is inundated with phone calls from the board members and maybe the police department, so I need to be with her. I'd like to come back here before visitors' hours end and check on Mitch, okay?"

"Sure. You haven't eaten since lunch yesterday, and Mrs. Ketchum has made herself available to move in for the next few weeks to help you and Prissy as much as possible."

As Mitch gradually improved, Bree's mood got brighter. On day three, she entered his room to find him slowly coming around. His eyes squinted, and he covered them with his arm. Bree turned off all the lights. When he mumbled something, she rang the nurse.

"Mr. Strong, I'm Joyce, your nurse today. How are

you feeling?"

"My head hurts. My throat is scratchy, and my lungs feel like they're half full of something heavy… It hurts to breathe."

Bree's stomach churned. Nausea threatened to appear. "Can the doctor give him something?"

Mitch turned to see Bree for the first time. "Bree. Sweetheart… why is your hair gray?"

The nurse and Bree shared looks. "I need to call the doctor. Be right back."

After a long examination and more bloodwork, the doctor explained that Mitch had been exposed to large amounts of carbon monoxide and other gases that would slowly be flushed out of his body, and based on his progress so far, thought he would recover fully. However, after testing his vision, the diagnosis was acquired dyschromatopsia. Mitch was colorblind.

Mitch confirmed that the colors appeared faded. Not just red and green, but blue and yellow seemed grayish as well. Overexposure to carbon monoxide had deprived his retinal cells of oxygen. The doctor explained that this was usually a temporary condition that could last anywhere from a few days to several weeks or longer. Treatment included high-flow oxygen therapy and rest. Unfortunately, if his condition didn't improve, he would face restrictions on operating machinery and would be unable to fight fires. The last part plagued Mitch's brain, and he refused to talk to Bree, no matter how she prodded him.

Mitch spent two more days in the hospital, then the doctor suggested that he convalesce at home. "I've told you before, it's no imposition for you to move into my home," Bree insisted. "There's a spacious bedroom down the hall from mine and Chewbarka, and I can look after you."

"Yeah, just like I'm a sick child and you can check

on me at all hours of the night."

Bree rolled her eyes. If his lip stuck out any further, he would trip over it. "Let's get you settled there. Remember, I have a company to run, and the waiting room isn't conducive for research. However, if you feel that you need to go to a nursing home and eat institutional food rather than Prissy's, I'll make those arrangements. What's it to be?"

"Fine. I miss seeing Chewie."

Bree smiled behind his back. When they arrived at the mansion, Dirk, Hank, and Steve greeted him, then carried his things up to the bedroom. For about an hour, things were calm, and then Mitch's yelling cleared the room.

"He's feeling sorry for himself," Dirk said as he led the others down the stairs. "I can't blame him. He thinks his firefighting days are over. Who knows? We'll stop by later. If you need anything, like a firehose to tie him up, let me know."

"Or I could bring one of my smaller drones, and you can watch him without risking his wrath," Steve said teasingly.

"Thanks, guys," Bree replied. "Come by for dinner and bring Darla. Surely, he won't be surly with her here."

Bree didn't blame Mitch for throwing a pity party for himself. Having an accident that traumatically changed your life wasn't a small thing. However, after putting up with his foul temper for a day and a half, she decided it was enough. She returned to her former self, doing what she did best: research. Two days later, she led someone into his room where Mitch lay on the bed, the oxygen tank on the floor next to him.

"Mitch, I'd like you to meet a colleague of mine, Dr. Walter Brennin. He's an ophthalmologist specializing in traumatic vision research. He'd like to see if you would benefit from color-enhancing eyeglasses."

"What's the use, Bree?" he asked listlessly. "Even if it restores some of my color vision, I still can't do my job properly. They'll bench me on a medical technicality, and I won't be a firefighter any longer."

"Mitchel Strong, stop whining." His eyebrows scrunched together. "What certification were you trying to get while working as a firefighter?"

"Arson certification."

She stabbed a finger at him. "Exactly. I checked the regulations, and even if you wear these glasses for the rest of your life, you don't need to have the same color vision as a firefighter does. Your dream job is still within reach."

Mitch straightened up. "Is this true?"

"Absolutely," Dr. Brennin said. "And there's also the possibility that your color vision will return to normal if you continue with oxygen therapy and rest."

For the first time in many days, Mitch smiled, and so did Bree. "Really? Then, let's do this."

She wiped away a stray tear.

The moment Mitch put on the glasses, he declared that the colors were apparent but muted.

"If your vision changes, it will be gradual, so be patient; it'll take some time to get used to it. I'll drop by next week to check up on you. Bree, I'll see myself out."

"Thanks, Walt." She handed Mitch a mirror.

"I look like Clark Kent. Dirk's going to be jealous."

ANOTHER WEEK WENT by. Mitch rested in bed, on the

couch, or on a lounge chair in the shade by the pool, with his portable oxygen tank and a cannula. Gradually, he had enough energy to toss a ball to Chewbarka, encourage the dog to corral the chickens with Prissy, read arson course materials, and spend quiet time with Bree. He was climbing the walls. Who knew lounging around could be so boring?

Every day, someone from the station would drop by to share the station gossip, which was usually about Steve and rumors about Darla. Even Hank dropped by. Dirk was always there for breakfast, after he got off work, and on his days off. He made himself indispensable to Prissy by helping with little chores, assisting in the kitchen, sharing his grandmother's recipes with her, and then watching television with her before heading home.

Mitch knew he wasn't the main reason for Dirk's visits, and eventually, he discussed it with Bree. "Have you noticed that Dirk's been hanging around every day. He's here for breakfast, after work, for dinner, and he goes home late. Don't you think that's an imposition?"

Bree choked on her coffee, and Mitch patted her on the back. "Before moving in here, you did the same thing," she said.

"Darn right I did." He grinned. "I told you from the very start how I felt. I couldn't stay away from you. And then there was Dirk's brother, Brandon. I couldn't let him take you away from me… You're not sad about that, are you? Because you're the love of my life, sweet cheeks."

"You're making me blush." She kissed him. "I'm so happy you didn't give up on me. I love you too."

Although Mitch was improving, he was still grumpy. If his vision was getting better, it was doing so very slowly. The doctor allowed him to return to the station for a few hours a day in an inactive duty capacity to file paperwork and "supervise." He wasn't allowed to lift anything heavy or exercise. Dirk drove him to and from work, but if he got tired, Joe or Bob picked him up to return to Bree's house. The empty hours allowed him to work on the courses left in his arson certification. When those were finished, he would apply to take the North Carolina exams: the Fire Investigation Technician (FIT) certification, the Certified Fire Investigator (CFI) certification, and the CFI course exam. The coursework and being around the other station crew members boosted his spirits. Slowly, the old Mitch reappeared, and his crewmates didn't need to tiptoe around him.

He was thankful that Bree was so patient as a nurse. When his eyes tired, she read the newspaper to him, and they talked about local politics. She spoke to him about everything: her research, things she wanted him to teach her about cooking and grilling, and they even made plans to visit his good sister by Christmas.

"We haven't discussed the elephant in the room, who did this to me. I can take it, Bree. What do you know?"

She grimaced. "Not much. Even with Steve's drone taking videos, we couldn't find any clues. Bob's tech team reviewed the footage before handing it over to the police and sheriff's department but found nothing. The only cell phones being used were those of the EMTs, and surprisingly, Darla's. She took a few photographs of Steve holding the drone, but nothing else was on her camera. We all suspect Frank, but we can't prove it. I'm sorry, Mitch. However, there may be a way to smoke him out."

"Please don't tell me you're going to be used as bait, because I'll lose my mind with worry."

"Bob, Joe, Prissy, and I have talked about setting a

trap for him at the Founder's Day Picnic. The Chirp results have come back better than expected, and I promised our employees they would see the prototypes and find out what they could do. This is the only time Frank can legitimately obtain access to the information after the board is informed. Before you argue with me, arrangements have been made to have extra security agents and off-duty Station 18 crew present. He's going to make a mistake."

Chapter 27

BEFORE HEADING BACK to NCSU, Anna and Scott had examined all the warehouse remains, analyzed the data from each Chirp prototype, and prepared a comprehensive report. They concluded that every unit performed as hoped or better and suggested it was time to apply for patents and begin manufacturing. This was terrific news. Prissy and Bree danced around the kitchen, singing at the top of their lungs until Chewbarka howled and bayed.

There was so much that had to be done: wait on the patents, but the labels would indicate that they were "patent pending;" the manufacturing facility wasn't finished, and it would probably take another six months before it was ready; and a marketing team needed to be in place when it started. Neither Prissy nor Bree knew the marketing side of the business, so they had to hire a firm that would keep everything secret. They decided to ask Katherine Gates, SEcure Well's COO, for advice and not to divulge their conversations when she came to the house.

FRANK NOTICED KATHERINE leaving SEcure Well's office twice with a heavy computer bag, only to return late in the afternoon. He casually asked her about her activities, but she was tight-lipped. On the third day, he followed her to Bree's house.

From across the street, he watched Bree and Katherine go into the mansion. "Bree, Bree, Bree. You can't fool me. The Chirp tests were successful, and you think you can hide it from me? Of course. Katherine was there to advise you on the next steps for manufacturing. Tsk, tsk, tsk. I'm onto you. You're going to brag about this at the board meeting, then make us an offer we can't refuse, probably three times what you told me you needed. I'm going to fight fire with fire." He laughed at his own pun. If she didn't bring working prototypes to the meeting, most likely, she'd bring some to the Founder's Day Picnic to gloat. "That's where I'll steal it." He pulled away from the curb and drove off whistling.

PRISSY, BREE, AND Bob entered the boardroom a few minutes before the meeting was scheduled to start. Bree placed a packet of information in front of each seat. At the same time, Prissy laid several platters of homemade pastries down the middle of the table—accompanied by little plates and napkins, as well as coffee cups and carafes with creamer and sugar nearby.

In this arrangement, Bree sat at the head of the table with Prissy to her right and Bob to her left. He placed a box to the right of her paper packet, which contained inactive and spent prototypes from the fire for the board's perusal.

As other board members arrived, Katherine and David walked in wearing huge smiles. Prissy leaned over and whispered to Bree, "They're awfully chummy. Do you think they're doing the horizontal tango?"

Bree grinned. "I think it's called 'mambo', but you're correct, and I'm so happy for both of them."

Everyone took their seats as Frank made an entrance, arriving late.

Prissy started the meeting. "Good morning. Bree and I are pleased to inform you that the warehouse fire testing was a complete success, and Mitchel Strong has fully recovered from the injuries he sustained during the fire. However, breathing in large amounts of carbon monoxide had residual effects on his throat and lungs, and sadly, he developed acute acquired color vision deficiency. The colors red, green, blue, and yellow now have a gray tint. Fortunately, he's wearing specialized glasses that help correct this, and we hope his vision will continue to get better."

Bob stood. "I'd like to add something to what Ms. Matthews said. Our firefighters are trained experts, and this warehouse fire was planned meticulously so that Mitch and Dirk would have minimal exposure while monitoring each Zone as it was being tested. However, what Mitch experienced was not by accident. His regulator hose was cut before he entered the building. The authorities are treating this as attempted murder."

The entire board gasped in disbelief. The loudest

gasp came from Frank.

"SEcure Well is assisting the authorities. We have provided drone footage and cell phone photos from the Station 18 crew. If you saw or heard anything, please let me know. We also suspect that the saboteur of the company's fire extinguishers may have cut Mitch's hose."

More gasps and angry voices filled the room.

"Again, if you have any information, please let me know. Thank you." Bob sat down, then nodded to Bree.

Bree stood on unsteady legs. Listening to Prissy and Bob was difficult as flashbacks flooded her mind. She flexed her hands twice, took a deep breath, and exhaled. She knew someone in this room had nearly killed Mitch. "SEcure Well has been a major part of my entire life, and I've always been proud to continue my grandfather's work. I think he would be just as excited as Prissy and I am to introduce The Chirp in all its variations as the next-generation heat source monitor."

The room erupted in applause.

"You have a packet of information containing the research data from the warehouse fire. The prototypes' effectiveness in various situations is demonstrated in the tables on pages seven through twenty-one. Two independent researchers from NCSU helped fabricate the prototypes with David Weisman and me."

Frank yelled, "You used David's assistance while this was all done in secret and without notifying the board or the research and development department? I must protest. This is just another reason why you should not be in a leadership position for this company."

David and Katherine said together, "Shut up, Frank."

Bree continued, "As I was saying before being so rudely interrupted, from pages twenty-two to thirty-five, the independent researchers provided a detailed assessment of each unit and offered recommendations for improving a few models. The rest of the information packet covers Two Chicks, LLC's investment in producing The Chirp, along with marketing details on pages forty-one through fifty. Pages fifty-one through fifty-eight show the approximate production cost for each unit and the projected market price. It's suggested that our initial investment will be recovered within the first eighteen months."

Board members nodded and smiled. "Looks good."

"Bob will pass out some of the used prototypes so you can see how compact and lightweight they are, and then collect them before you leave. Now, please look at pages fifty-nine through sixty-one. I want to reiterate that what we developed was always meant to belong to SEcure Well, but we were *convinced* to take this route." She and everyone in the room stared at Frank. "So, Prissy and I would like to sell The Chirp to this company. The price is on the last page."

Everyone flipped to the last page. Frank yelled, "This is outrageous. Your profit is scandalous!"

Prissy stood as Bree gathered her belongings. "You might notice that Bree's salary for the conception and development was not included in the initial investment, not to mention the numerous problems that have arisen over the past three years that she's single-handedly addressed. This offer is non-negotiable, and if the board doesn't approve, Two Chicks, LLC, will proceed on its own. Please give us your decision by Friday. We will announce The Chirp during the Founder's Day Picnic on Saturday. Thank you for coming."

Bob collected all the prototypes and then followed

Prissy and Bree out.

BREE TOLD BOB to go through the Sonic Drive-in for a garbage hotdog, large onion rings with ketchup, and a large cherry limeade. Prissy stared at her with her mouth hanging open. "Fine. I want the same thing. Don't you dare tell anyone."

"There's hope for you yet," Bree said.

By the time they finished their lunch, Bree's cell phone rang. It was Katherine, so she put it on speaker. "Bree, the board voted to accept Two Chicks, LLC's offer. The only caveat is that we would like to make installment payments over the next four years, rather than two. Would that be acceptable?"

"Hold on. Let me check with Prissy." Bree muted the phone and danced in her seat. Prissy squealed. Bree placed her finger over her mouth and said, "Shhh," while smiling.

Taking the phone off mute, she said calmly, "Katherine, we accept your offer and the contingency. Our lawyer will draft the papers and send them by courier for everyone's signature by Friday, so we can announce it on Saturday. And Katherine? Thank you for helping us get this done. We sincerely appreciate it. See you Saturday."

There was so much noise in the back seat as the vehicle rocked back and forth that Bob had to step outside to call Joe to share the good news.

BREE AND PRISSY walked into the kitchen arm in arm, singing Queen's "We are the Champions" at the top of their lungs. Bob followed, singing along. Chewbarka joined in, doing her version of a happy dance, prancing on her hind legs in circles, while howling.

Joe appeared with a chilled Brut Champagne and glasses, while Mitch plugged his ears with his fingers, grinning from ear to ear. The cork popped, and the glasses were filled. Bree handed Mitch a large container of onion rings, while Prissy pulled out a raspberry-and-chocolate truffle cheesecake. Just as she brought out plates, forks, and a super-sized knife to slice it, Dirk and Steve appeared at the back door. "I heard there was cheesecake," Steve said, holding out his hands.

Mitch laughed, eyeing Bree. "I guess Hank told them the good news about SEcure Well buying The Chirp. Yep, it's a great day to celebrate. I've got some news, too." He removed his glasses and looked at each person for a moment before moving to the next. "I can see almost all the colors now. There is some gray in the yellows, but Dr. Brennin said he thinks I'll fully recover."

Bree rushed into his arms. "That's definitely worth celebrating."

Chapter 28

STARTING AT EIGHT o'clock in the morning, it was an all-hands-on-deck affair, setting up for the Founder's Day picnic. Family-friendly activities took place throughout the estate's large backyard, featuring a big bouncy house next to a small petting zoo and a pony ride. Cornhole, bocce ball, a giant Connect Four game, and lawn checkers were set up in various areas. Visitors were encouraged to bring chairs or large blankets to sit in front of the large outdoor screen, which was set up to display cartoons and movie shorts. A taco food truck and a pizza vendor were on-site, and thanks to Bree's new grill, hot dogs and burgers kept people fed.

A fire truck with an EMT unit was set up on the street, ready for kids to climb on and talk about emergency preparedness, while passing out bags with little first-aid kits and refrigerator magnets listing the city's emergency numbers. Sparky, the fire dog, and his handler roamed the area, distributing plastic firefighter hats and having their photos taken, while fire safety coloring sheets and crayons kept kids busy at two other tables.

Once the mad rush to eat was over, Bree and Prissy welcomed their guests and then introduced The Chirp via a small video shown on the outdoor screen. Steve had previously asked Bree if he could put together a PG-friendly version of the testing process for the prototypes. To her surprise, it was very well done. So, she asked him to take charge of creating and playing the whole video segment. The last part included a thirty-second announcement indicating that SEcure Well would begin producing the prototype in the next few months as the newest line in fire safety protection. The video ended with a thank you for everyone's attendance.

Bree and Prissy congratulated Steve for a job well done. Bree stared at Steve as if she were seeing him for the first time. Her eyes twinkled, and a smile lit her face. Prissy recognized the look immediately. "You're on to something, aren't you?"

"I believe so. Steve, why don't you meet Prissy and me in a week or so? I think we might have something that would interest you. Okay?"

"Sure, no problem. Will Prissy feed me?" Dirk slapped him on the back of the head, and everyone laughed.

"I think that can be arranged… And thank you again, everyone, for joining us today. Your support means everything."

Out of the blue, Frank walked up to Bree without acknowledging the others. "We need to talk. Now is preferable, and perhaps in your office?"

"Can't this wait?" He shook his head. "This better be important because I don't appreciate you taking me away from all my guests." He stared at her without speaking. "Fine. This way."

From the cornhole area, Mitch watched Bree lead Frank through the kitchen door. He joined Steve and

Darla, hoping Frank wouldn't do anything stupid that he'd have to rectify.

Darla elbowed Steve. "That's him! Remember, I told you I saw someone in a white jumpsuit bend down and then, a minute or two later, casually drop something into a garbage bin? That's the guy."

"The guy was Frank?" Mitch asked, his heart pounding. "Are you sure, Darla?"

"I'm positive. He looked around to see if anyone was watching him, and I saw his face. I didn't get a photo of him, but that's the guy."

"WHAT IS SO important that I need to leave my guests, Frank?" She touched her watch.

He followed her through the kitchen into the hallway leading to her office, passing Mrs. Ketchum on the way. Once in the office, Frank closed the door.

With great effort, he kept his voice low, calm, and even. "You have managed to insult me once more. Why you would do this to me, I'll never know. I've given you many years of my expertise and service, and you throw it in my face with that video. I still think you've pulled the greatest scam by selling those chirping parts to SEcure Well. First, you give me a burned-out prototype with bogus paperwork, and then you give us used ones at the board meeting. If these really work, I demand that you provide me with a real one, complete with the proper documentation, so I can have it verified."

Bree narrowed her eyes at him. "How dare you insinuate such a thing. My professionalism, motives, and intent are beyond reproach. And you demand that I give you something so valuable to appease your vanity? Think again." With lightning speed, Frank covered her face with a handkerchief. Bree gagged and then sagged into his arms.

Frank took her laptop from the desk and used her index finger to gain access. When the screen saver popped up, it was an image of The Chirp. "How quaint. Let's see what files are on the desktop. Ah, The Chirp. Well, that makes it easy. Hmmm. What a lovely little package: schematics, testing, expenses, marketing… It's all here." He pulled out a thumb drive and downloaded everything to it. Then he searched the room for any prototypes. In her bottom desk drawer were three, each in a different color. "Might as well take them all." He stuffed them into his pants pockets along with the thumb drive. Then he made a snap decision. "If I'm going to get out of here, I'm going to need a shield. Thank you, Bree, for volunteering."

He slapped her cheeks and shook her until she moaned. "We're going for a ride. You always loved riding with me, and I'm so glad you want to go now. Isn't that right?" She moaned again. "I'll take that as a yes." He pulled out a syringe, uncapped it, and stuck her with it. Bree's eyes fluttered open. "I'm sorry you don't feel well, but perhaps some fresh air will help. Let's walk to my car and go for a drive. What do you say?"

"Xena would like that," she mumbled.

"Xena? Whatever. Stand up straight, and I'll put my arm around you like old times."

He half-carried her to his car and shoved her inside. "I'm not going to hurt you, Bree. But I need to get away from here quickly. By the time your security dogs and that firefighter boyfriend of yours realize you're not at home, we'll be far away."

He hightailed it out of the neighborhood and to a local park, where he tossed the prototypes and thumb drive into a small pizza box, dropped the box into a garbage can, then sent a voice text.

"There's a small package for you to retrieve. Send the money now. Once I have confirmation, I'll send you the location."

While Frank waited for a reply, he headed out of town into farm country. Looking over at Bree, he said, "It's about time you learn your place. We could have had some fun for a long time, but you have no class. One day, you'll wish you had listened to me and picked me over that has-been firefighter. Oh, well. I'm moving on to much bigger and better things. So, consider this my resignation as CFO to SEcure Well. Now, be a good little girl, and take a nap." His maniacal laugh reverberated off the windows.

The deposit confirmation pinged on his phone, and he sent another voice text.

"Thank you. Two separate emails will guide you to the precise location. The first one has been sent. When I'm sure that I haven't been followed, I'll send the last one."

Frank bounced down a rutted, gravel driveway, pulled into the open doorway of a dilapidated barn, and turned off the engine. He took his suitcases out of the trunk, closed the barn door, handed the bags off to the driver of a black SUV, and climbed into the backseat to sip champagne while riding away. He only had to wait another forty-five minutes to arrive at a private airport outside of Raleigh for the next leg of his journey.

His suitcases were transferred to a Gulfstream G280, and then he boarded the sleek private jet to meet the steward. "Welcome aboard, Mr. Wainwright. May I take your computer bag?"

"No, thank you. I need to send an email before we take off."

"Very well, we have fifteen minutes before we taxi. The flight to Teterboro will take about an hour. A personal transport and concierge will escort you directly to your gate, speeding up your passage through customs. The wait should be around an hour before boarding your connecting flight, and your first-class seat has been confirmed. If you fasten your seat belt, I will bring some refreshments."

Frank nodded, appreciating the attention he deserved. While he waited for his laptop to boot up, he accepted a flute of champagne with a cheese-and-fruit plate. Congratulating himself for getting away with what he'd done, he pulled up a prewritten two-line statement addressed to Mark Stokes and James Fuller:

"You'll find what you want in a black trash can on the northeast corner of Ashley Bay Park by the bathrooms, inside a pizza box. Now, we're done."

He hit send, then closed the laptop as the jet engines roared to life. Looking out the window, he noticed that instead of moving toward the runway, the jet was moving toward the hangar.

Frank pressed the buzzer for the steward. "Is there a problem?"

"I'm sorry, sir, but one of the engine emergency lights flashed, and the pilot has requested a maintenance check. The plane underwent a check yesterday, so it may be a minor glitch, and it shouldn't take long. In the meantime, feel free to use the Wi-Fi and enjoy your snack."

Once the plane had come to a stop, the stairs were lowered to the ground. The steward asked Frank to deplane. "Maintenance has requested everyone except the captain to exit and wait in the lounge area. Please take everything with you as you leave. As soon as the problem is fixed, I will personally escort you back on board. Thank you."

Picking up the computer bag, Frank straightened and found it difficult to walk toward the open doorway where the steward directed him to leave. His head was fuzzy. *Probably the cheap champagne.* He managed to climb down the stairs, and a man dressed in black helped him into the hangar. He didn't recognize him, but there was a familiar emblem on his polo shirt. Suddenly, Frank's vision failed, and he felt his body being maneuvered into the backseat of a large, black vehicle. Then total darkness.

He woke up hours later with a throbbing head, lying on a thin, foul-smelling mattress inside a small room with heavy metal bars. People shook the bars, shouting insults and curses his way. As he tried to sit up, his stomach churned a few times before he vomited into a stainless-steel toilet. Looking around, he saw the two men he had emailed earlier in the adjoining jail cell. *No, it couldn't be!*

BREE WAS BETWEEN the real world and the ethers, in a long tunnel surrounded by mist and heat. She resisted opening her eyes; it felt good to be quiet, not having to think. She was floating toward something that smelled familiar… heavenly. It smelled like… Mitch. She smiled, wanting to get as close to it as possible. *Mitch.* She could always be free around him and his touch. She snuggled closer, enveloped in the scent and longing to be held tight. She imagined Mitch calling her; she desperately wanted to answer him, but this was enough for now.

MITCH TOUCHED HER neck with a shaky hand. "Bree, sweetheart, can you hear me?" There was a strong pulse, and she was breathing normally. He gently felt her head and found no injuries; then, he checked her pupils. They were slightly dilated, but they reacted to the light he shone in her eyes. Good. "Baby, please wake up. I need to hear that you're okay. Come on, Bree, talk to me, sweetheart." Bree mumbled as her eyes fluttered open. "That's it, darlin', I've got you. You're safe." Mitch placed a sweet kiss on her mouth. "I've been worried sick. You're going to be alright." He picked her up off the back seat and cradled her in his strong arms, then carried her to the back seat of Bob's SUV.

Prissy got in beside her. "Brianna. Bree, are you okay?"

Bree's eyes finally fluttered open. "What happened? How did I get here?"

"Oh, no." Prissy took both of Bree's hands in hers. "What do you remember?"

"Um… Mrs. Ketchum and then going into my office."

"Cousin, it was just as we suspected, it was Frank all along. He must have drugged you and then used you to get away. Give me the word, and I'm going to castrate that asshole."

Bree tried to smile.

Prissy dropped down on the seat next to her and cried on Bree's shoulder. "I didn't know what I'd do if you… you… left me. Thank God you're alright. From now on, I promise to take our security more seriously. And I don't think you should go anywhere or do anything without a shadow. I'll even agree to another dog if that's what it takes. Don't ever leave me again."

"Okay," Bree said weakly.

Chewbarka jumped up on the seat and licked

Bree's face. She patted the dog. "She came too?"

"She's the one who found you inside the barn in Frank's car. I think she'd have clawed the door off if we didn't open it," Mitch said. "She loves you as much as I do. Don't ya girl?"

The dog barked, and everyone laughed.

Chris ran toward the SUV. "Frank's connection to Guardian Systems has been verified. The authorities were at the drop when the stolen prototypes and a thumb drive were recovered, and two emails sent from his laptop to Mark Stokes and James Fuller revealed their involvement in the espionage. The transfer of funds from them to Frank has also sealed the company's fate. They're dead in the water. Frank was picked up at a private airport using a different passport, with the Maldives as his destination, a country with no extradition. Add the attempted murder and kidnapping charge to his extensive list of crimes, and he'll face a long prison sentence."

Bob rubbed a hand over his face. "Bree, you took a considerable risk letting Frank into your office. I shouldn't have let you do that, and I'm sorry. I didn't anticipate him drugging you, especially after what he did to Mitch."

Bree shifted to face Bob. "None of us did, but it had to be me in there. I knew you all had my back."

"When Mrs. Ketchum saw Frank drag you out of the house, we followed him. We knew where you were at all times. It wasn't an ideal situation, but you're Xena," Joe said. He leaned over the seat and patted Bree's hand. "Anytime you want to stop inventing and become an agent, just let me know."

Bree smiled. "I'll do that."

Not wanting to ever be in the doghouse, Mitch wisely didn't say anything; he kissed her.

Chapter 29

SLOWLY, EVERYTHING RETURNED to normal. The days got shorter, and the temperature dropped by a degree or two. It was perfect for a backyard cookout, and Bree was learning the finer points of grilling. She had stopped by the station to pass out her latest creation, pineapple bread pudding casserole with caramel sauce and vanilla ice cream. Instead of shyly avoiding the treat, her volunteer taste testers, Mitch, Dirk, Steve, and even Hank, eagerly stepped forward.

Hank savored the dessert with his eyes closed. "This may be the best one yet, Bree. Did Prissy show you how to do this?"

"Not exactly. She made something similar with apples and pears, but I craved the pineapple, and it came out perfectly."

"Maybe we should change up our chili cookoff to a dessert cookoff," Steve suggested, going back for his third helping.

"I'll think about it," Hank said. "But keep bringing these in. My wife is dying for some new recipes, so I'm taking home a little piece… that is, if it makes it out of my office."

Bree beamed. It was good to be known for something other than setting fires in the kitchen. Grills were self-contained, and she could always close the lid, close the air vent, and if need be, a fire extinguisher was always handy.

Mitch raved about the new dessert. "I think I've gained a few pounds from yours and Prissy's cooking." Bree smiled brightly.

He pulled her away from the others. "I have something I'd like to show you. But you might or might not think it's interesting, who knows?"

"Now I'm intrigued. Bring it over when you get home."

Several hours later, Mitch found Bree in her office looking at the Hot Shot information. She hadn't had time to work on it while trying to get The Chirp into production. She smiled at him. "Hi. Is it dinner time already?"

He snorted. "I brought several steaks, potatoes, and beer. I thought you'd cook for all of us tonight."

She leaped out of her chair, leading the way to the kitchen, elated that someone was requesting her to cook. "Absolutely, with your help, of course."

Mitch stopped beside the island and moved from foot to foot. "While I was recovering, I had a lot of time to think. You and I differ in that regard. You're the thinker. You see things, ask questions, and then create inventions that work. I prefer to assess a situation and implement a solution immediately. With lots of time to think, my brain migrated into places that I'd never go, and it drove me crazy." He paused. "Gee, that makes me sound dumb—"

"On the contrary." She giggled. "I understand what you're saying, and I appreciate the compliment. But now you've elevated my curiosity. What's up?"

"I've been thinking about the grill you built, what

you said about Dirk's grill, and fires from grills that aren't properly maintained. Not every grill is manned by a guy. Women are grilling or want to learn how. It's a market that manufacturers are ignoring. Why not create products that give women confidence and safety?" He picked up a large canvas boat bag, pulled out a rectangular wooden box, and placed it on the kitchen island.

"Every top grill manufacturer has its own line of products and accessories, but they lack fire safety items. You're developing the Hot Shot, but what about other products, such as gloves, mats, and grill blankets? I believe that SEcure Well could lead the way in developing a product line. So, I've designed a fire blanket box that can be attached to most grills or placed nearby. The heavy-duty, flame-retardant fiberglass blanket is quickly deployed by pulling one or both handles and tossing it over the grill. The case could be decorative, suitable for different grilling areas."

Bree carefully inspected the box and the blanket. Then she tossed it over one of her kitchen barstools and stood back, silently staring at it. It was like throwing a Frisbee, but then it opened like a flexible umbrella, taking the shape of the barstool.

Mitch quickly added, "It could be used over a fire pit, a campfire, or even an industrial stove with lots of burners." Bree continued to stare. "With flexible materials, it could also be used as a personal blanket to escape house fires."

She studied the design from every angle. "Does this have a name?"

"I was thinking… Ember Shield."

"No," she shook her head slowly. "This is your baby… Strong Guard. *Engineered by a firefighter. Designed for grillers.* Or something like that."

The corner of Mitch's mouth turned up. "It sounds…tough."

"It's perfect, and your ideas are perfect. Once our lawsuits are settled, I would like you to pitch this to Prissy and the board with my full backing."

"You're not just saying this because I'm your boyfriend, are you?"

"No. I see a product that can fill an unfilled niche, and you've just scraped the surface. If I didn't think it was product worthy, I would have told you as gently as possible." She held up a finger. "However, to be part of the SEcure Well family, it will require an NDA until we can get through negotiations. Agreed?"

"Agreed. Let's seal this with a kiss." It was slow, long, and passionate. "I love your incentives," Mitch said, reluctantly pulling away.

"Don't forget we still need to do the research and testing on Hot Shot. And some other things."

He stopped her with another kiss, then said, "While we're negotiating, there's something else we should discuss." She studied his face, which had gotten serious. "I'm thinking of a merger. Like a Kelly with a Strong. How would you feel about that?"

"Are you asking me to—"

"Not yet, but I'd like for you to think about it after you meet the good sister."

Her smile lit up the room. "It sounds like the perfect merger. I'd love to meet your sister and the rest of your family. I love you."

"I'm so relieved, and I love you too."

He kissed her slowly, full of promise, and sparking a flame that would never burn out.

Additional Books

Nonfiction:

It Happens Series:
It Only Happens To Me…2025
It May Happen To You…, 2026

Fiction:

Blame It On Series:
Blame It On Paris, 2025
Blame It On NYC, in 2026.

Chasing Sparks Series:
Love At First Spark, 2025
Chasing the Perfect Spark, 2026

If *Love at First Spark* made you smile, I'd be grateful if you left a review on Amazon or Goodreads—it helps new readers find their way to the story. You can also subscribe to my monthly newsletter at www.helen aitkenbooks.com for more sparks, surprises, and rom-com fun. I'd love to hear from you, too. Feel free to drop me a line at helen.aitkenbooks@gmail.com

Helen Aitken is a former science educator and award-winning writer who lives in coastal North Carolina. Freelancing since 2006, she spent nine years as a magazine columnist, writing about boating safety and environmental issues. She's also a lifetime member of the National Society of Newspaper Columnists.

While in Japan, her husband, Scott, served as a commanding officer and gave Helen strict orders to stay off the "blotter"—the military police activity log—and avoid causing any international incidents. She will neither confirm nor deny how well she followed those instructions.

Despite having a "black thumb" in the garden, Helen is a Fourth Degree Master of Ohara Ikebana (Japanese flower arranging) and has exhibited in Japan, Washington, D.C., and North Carolina. She's also taught countless workshops and given demonstrations.

Helen loves the beach, classic wooden boats, sweet tea, chicken salad, and her husband and son, Scott and Will—but not necessarily in that order. These days, she divides her time between writing, spoiling a very entitled cat, getting into mischief, traveling, and occasionally putting out kitchen fires… her inspiration for *Love At First Spark*.

Website:
www.helenaitkenbooks.com

Email:
helen.aitkenbooks@gmail.com